JILL NORRIS

Room 1210

This book is dedicated to my amazing friend Lynn. Your kindness and never ending support helped me accomplish my dream. I will forever be grateful for your help and being my cheerleader throughout this journey.
It's also dedicated to an amazing, fearless woman, who taught me to never have regrets and to never let fear win. Your courage through everything you're going through gave me the courage to finally finish this book, thank you Diane. You will forever be in my heart.

The oldest and strongest emotion of
mankind is fear, and the oldest and
strongest kind of fear, is fear of the
unknown.

H.P. Lovecraft

I

Part One

Chapter 1

Summer of 1928

Jacqueline sat in complete darkness with this heavy feeling sitting on her chest. She could hear the slight rattles of chains, and she could feel this immense sadness that engulfed her entire body and her body trembled. She knew the feeling didn't belong to her but to the space that surrounded her. The darkness around her seemed to deepen as if someone had put a blanket on a window to the already dark area. Her heart started to race, and she hated that she could not see anything. She felt like her body would break apart from the strong feelings of fear and sadness, it was as if she were having the worst panic attack. *What was this place and why did she feel this way?*

This horrible laugh broke through the silence.

It was deep, guttural and echoed from all around her, it sounded like something out of your worst nightmare. Jacqueline's body trembled even more, her heart racing so fast she felt it would give out.

Jacqueline jerked back quickly, as something touched her arm, but the touch persisted, unrelenting, firmer this time. It felt as if slimy frog hands were pushing down on her shoulders. Instantly, her joints ached as if she had a fever. The immense sadness she had in her head grew stronger. She could feel the lump in her throat and knew if she gave in she would burst into tears that would never stop. It would not be long before her body finally said that it could not handle anymore and would fail her.

The thing that was touching her spoke in this evil whisper that made her skin crawl, and her hair stand on edge. "You are perfect, your fear has a potent smell."

"Who are you? Where am I?" Jacqueline said, her voice cracking.

The thing laughed again, sounding even worse than before, although she wasn't sure how that was possible.

"I am fear itself my love," it said in an eerily cheerful tone. "I feed off it. You beckoned me and I came running."

Jacqueline's eyebrows furrowed. She had never beckoned this thing to her. "I did not call you, why are you here?"

The voice chuckled. "Oh, but you did. You and your friends thought it would be fun. Inviting things in, playing with that little talking board at recess."

Jacqueline's mind flashed back to that day at school.

She had sat in a circle with her friends in the grass. Poppy had taken a paper out of her pocket, on it letters were written in crayon and the words yes, no, hello, and goodbye. A makeshift talking board. Poppy had said you could talk to your loved ones who had passed on, or anyone that had passed on that were in the area.

Jacqueline had been curious since they had just lost their favorite teacher, Mr. Davidson. He was a bit older, walked with a cane, and had a distinct smoker's cough. He would always make everyone laugh, telling jokes to break up the monotony of schoolwork. If you had trouble with something you were learning, he would have you stay after class and teach you one on one until you understood... he was so patient and kind. When he passed, everyone was devastated, they had lost more than a teacher but also a friend.

Jacqueline could remember one time with Mr. Davidson that was very special to her. She was failing math badly. Her parents couldn't help her, numbers weren't their world. Their world was rows of corn and grain, farm animals and fixing fences. This had been Jacqueline's grandfathers farm, and her dad had taken over when he passed away. Jacqueline's dad only knew farm life. He sadly had only made it to the seventh grade before he was forced to work on the farm full time. Her mom had never gone to school. Jacqueline's mom's parents believed anything could be taught by being in the real world and not sitting in class. Jacqueline's dad had taught her mom how to read when they got married. Jacqueline refused to ask her parents for help. Deep down, she knew it would only hurt them, it would remind them of the education they never had, and of the gap they couldn't close for her no matter how much they wanted to. She tried to study all night, making flash cards and flipping them all night. No matter how many times she flipped them she could not get the answers correct. She came to school the next day completely exhausted and defeated. Mr. Davidson had seen her and came over quickly, looking very concerned.

"Jacqueline, are you OK?"

Tears stung Jacqueline's eyes. "I was up late last night. I'm having trouble with my math. I have tried everything to learn but no matter what I do, I can't get the answers to stick in my head."

Mr. Davidson had smiled at her and squatted down to her level. "I wasn't very good at math at your age either, but my mom taught me little songs to help me. It really worked. I can teach them to you, if you would like."

Jacqueline smiled as she wiped her eyes, "Could you?"

"Of course, come after class and we will go over it all. I will have you solving problems in no time."

Mr. Davidson had taught her a song that stuck with her and helped her so much.

> *"One plus one will always be two,*
> *Add them up it's easy to do.*
> *Two times two is four, you see,*
> *Three times three makes up nine for me.*
> *Four times five is twenty, true,*
> *Practice math and it sticks with you."*

And he was right, soon after that, Jacqueline was solving math problems like a whiz. She no longer felt like a failure. She enjoyed doing math now and didn't feel like she was falling behind. She would make up more songs to keep math fun and easy to remember. She remembered showing her parents what she learned and helping them as well. She had never been so proud of herself but was also very grateful for Mr. Davidson and his math song.

Jacqueline stared at the speaking board and then at Poppy. "Ok, let's do this." she said, thinking nothing bad would come from doing this.

Jacqueline knew she was different than the other kids. She could see things that normal people couldn't, people who had passed away. She looked towards the road and saw Mr. Davidson standing off in the distance, just watching the kids as he always did when it was recess time. She loved that even after death he was always watching them. Yet this time was different. Once they pulled that paper out, he seemed to float closer, with a worried look on his face. She had never seen a spirit come that close before. They usually stayed off in the distance just enough for her to understand they were no longer living but not enough to frighten her.

She jerked away, a little frightened with how close he had come. He now stood right behind Poppy, shaking his head. Most spirits could speak to her, but her teacher did not seem to have enough energy to do so. No one else ever heard them speak because the spirits didn't speak in the traditional sense, they seemed to talk right into her mind, almost as if she was thinking the words, but it wouldn't be her voice. Others would show her pictures in her mind if they didn't have the energy. Flashes of a dark mist passed through her mind with piercing yellow eyes, and these long-jagged teeth. She was terrified by the images but didn't understand what he was trying to tell her, and why he would be trying to scare her.

She looked away and pushed the thought from her mind. She did not want to see that image anymore.

The girls held their fingers to a coin, and Poppy asked the first question.

"Is Mr. Davidson here with us now?"

The girls sat there eagerly waiting for the coin to move, fingers lightly touching it, all on the edge of their seat, hoping and praying something would happen, but the coin did not move.

Jacqueline looked back up to see her teacher, Mr. Davidson, but he was gone.

"I swear, the coin moved for me last night." Poppy said.

Jacqueline was starting to get an uneasy feeling in the pit of her stomach. "I don't think we should be playing with this."

Poppy rolled her eyes. "It's harmless guys, I saw my parents play with one at their party the other night. They talked about it all night, saying how real it was."

As Poppy finished her sentence, the coin started to move. The girl to the right of Poppy lifted her hand quickly off the coin. "Ok poppy, I know you're moving the coin because you're mad we didn't believe you."

"I swear, I'm not doing it." Poppy insisted.

The coin slowly moved to the word hello and all the girls screamed. They quickly jerked their hands away from the coin, and all but Jacqueline and Poppy ran towards the school.

"See Jacqueline, I told you it works."

Jacqueline sat there, now feeling more nervous, as if what they had spoken to was in fact not Mr. Davidson but something else, but she didn't want her friend to be upset. "You're right, that seemed real. I think we should put it away now and get back to class."

Poppy shrugged and folded the piece of paper back up and shoved it back into the pocket of her dress.

* * *

Jacqueline's heart pounded in her chest. She was now back in the darkness, her body aching even more than it had before, her head was pounding, the pain so excruciating she felt like her skull was going to crack open. Her hands flew to her head as she screamed in pain, "make it stop, make it stop."

The creature slid its slimy hand down her arm, leaving goosebumps in its path.

It whispered into her ear, so quietly, she almost did not hear it. "You are free for now, but I am coming for you."

Jacqueline shot up in bed, her heart still going a mile a

minute, nausea filled her gut, sweat drenching her, and her head felt like it was about to explode. She ran out of her bedroom and to the bathroom as quickly as she could. As she reached the toilet, she vomited what felt like her entire insides into the bowl. Tears streamed down her face as her stomach kept wrenching but nothing else was coming out.

After what felt like an eternity, her body finally calmed down and she sat on the floor, her back resting on the side of the toilet, tears streaming down her face. She brought her knees to her chest and hugged herself tightly as she let out all the sadness that she had felt in that dream. Her body shook, her head ached, and the tears wouldn't stop. She felt as if her heart was breaking in two.

Her mother appeared moments later, panic on her face. "Oh my god Jacqueline. You look awful, Are you OK." Her mom placed her shaky hand on Jacqueline's forehead and then her neck. "You're burning up, let's get you back to bed sweetie."

Jacqueline didn't want to tell her mom about the nightmare, or the speaking board they had played with. She didn't want to tell her mom that she could see things others could not. She knew her mom wouldn't believe, and they would probably have her tested for insanity. She didn't want to worry her mother any more than she clearly already was, as she sat there fussing over Jacqueline's fever.

Jacqueline sat alone in the library the next day, many books stacked on the table in front of her. She needed to understand her experience and what these creatures were. She read book after book about mythical creatures, witches, haunting of demons and things that should not exist. She flipped page after page, and book after book, eyes scanning words that offered no answers, only more questions. Every passage ended in frustration. None of the stories matched the horror that stalked her dreams. Her hope began to fade.

She went back to the bookshelf about mythical creatures and slid her finger down the spines, reading the names of the titles silently as she went. None of the book titles seemed like they would have anything to do with what she was looking for. Her heart sank as her fingers touched the last spine, realizing she may never know what these creatures were that haunted her nightmares. She felt the lump in her throat again, but she did not want to cry.

As she went to turn around, something shiny caught her eye on the bottom shelf. It seemed to be sticking out farther than the rest of the books. Hollow Ground was inscribed on the front in gold letters. She picked it up and seemed confused because she had looked over these shelves a couple of times and this book had not been there.

Intrigued, she returned to the table, the book clutched tightly in her hands. Setting it down, she hesitated, fear prickling beneath her curiosity. For a long moment, she simply stared, afraid of what waited inside. Finally, with trembling fingers, she opened the first page and froze. The image staring back at her was all too familiar. A figure shrouded in swirling mist filled the page, its form half hidden but its eyes unmistakable. Two burning orbs of yellow cut through the darkness. Below, a mouth stretched impossibly wide, filled with jagged teeth. Her hand trembled as she turned the page, her eyes scanning the text. Her fingertips drifted across the words, needing to feel them as much as see them. It spoke of creatures called Hollow Ones. They only fed on those who summoned them. Once you did, they filled your life with terror, fear was what made you taste sweeter to them. They would torment you until you were consumed by it, then they would feed until there was nothing left. Your body would remain, but your soul would be dragged to Hollow Ground, devoured piece by piece until you vanished completely... erased from existence.

Jacqueline read on as the article quoted someone they had interviewed who had seen one of the Hollow creatures and lived to talk about it. The article talked about a man named Jeffrey from Pennsylvania, who used a talking board to try to speak to his mother who had passed. He stated, "After I used the board, I started seeing shadow figures around my house when I would be outside. I would swear yellow eyes were peering at me through bushes. Everyone told me it was just wild animals, but the feelings that engulfed my body when I would see these things, you wouldn't get that from an animal. One day I started hearing whispers and tapping sounds around my home, as if it was playing with me. I would feel things touch me in the night. Then one night I felt it grab my leg as I was walking up the stairs. When I turned around, I saw this large misty figure, piercing yellow eyes and long jagged teeth that had drool dripping from them. I was terrified. I ran down the stairs, right through the creature. My neighbor Jeb gave me a talisman to keep it away and told me to always have it on me. Sometimes I would still see this thing from a distance, but it never scared me again. You shouldn't play with tools of the dead if you don't know what you're doing, learn from me."

As Jacqueline scrolled, she saw many accounts from people's families stating that their sons or daughters had claimed the same things were scaring them, but no one believed them until their untimely deaths. There were reports from all over the U.S.

Jacqueline hands shook as she read the next page. It spoke

about the effects these creatures have on your physical body. The feelings she had in her nightmare, the immense sadness she had felt, the aching joints and fever she would feel, that was all real. They had called to these beings and now they too were being attacked.

Jacqueline flipped through the pages faster, looking for a way to defeat them. She did not want her and her friends to be the next victims. As she flipped to the last page, thinking she had failed, that there was no way to fix this, the last sentences gave her hope.

'The only way to save your soul is to show no fear, do not believe anything you see or hear once you have called on them. They need to feed to stay alive.'

She figured the only way to do that was to treat them as if they were just a bully at school or a lost soul looking for help. She knew most souls were nice and just needed help. If she could envision them as a soul who was just scared, she could trick her brain. That's when she recalled to mind her very first spirit she had encountered.

The first spirit showed up when she was seven. She was outside on her way to the barn to feed the newborn calves. She hated that farm, hated the chores, hated the responsibility, hated the isolation, but she loved the new calves, and she did not mind feeding them. She had two bottles in her hands ready to enter the barn and that's when she saw him.

He was just standing at the entrance of the barn. He appeared to be no older than eight. His skin was pale, drained of all warmth, and his cheeks held no trace of life. Deep, sunken eyes stared at her. He wore a thin linen shirt and trousers, the kind that might have once been white but now looked dark and torn in places, and a straw hat sat on his head. He looked so tired... and so very cold. She dropped the bottles and tried to scream but nothing came out, as if she was frozen. *Who was this boy and where had he come from.*

She closed her eyes and took a couple deep breaths. Once her breathing evened out, she bent down and grabbed the bottles, the warmth from the milk snapping her back to reality. When she looked back up, the boy was gone.

She thought she had imagined him but the next day when she got to the barn, he was in the same spot. He never tried to point to anything, never said anything, but she could feel this deep sadness anytime he showed up. She often wondered why he was so sad and tired. She left a pen and paper on a hay bale in hopes he would communicate that way and a blanket for him since he always looked so cold. Each day she checked them, the papers were always still blank and the blanket never moved. After about three weeks, he showed up in her room one day. She was reading the voyages of Dr. Dolittle when she felt this overwhelming sadness come over her and she immediately knew who it was. She looked up and in the corner of the room there stood the little boy. And in her mind, as clear as spoken words, came a single name. Timmy.

He would come around when he felt like it. No specific time of day, but once a day he would always show his face, and weirdly enough it made her happy when he showed up.

After about a month and a half of seeing him, he finally spoke up, but not out loud. She could hear him speaking in her head and she was shocked because it was like she was thinking the words, but she could hear his voice. She had no idea how this was possible, but she was so happy that he was finally communicating with her, so she didn't question it for long. He told her he was lonely and that he loved the farm and loved hanging quietly in her room with her. That even though things looked different now he felt like he was home. She did ask him why he was so tired and where his family was. He said that he was tired because he had been playing in the woods near the barn when he got lost and he has been searching for his family ever since. After telling her his story, he stayed quiet. He would follow her into the barn to watch her feed the calves or he would just sit in the corner of her room and watch her read.

Jacqueline felt bad that he was lonely and wished there was more she could do for him and wished she could help him find his family, but he seemed very content just sitting with her.

She loved seeing him and knew if she treated the Hollow Ones the same way she would be fine. She saw a Hollow One a couple of times after that, lurking in the corners of her room, but she had learned to calm her breathing, and not be scared, realizing they could not harm her if she wasn't scared. After a couple of nights, she never had issues again. She had asked her friends if they had any troubles sleeping or being scared at home, but they all said no. For some reason it had only been after her, and the thing had failed.

Then one day she saw a spirit that changed her and her gift. She was at the grocery store with her mom. It was a normal Sunday afternoon. They rolled through the isles as she snuck snacks into the grocery cart hoping her mom wouldn't see. She snuck to the next isle and grabbed a bag of cookies but as she went to turn around she saw a woman. The woman's dress was tattered, her hair long and tangled and Jacqueline swore she could hear her crying.

"Are you OK?" Jacqueline asked, but the lady did not answer. Jacqueline looked at the other people in the isle, but no one seemed to pay this woman any mind. That was when Jacqueline realized that the lady wasn't alive. The lady looked up with tears streaming down her face and started screaming for help repeatedly. Suddenly the spirit ran towards her quickly, crying and screaming louder. Jacqueline put her hands over her eyes and backed up into a shelf, lightly mumbling go away repeatedly. She felt someone shaking her but was too scared to open her eyes, not wanting to see this woman's face again. Finally the screaming faded and she could hear her mom's voice coming through. She opened her eyes, and there stood her mom, looking scared to death.

Jacqueline sobbed and her body trembled as she tried telling her mom what she saw, and why she was so scared. But whatever softness had been in her mother's eyes hardened at once, replaced by a hard scowl. Her mother seized her by the arm, yanking her off the floor. "Get your shit together." She hissed.

Jacqueline froze, staring up at her mother's flushed face, confusion twisting in her chest. That's when she realized the red on her mother's cheeks wasn't anger. It was shame. Her mother's voice filled the car all the way home, sharp and bitter. "You made a fool of me in there. Enough of this nonsense. No more stories, no more imaginary friends. I do not want to hear about Timmy ever again."

After that night Jacqueline buried her gift. She ignored the whispers, the shadows, and the flickers in her peripheral vision. She knew she couldn't embarrass her mom again. She had been grounded for a month after the grocery store incident, and she had learned that some truths were too uncomfortable for the living.The next day when she came home from school, Timmy wasn't there, and he never came back to see her.

* * *

Summer of 1931

Jacqueline and her mother didn't have a lot of money, farm life was unforgiving and money was tight, especially after her dad passed away a year ago. At the age of thirteen, she was forced to stop school and took a job cleaning houses for the wealthy in Greenwich, Connecticut. She had four houses she cleaned for. Every house looked the same. Grand colonial homes with beautiful gardens and picket white fences that looked like they were straight out of Eden. Inside, the homes were pristine and so clean she wasn't sure what she was actually cleaning. She never saw the man of the house and the children would be in school, so she was usually alone inside these huge houses, the wife out spending all her husband's money or hosting tea time. The women of the houses were always nice to her and never looked down on her but you could see the pity in their faces when they talked to her and that made her mad. She was fine, and happy for the most part. She didn't need their pity.

Then one day she met a woman who would change her world for the better. It was like the lady was a puzzle piece she had been missing for a very long time. She was cleaning the Johnson's home when a lady came over for tea.

"Jacqueline," Mrs. Johnson said. "I need you to set up a table for tea. The other maid is out doing the laundry, and I have a friend over."

"Yes Mrs. Johnson, right away." Jacqueline ran off to the kitchen to grab the needed things for the table.

When she returned to the table a woman sat across from Mrs.

Johnson that she had never seen before. She was wearing this beautiful purple dress, a black shawl covered her arms. She had long black wavy hair and a purple velvet piece of cloth that wrapped around her head. Beautiful beaded bracelets covered her arms, and her fingers were adorned with many rings. To Jacqueline she was absolutely stunning and mystical.

She turned towards Jacqueline and looked at her for what seemed like an eternity, her eyes piercing right into Jacqueline's soul. "And who is this?" The lady said to Mrs. Johnson.

"This is one of our house maids, Jacqueline Zodo." Mrs. Johnson said politely.

"Well hello Jacqueline," she said in a buttery tone. "It's nice to meet you. My name is Madame Lynette. I feel we may need to talk later. You have been hiding something."

Jacqueline frowned, not understanding at the time what she meant. She hadn't been hiding anything. She felt she was a very trustworthy girl.

"Jacqueline, is there something you want to tell me?" Mrs. Johnson said, crossing her arms.

"N...no Mrs. Johnson." Jacqueline said as her voice trembled.

"Oh no dear" Madame Lynette said chuckling lightly. "I did not mean it like that. I meant that you have a beautiful gift Jacqueline, but you keep it locked away."

Jacqueline's eyebrows scrunched together. She felt she was quite ordinary. She had no amazing gifts or talents. If she did, she certainly wouldn't be cleaning houses for these women. She would be living in them.

"Well," Mrs. Johnson said, clearing her throat. "Jacqueline needs to get back to work. We have things to discuss." gesturing for Jacqueline to move along.

As Jacqueline dusted the imaginary dust in the den the words from Madame Lynette kept running through her head. *Was there something this woman could see that she couldn't? Did she have a gift?* She was definitely hiding it pretty good because even she didn't know she had whatever gift Madame Lynette said she had.

Jacqueline's head shot up as she heard excited squealing coming from the parlor. She snuck over to the wall in hopes of getting a glimpse of what was going on.She saw Madame Lynette and Mrs. Johnson sitting at the table. A stack of cards sat before Madame Lynette, and Jacqueline could see her flipping them and whispering. Then Mrs. Johnson would get excited. She was so confused and had never seen anything like this.Why was Mrs. Johnson so excited about a card game? Was she a betting woman?

"Oh, thank you Madame Lynette, you have made me so happy. I knew you would only have good things to say about my future."

Then Madame Lynette bowed her head and got up from the table. She turned towards Jacqueline and Jacqueline quickly hid, hoping Mrs. Johnson had not also seen her.

As she dusted a random sconce on the wall next to her, she smelled the aroma of frankincense. Jacqueline turned and jumped back as Madame Lynette stood before her.

"Child, we need to talk. I can feel your gift. Why do you suppress the ones from the other side?"

Then it all made sense to Jacqueline, she was talking about her ability to see and hear spirits. That wasn't a gift to Jacqueline, it was a curse that brought embarrassment to her mother.

"My mother told me I had to. She told me that what I was seeing were things I was making up because I was lonely and that my imagination was making them real to me. She said it wasn't healthy for me to keep making up stories and that I needed to grow up."

"Oh, my dear," Madame Lynette said as she caressed Jacqueline's cheek. "They are very real. You need to embrace your gift. Sometimes spirits come because they need you, others come to warn, and others come to you because they just need a friend... like Timmy needed you."

Jacqueline's eyes grew wide, and she stood there shocked. *How did she know about Timmy? Could she see Timmy? Oh, how she missed him, she never forgot and always wondered if he was OK.*

Madame Lynette chuckled lightly. "Yes Jacqueline, I can see him. But not in the way you could. I can only see the memory of him and the feelings he had, and when I touched your arm, your memories came to me. I can feel how very grateful he was for your company. Please do not be afraid of your gift."

"Like you, do I have your gift? Like what you did for Mrs. Johnson?"

"Yes love, I am able to read people's future through my cards and other objects. I can answer questions for people who need help, or who are struggling, and need to know they are on the right path. You have that ability, I can feel it. Do not suppress it, you could do amazing things. I can also feel that your power is very strong, you will be able to see scary things as well and can warn people before destruction hits them." Then Madame Lynette got closer to Jacqueline. Her voice got quieter as she spoke the next words. "But I must warn you, do not ever be afraid of the Hollow Ones. They are not human but can take many forms."

"I read about the Hollow One's once, but I didn't know they

could take other forms."

Mrs. Johnson's voice interrupted their serious conversation. "Madame Lynette, I have your payment. You must go. My children will be home soon."

Madame Lynette placed her hands on Jacqueline's shoulders. "I must go darling, be safe, and do not be afraid. We need to talk more. I can help you with your gift and help you tap into your powers. Come find me."

Jacqueline was very intrigued as she watched Madame Lynette walk out the door that day. She knew she needed to find her, even if it was just for more answers.

Jacqueline did ask Mrs. Johnson if she knew where Madame Lynette lived but sadly, she had no idea. She tried asking around town, but no one knew. Anytime people did get a reading from her it was only because they happened to see her around town and they were able to snag her and ask for a reading. Madame Lynette would oblige, and they would set up a time for Madame Lynette to come to their house.

If that was the case, how was she ever going to find Madame Lynette so that she could learn more about this gift she possessed?

She went to the library one day to pull a book about magic. She figured she could try to learn it on her own since she didn't think she would ever find out where she lived. As she handed the book to the librarian to check it out a thought tugged at her, it wouldn't hurt to ask. "I have a weird question." she began carefully. "Do you happen to know where Madame Lynette resides?"

"No, I'm sorry dear. She is an elusive one. She likes her privacy. All I know is that she lives far in the woods, so far if you weren't careful, you would get lost, and legend has it the woods take you."

Jacqueline felt a chill run down her spine. She thanked the librarian and quickly grabbed the book. *Was this a test from Madame Lynette to see if she could find her way without getting lost?* She decided that she was going to take the trek into the woods and hoped the woods didn't win.

Jacqueline went home and packed a bag with some bread, and a canteen of water. She decided she would take the trek into the woods behind her farm. If this was meant to happen, she would find her.

Jacqueline's legs trembled. She had walked farther than she realized. Doubt crept in as she turned in a slow circle, searching for any sign of where she had come from. But all she saw were trees, endless and silent. The familiar sounds of farm animals had vanished, and even the sweet scent of drying hay no longer lingered in the air.

She started to get nervous as she walked further into the woods. It was now late afternoon, the sun was starting to go down, and the forest seemed to look a little eerie. As she walked on, she heard twigs snapping near her. She spun quickly, heart racing, and chuckled with relief as she saw a squirrel bouncing along the forest floor.

"OK, get yourself together, you cannot get scared. You need to think clearly." Jacqueline said out loud to herself.

As the sun dipped lower in the sky, Jacqueline sank down beside a tree, her legs aching with the strange, popping stiffness that comes from walking to far. She set her sack on the ground and pulled out a small piece of bread, taking a moment to rest. The water she drank was warm and stale, but it soothed her dry throat. She forced herself to ration it, eating and drinking just enough, because if she truly was lost, she knew she would need what little she had left. "Why would someone want to live all the way out here?" She thought to herself.

Once she had rested for a minute she got back up, but as she did, she realized she couldn't remember which way she was going. Everything looked the same to her. She spun around hoping something would catch her eye and show her the way. Nothing. Just tree after tree.

She rubbed her hands on her pants to dry the sweat, her clothes sticking to her from how hot the day was. Her heart now beating faster. It felt as if the forest was spinning. She shook her head and stared into the forest, determined to see something familiar. She looked in front of her and through the trees she swore she saw yellow eyes staring at her. Her eyes went blurry. She tried to blink but it didn't seem to help. She felt as if the forest was spinning. She shifted her feet as she tried to balance herself, but her ankle shifted wrong and her body slammed into the rough bark of a nearby tree. Pain shot up her arm as she grabbed it. Her heartbeat thundered in her ears now and her stomach turned. She bent forward, her hands braced on her knees and lowered her head to her chest, trying to calm herself down. Fear flowed throughout her body, her joints trembling and aching. Then, cutting through the silence, came a soft, light chuckle that seemed to come from all around her.

Her head snapped up. "Nope, you know you can't show fear. That's what these things want. Clear your mind and find your way." She said, calming herself down. She closed her eyes and used her breathing techniques. Breathing out for three seconds and in for five seconds. After a couple of minutes she opened her eyes, feeling better. The eyes had disappeared. Her shoulders relaxed. She looked up at the hill in front of her, buttercups filling the hill. They were so pretty but it seemed weird that they were only growing in this spot. Her feet crunched on the dry leaves and pine needles as she made her way to the buttercup trail. As she got closer she noticed the flowers were parted perfectly on either side of her as if the path had been curated just for her. When she got to the top of the hill, the buttercup trail stopped and in the clearing of trees stood a very weird house. Tucked away behind a crooked wooden gate stood a brown cottage with steep jagged roof lines that twisted at odd angles. There were diamond paned windows, and a small wooden door with ivy growing around it. It looked like a house out of one of her fairy tale books. If a witch could ask for the perfect house, this was it. She knew she had found it.

The door opened and there was Madame Lynette, a huge smile on her face. "Oh good, you found me."

Jacqueline wasn't going to tell her how hard it had been to find, she wanted her to be proud and think she was competent to teach.

Madame Lynette ushered her into the cottage and closed the door behind them. Jacqueline's eyes widened as she stared into the very cluttered home. Brooms leaned against the walls, candles burned on every surface, shelves sagged beneath the weight of old books and jars filled with oddities. Everywhere she looked there was something and her house smelled of all types of herbs and incense. She felt so at home here, as if she could be herself and she wouldn't be judged.

Madame Lynette stood before her now, a gentle smile on her face. "You carry great power Jacqueline. I've known it since the first time I saw you. It radiates from within you." Her eyes softened, though there was a glint of curiosity behind them. "But before I show you anything, I need to see how much you already know."

Madame Lynette led her to a round wooden table draped with a midnight blue cloth. An ornate crystal ball sat in the center, large and oddly clouded, nothing like the pristine ones she saw in books.

"Close your eyes Jacqueline," She instructed gently. "Open your mind and tell me what you see."

She tried to open her mind but all she saw was the image of her mom yanking her off the store floor, cheeks red, eyes angry, scowling at her as she pulled her violently towards the entrance. Jacqueline squeezed her eyes and tried to focus harder, but nothing came. Her shoulders slumped and she opened her eyes.

"Jacqueline, you need to quiet your mind, let them come to you. Do your breathing techniques."

Jacqueline did as she was told. Letting her mind clear of everything, breathing in and out, feeling her body seem to float into a trance like state.

At first there was only silence. Then... a vision surged forward. She saw a girl, no older than seven, sitting on the edge of her bed, clutching a stuffed animal so tightly its stitching strained. Her room was dim, the single bulb above casting long, unnatural shadows. But it wasn't the room that stole Jacqueline's breath.

It was the corner.

A thick, rolling fog lingered there, curling unnaturally. Whatever it was didn't move, it was watching, waiting.

In her mind, she could hear the thing whisper.

"You don't know fear yet, little one."

Jacqueline's eyes flew open, her breath hitched.

Madame Lynette said nothing... only studied her.

Jacqueline's voice trembled. "There was a girl, she wasn't alone. Something dark was in the room with her, something evil. It looked like fog, but it spoke."

Lynette's expression darkened, and for the first time Jacqueline saw fear in her eyes. Madame Lynette pointed to the crystal ball. "Now that you have opened your mind, look inside, tell me what you see. And Jacqueline, do not just stare, concentrate and reach for the vision again."

Jacqueline leaned close to the crystal ball, heart racing, nervous to see the vision again. "It's just fog." She said confused.

"You saw the girl in your mind," Lynette said gently. "Now see her again. You need to focus, really see the vision in the crystal."

Jacqueline took a breath and shut out everything around her until all she saw was the ball. She let herself think of the little girl on the bed, the way her hands trembled as she clutched the stuffed animal. She thought about the fog swirling in the corner of the room, the sound of its voice.

The mist in the crystal began to swirl. Slowly, the scene began to emerge, first as smudges, then as shapes, then terrifying detail.

She saw the girl clearly, the bed, the fog.

This time the entity was clearer, taller, closer. Yellow glowing eyes, teeth that were white and jagged. It smirked at the girl and then its mouth opened wide, showing more jagged teeth in multiple rows.

It crept forward slowly, hungrily, and the girl opened her mouth to scream but no sound came out. Her eyes were wide, unblinking, and she was frozen in fear.

The creature seemed to feed off her, and became more solid as it fed. The fog tightening around the entity now instead of curling around the room.

Thick strands of drool hung from its teeth, and then the girls body sagged, her energy evaporating, and she fell back onto her pillow.

The fog retreated, and the ball went dark.

Jacqueline recoiled, a gasp stuck in her throat, tears burned her eyes. She looked up at Madame Lynette, whose face was drawn in sorrow.

"Could you see what happened?" Jacqueline asked.

"I didn't need to, I have seen these creatures in my visions before."

"What... what happened to her?"

"The Hollow One's have taken her." Madame Lynette leaned in closer. "The thing you saw, it was not a ghost. It was not human, never was. These creatures are born from a place of darkness."

Madame Lynette moved to the fireplace and threw another log in. Then she turned to face Jacqueline, her head bowed a little. "They dwell beneath us. Not in the ground as you know it, but in a world beneath the world. A hidden realm called Hollow Ground. A place where light cannot reach. A place built on rot and despair."

Jacqueline's breath faltered and her heart hammered in her chest. She had read about them but hearing Madame Lynette tell her made them more real and terrifying.

"The Hollow One's are parasites. They do not feed on flesh, nor on blood. They drink fear. Slowly. Methodically. They draw out your life force with every moment of terror you endure.

The more frightened you become, the more power they gain... There's no telling how many times they visited that poor girl, torturing her."

"They create fear," she continued. "They bend your reality, warp your senses, twisting your memories, making you question what's real and what's illusion. They will mimic loved ones. Speak in voices you trust. Show you things that never happened, or hide things that did, until you do not know what or who to believe."

Jacqueline sat there, frozen. A tear slid down her cheek as she thought of the little girl in the bed. The fear on that poor little girls face.

"They wear faces," Lynette hissed. "Faces you either already trust or people you could trust easily. And when you can no longer distinguish friend from foe, when the fear finally breaks you..." Her voice faltered. "That's when they finish the job."

Madame Lynette got quiet, her head bowed. Jacqueline didn't dare talk or move, as she could tell Madame Lynette was probably remembering a vision of someone she had seen come against these creatures and lose.

With a quiet voice Madame Lynette continued, "When they take the last bit of life out of you, they drag your soul down, into Hollow Ground."

Jacqueline's lips parted, her voice barely audible. "And what happens to the soul?"

Lynette's eyes darkened. "They chain it. Bind it to stone and shadow. There, you are tortured, repeatedly, for eternity. Not because they need to. But because they enjoy it."

She took a breath collecting herself. "But... not all is hopeless. Most Hollow Ones require fear to feed. If you resist, they will usually move on. They are hunters, they prefer easy prey."

Jacqueline nodded, but her gut told her there was more.

"However," Lynette said, her voice turning grim. "There is one unlike the others. A Hollow One so ancient, so clever, that even the others fear him. He doesn't just feed on fear... he feasts on sorrow, despair, and loneliness. He breaks your entire soul by breaking your heart and drinks from your pain. Unlike the rest he doesn't need to drain you slowly, if he wants you dead, he can kill you with just a thought. Snap your spine like a twig, crush your lungs without even touching you. There's only one thing that can make him stop. You have to find his name."

"You don't know his name?"

"No, He is so ancient and powerful, to find his name would take way more power than I have. But I know that you could."

"Me? Why me?"

"You have a gift, stronger than mine ever was. You can see them clearer than anyone I have ever trained. That's why their circling. They fear your strength, they know that you could figure it out. But know this child, finding its name doesn't kill it. It only banishes it. When you speak its true name aloud, it is dragged back to Hollow Ground. But the name only protects you, and perhaps those tethered to the place it haunts. But you will never save everyone. You must accept that."

"How do you know so much about them?" she finally asked.

Madame Lynette didn't respond right away. Her gaze drifted toward the flickering candle on the table, her face tightening with something Jacqueline hadn't seen before from her, fear. Real, lingering fear. When she finally spoke, her voice was quieter and distant.

"Let me tell you how I know they can't be destroyed... only avoided."

She exhaled slowly. "It was thirty years ago, Jacqueline."

* * *

Madame Lynette sat at her altar, the candlelight dancing gently across her small room. A piece of paper lay before her, the words "yes" and "no" scrawled in black ink. She held her pendulum over it, steady and focused.

"If anyone is here," she whispered, "move the pendulum to yes."

The crystal began to swing, slowly at first, then pulled left toward the word yes. Lynette smiled softly. "Thank you. Is this my grandma?"

Again, the pendulum moved to the left.

"Oh, Grandma... I've missed you. Are you safe? Are you happy where you are?"

"Yes."

She asked a few more questions, ending with a gentle goodbye and gratitude for the connection. The moment felt peaceful. Sacred.

That night as she lay in bed, she felt something watching her. She rubbed her eyes, her vision a little blurry but she swore she saw yellow eyes watching her in the corner. She blinked a couple of times as her vision focused. The eyes seemed to move closer, she blinked trying to refocus but when she did the room seemed to be foggy. She rubbed her eyes and when she opened them nothing was there. The room was clear, the eyes were gone.

But then the bed began to shake violently. She screamed and jumped up, only to be grabbed by something unseen. Fingers, ice cold and strong, wrapped around her ankle and yanked her to the ground. Her knee slammed against the floor, pain shooting up her leg as she cried out.

She scrambled to get away, but it dragged her, clawing her backward across the wood. She screamed louder as she felt her body being flipped over. What stood before her scared her more than anything. A tall, misty figure bent over her, piercing yellow eyes glowed from a face that barely had shape, and a grotesque mouth of jagged teeth stretched wide in a snarl.

Lynette clutched her beaded seeing eye necklace and squeezed her eyes shut.

"You aren't real. This is a dream. You aren't real. Protect me, Grandma," she repeated over and over.

And suddenly... it stopped. Her mind started to relax. When she dared to peek, the room was empty. The fog had lifted. She wanted to believe it was just a nightmare. But it returned the next night, and the night after that, scaring her more every time. Each time, she woke weaker, more drained. She went to the doctors, but the doctor told her nothing was physically wrong other than the fact that she was lethargic. Still, she lost weight rapidly. Her face was sunken in, her nails were brittle and cracked. Her hair was falling out in clumps.

It felt like something was feeding off her life and she was terrified.

Desperate, she went to the library to search for answers. Books on illness told her nothing, none of her symptoms added up. She felt defeated and decided to look around. One book caught her eye. An old leather-bound book tucked away on the bottom shelf: Hollow Ground.

Her hands trembled as she turned the pages. Inside, she read about beings called Hollow Ones. Creatures that fed on fear until nothing of the person remained. The pictures it showed looked just like the creature that had been in her room. All her symptoms added up to what this explained would happen to a person being fed from. Then they dragged the soul into the cursed realm they came from, where you are tormented for all eternity.

She slammed the book shut, horrified. The dreams weren't dreams. She had been hunted. She knew she needed to protect herself. She enchanted her necklace, practicing calm breathing, and learned to control her fear. Over time, the creature stopped coming. Her strength slowly returned.

Years passed. Then she discovered tarot. At first, it was harmless. But eventually, the visions returned. They were worse than before, darker, scarier. The necklace didn't seem to work this time. The creature seemed to be immune to the amulet. It had adapted.

She decided to move to a remote cabin deep in the woods, hoping moving would protect her.

One night, it appeared again. It didn't snarl this time... It laughed. A low, echoing laugh that sent shivers down her spine. "Missed me, friend?" it whispered, close enough to feel its breath.

"No!" she cried, voice breaking.

She was physically deteriorating, and emotionally unraveling, she felt completely defeated by this creature. She went back to the library and found that same book again. She flipped frantically through its worn pages needing answers. She had become even more sickly. She couldn't eat anymore, she could barely walk from loss of energy, she was at the end of her rope, and she knew it wouldn't be much longer before it finished her off. In the final pages, she read something she hadn't noticed before:

They cannot be killed. But speak their name, and you steal their power. Call them by their true name. When you do, they are pulled back to Hollow Ground... and the souls they've stolen from that place are set free.

But how was she supposed to learn its name?

Divination had opened the door, surely it couldn't close it. And yet... she had no choice. She returned to her altar, lit some candles, cleared her mind and pulled out her pendulum and the paper with the words yes and no scribbled on them.

"Grandma," she whispered, "if you're here... I need help."

The pendulum swayed and pointed to yes.

"Do you know this thing's name?"

Yes.

"Can you give me a clue?"

No.

Frustrated, Lynette dropped the pendulum without closing the session. She blew out the candles, crumpled the paper, and hurled it across the room.

She remembered that the amulet had protected her once before. Heart racing, she snatched her mother's necklace and ran to the altar. Her fingers trembled as she lit the white candle for protection. She reached for the small glass vial, a mixture of mugwort, lavender, and frankincense. She uncorked the vial and let a few drops fall onto the candle and necklace. The mixture shimmered faintly in the candlelight, smoke curling from the flame as if the oils themselves breathed.

She spoke the spell, and the air grew warmer. The candle flickered once, then straightened, its flame burning taller. She quickly placed the necklace around her neck. She exhaled, her eyes flickering towards the shadows. The protection had returned... but so had the feeling of being watched. She knew the cost, to keep the creature at bay, she could never remove the necklace, or she would have to learn its name.

* * *

"That's how I survived," Madame Lynette said, her voice grave. "I still wear the necklace to this day." She pulled the necklace out from underneath her top for only a second, the crystal glinting, before she put it back. "Not everyone gets out. You can't kill them. You can only hope to force them back and keep them there. For most, all I can offer is a small bit of protection."

She looked at Jacqueline.

"But you..." Madame Lynette's voice softened, almost reverent. "You've already seen them, and you were wise enough not to show fear. That's the only reason they didn't take more. Your power is much stronger. I know you can find the name and help others."

She leaned forward, her eyes sharp with conviction. "Over the years, I've learned how to protect myself. I've studied, practiced, and made mistakes I'll never forget. Now I know how to cleanse the space, how to seal the energy, how to keep them from slipping through when I use divination tools, and most importantly, how to close the door when I'm done."

She reached for Jacqueline's hand. "And I'm going to teach you everything I know, including how to make protective amulets for yourself and others."

Jacqueline learned to embrace her gift once again. Madame Lynette taught her how to draw protection circles, making sure that Jacqueline really manifested what she wanted, envisioning the protection as a bubble all around her.

Then she brought her outside, taught her how to ground herself, they walked barefoot through the woods as Madame Lynette taught her how to push energy she didn't want away from her body, only allowing what you wanted in, to come near.

She showed her how to really read tarot, letting the cards do the talking. She taught her to focus on the card and what images came to her, while other parts of the card seemed to fade in the background.

Then she taught her white magic spells, and how to protect objects that you could give to others to keep them safe. They went over herbs, crystals, oils, candles, and much more, making sure Jacqueline understood how everything she did needed to be done with full concentration and understanding of what she was using.

The weeks flew by. Jacqueline stood alone in the woods behind Lynette's cottage. The time had come, she could feel it. She knew she was ready to start this journey on her own.

Spirits came and went. They were usually asking to give someone a message. Most people were very skeptical when she was telling them about what their dead loved ones were saying but others listened and cried. Hugging her and thanking her for giving them closure and comfort.She loved being able to help people and the spirits who needed their voices heard. Though she never saw Timmy again, she hoped it was because he had finally found his family. She guessed he had stayed for as long as he did because he was the one who knew that she needed help in believing in spirits and that they were good and weren't there to harm her.

Years went by and her gift grew. She was now 38 years old, and she was well versed in how to read tarot and use other divination tools, she could speak quite well to spirits and understood most hints they gave her. Some spirits wouldn't speak but would only show her images she had to decipher. It made it a little bit more difficult but usually the grieving family or friend knew, and it made perfect sense to them.

She had become very good at crafting spells for people who needed them as well. She only crafted good spells for healing, protection, and clarity. She always remembered what she had been taught about dark magic and never played with it. She loved the person she had become and was so thankful for the moment in time she had met Madame Lynette.

Jacqueline also helped get Demons out of people's homes. She would cleanse the area and then she would call upon demonologists who would come into the house. They would help them get enough evidence so the church could help expel them out of their homes.

The only thing she wasn't good at was helping people when Hollow Ones came and terrorized someone's home. She wasn't afraid of them, but she couldn't help give the homeowners that same calmness and so the hauntings would continue. She would give them the wearable items she had put protection spells on, but most people never listened and would not wear them. These beings were very strong, and the more people feared them the stronger these Hollow Ones got.

When she would ask the family what they may have done to get a Hollow One to be welcomed into their home it was always the same. They thought it would be fun to have a seance or use a talking board as if it was a cool party trick. She hated that. People should never use them. They never cleansed the area before or closed the connection afterwards properly. Then their negligence would invite the Hollow Ones in, and they would feed on them until they eventually disappeared.

Chapter 2

Summer of 1958

Jane stood in the lobby of the old hotel, soft jazz played softly, and the scent of polished wood filled her nose. It was early evening when she arrived, stepping through the tall wooden doors like she had done countless times before. Jane Chapman was a vision from another world, one bathed in red lipstick, curled brunette hair pinned just right with bobby pins, and grace that turned every head. Her black swing dress hugged her curves, the red belt cinching her waist like the ribbon on a gift. Red saddle shoes clicked against the marble floor with charming authority. At just 5'4, she was not towering, but her presence made her seem taller. Glamorous, confident, and magnetic.

The front desk clerk looked up, face lighting up in recognition. "Oh, Miss Chapman, we are delighted to see you," he beamed.

Jane gave a coy smile. "Why thank you. I'll be staying in my usual room."

"Room 1210," he said with a knowing nod. He turned to the row of mailboxes behind him and plucked a single skeleton key from the slot. "Enjoy your stay, Miss Chapman. Oh, and before I forget, Miss Winchester will be visiting you tonight. She says she has someone with her you've been dying to meet."

Jane's smile widened, eyes glinting. "Oh, I can't wait." She always had a curiosity for the taboo and Miss Winchester was bringing a psychic tonight to read her cards. Jane and Betty had always dabbled in this kind of thing, doing seances here, or the last time playing with the Ouija board, but it would be exciting to have someone tonight that really knew what they were doing.

She took her key and made her way to the ornate elevator. Its dark Victorian charm always made her heart skip. Matte black walls surrounded the space, their surfaces subtly textured with deep set paneling and soft shadows that danced beneath the glow of two vintage sconces. She loved that it gave the illusion of candlelight, though her real obsession was the elevator door. An ornate design that looked like something plucked from a forgotten European manor. Intricate swirls and floral patterns curled like ivy across the black metal door. It gave Jane a feeling that the doorway was opening to a confessional.

To the left of the elevator, she saw the small control panel glowing faintly red, the arrow pointing up, waiting for its next guest. The entire space radiated a dark, opulent charm, inviting and foreboding all at once.

When she stepped inside, she felt like the mirrored walls watched you, and the soft notes of swing music floating from a hidden speaker made it even more mysterious.

The bellman tipped his cap. "Miss Chapman, happy to see you again." Jane walked in smiling back at the bellman. He tapped the number 12 on the elevator and the sound of the elevator coming to life whirled inside, then the cart bounced for a second and started to ascend.

"Thank you, Charles. How's the family?"

"Oh, just swell. Baby Bonnie's learning how to crawl."

"How darling. I'm sure she is just the cutest thing."

"She is the apple of our eye." Charles said proudly.

The elevator chimed, the number 12 glowing overhead.

"Well, this is my stop. Have a good evening, Charles."

"You too, Miss Chapman." He bowed his head, and the door slid open.

She stepped onto the familiar twelfth floor, her heels sinking slightly into the plush carpet. Swirls of gray, red, and blue threading through a pattern of birds. The wallpaper was flocked velvet gold, with floral designs that shimmered in the light. It made her feel like she was home.

She reached Room 1210 and inserted the key. The lock gave a soft, satisfying click. But as she opened the door, a strange thickness in the air wrapped around her like a damp shawl. Odd, she thought. Maybe they had the heat on too high.

She flicked on the light and set her suitcase by the door, then crossed to the window, cracking it open to let in the crisp night air hoping that would cool the room down. After slipping off her shoes, she curled up on the red velvet couch near the bookcase. The titles always amused her, especially one:*The Night Jane Would Never Forget.*It felt as though the room itself had curated that book just for her. She opened the book to find it empty. She shrugged and placed it back on the shelf. She figured it must be blank on purpose to make the bookcase appear full.

Even though it was empty, she hoped it would live up to the title.

An hour passed as she read a favorite:*Jules' Last Dip,*a mystery about an Olympic swimmer who drowned under suspicious circumstances. In the book, many speculated it had to have been murder even though it was ruled a suicide. She was a couple chapters in when a knock echoed at the door.

She opened it to find Miss Winchester, Betty, her best friend since childhood. Betty wore a lavender swing dress with a pink sash and her signature black saddle shoes that made her legs look even better. Her blonde bouffant hair was perfect, her makeup pristine, and her piercing blue eyes twinkled like mischief in a bottle. She had the perfect tiny waist but was voluptuous in all the right areas.

Beside her stood a woman Jane did not recognize. She was Jane's height, draped in a long ruffled black dress, a deep purple scarf with tasseled edges adorned her shoulders. Her matching turban bore a white feather and an opaque jewel, and her dark eyes seemed to look straight into your soul. Her arms were adorned with many beaded bracelets and a seeing eye necklace dangled from her long black fingernails. She made you feel uncomfortable, the way she looked at you with such an intense stare, as if she was staring into your soul.

"Jane! It's been so long," Betty said, hugging her friend tightly.

"Far too long. Do come in. Thank you both for coming."

The mysterious woman said nothing, only nodded.

"She doesn't speak much," Betty explained. "But what she says always comes true. She is amazing."

"Well then, where would you like us to sit....ummm... I'm sorry I didn't get your name?" Jane stammered to the mysterious lady.

"Her name is Madame Zodo." Betty said.

"Oh, well it's nice to meet you Madame Zodo." Jane said with a slight almost scared smile.

"There is someone else in this room," said Madame Zodo

in a hushed tone. She moved into the room further and stopped. "Are you going to talk to us or do you only carry hollow thoughts?" she said to the corner of the room.

Jane and Betty looked at each other completely confused. Madame Zodo turned to them, "I can see a dark figure in the corner by the bookcase. I tried to ask him why he is here but when I do, he darts away. He keeps showing me a Ouija board, but I don't know why. Hopefully the longer I am here he will trust us enough to let me in further."

Jane's eyes widen and she looked at Betty. She knew why. Betty smiled wide, "Oh, she can also see souls who have passed on. Isn't she great!"

Jane was not too sure she felt Betty's enthusiasm, but Betty was so excited it took away a little of her fears, and she decided to keep a positive and open mind to whatever Madame Zodo was going to say.

Jane had arranged the room for their little gathering, pulling a throne like chair from the corner for Zodo and setting up a small table. Madame Zodo made her way to the table setting things up as she went. Candles now glowed nearby, and frankincense hung in the air. Her Tarot cards lay in a perfect pile on the table.

Madame Zodo shuffled her tarot cards, each motion elegant and deliberate. Then she cut the deck in half and placed them back in a perfect pile on the table. Her heavily ringed fingers hovered above the table. Her eyes, dark and impossibly deep never leaving Jane's face. With a deliberate breath, Madame Zodo drew the first card.

*Flip.*Nine of Swords.

"You are plagued by worry," she said quietly. "Restless dreams. A secret clawing at your soul. You haven't been sleeping well, have you?"

Jane paled. Nightmares had tormented her lately. They were of a young girl, blonde, who was drowning. No matter how Jane tried to help her, the ending was always the same. Jane would then wake up in a heap of sweat, but she couldn't understand why it was always the same dream, and it always felt too real.

*Flip.*Knight of Swords.

Zodo frowned. "He charges in, reckless. Fast. Dangerous. There is no time to prepare."

Jane shifted in her chair. A chill crept up her spine, but it made no sense, the air was too warm, too thick. Madame Zodo's hand trembled slightly as she reached for the final card.

*Flip.*The Tower.

Zodo gasped. She leaned in, eyes fierce now. "The Tower warns of disaster. Collapse. Tonight, child. Not someday. Tonight. Something is coming for you. You must run. You must leave this place."

Madame Zodo's dark eyes never left Jane as she began to tremble. She didn't know what to do. *Is this real? Were her nightmares true, this ominous feeling in the room, was this an omen?*

Betty tried to laugh it off, "Well, this has been fun but maybe it's time to leave Madame Zodo."

Zodo just looked at Jane with this fierce sadness in her eyes. "Be safe my child. The energy in here has darkened further. Do not trust this shadow figure, he is not a lingering soul. You should leave, but as you do, show no fear or it will consume you." Then she handed her the necklace she had been holding. "You need this more than I do, it will keep you safe, do not let it go."

The necklace felt heavier in Jane's hand then she expected,

and she gripped it tight.

"Don't you worry about a thing Jane. I mean, she's usually right but there's a first time for everything," Betty said patting her on the shoulder. "Did you want me to stay for a while?"

Jane shook her head, "No, you go home. I'm sure there's nothing to worry about. This has been my room for years since I've been coming here. Nothing bad has ever happened before." But as Jane said it, she knew she was lying. The room had never felt like this before.

"Alright. Just know you can always go downstairs and hang out with the bellman if you get scared." Betty said trying to lighten the mood.

"Have a good night and thank you Madame Zodo for com-ing." Jane opened the door and waved her arm towards the exit. "See you soon Betty."

Betty kissed her on the cheek and Madame Zodo just looked at her for a quick second and then made her way into the hallway. The door shut and the click sounded louder than it ever had. It was an ominous loud echoing click, like a forever click. Jane sat back down on the couch.

The candle was still lit, and the flame was pulling ever so slightly towards the bathroom area. She turned her head but saw nothing. Now her imagination was going to get to her and freak her out at every turn. She rubbed the beads between her fingers as if they would keep her safe. She decided it would be better if she just went to bed now so morning would come quickly. She wasn't going to be staying for the week like she usually did. She was just going to leave once the sun came up. She placed the necklace on the couch and decided she would take a shower to calm her nerves.

The bathroom door creaked open, and she was greeted by

cool tile underfoot and the faint scent of lavender soap. With a sigh, she turned the knobs of the antique shower, listening as the pipes groaned to life behind the walls. Water splashed against porcelain, echoing gently in the tiled space. Steam began to rise, curling up toward the ceiling as the water warmed.

Jane's fingers fumbled for the zipper and she unzipped her black swing dress, letting it slip off her shoulders and down her body in a silken whisper. The red belt dropped beside it, a final accent against the cold tile floor. She removed her undergarments, placing them atop the dress.

She walked over to the mirror and picked up her floral-patterned shower bonnet, slipping it carefully over her pinned curls. The elastic hugged her head, securing the style she had spent so long perfecting earlier in the day. She gently adjusted it in the mirror, smoothing it into place. Her reflection looked back at her, still flawless, even in the dim light.

She took one final glance at the door, already half dreading the strange heaviness still lingering in the room and then stepped toward the rising steam. She proceeded to get in the shower and rinse off the night. The water was warm as it ran down her body, and she washed away the petrifying feeling from earlier. Her body froze in place when she thought she heard the door open. She wrapped her fingers around the curtain and tugged it open just enough to see into the bathroom, but nothing was there. She was clearly still on edge.

She grabbed her towel and wrapped it around herself before she opened the curtain. When she stepped onto the cold tile floor, she noticed a card slightly peeking out from underneath the door. She quickly grabbed it and realized it was one of Madame Zodo's tarot cards. It must have dropped when they were leaving the room. She flipped it over and stood in shock when what looked back at her was the tower card. Was this an accident, coincidence?

Her hand shook as she put the card on the sink, the shower had now done no good since she was sweating profusely. She did not want to die! She needed to leave this room now! She quickly grabbed her dress and threw it on, forgetting the undergarments entirely. She ripped the bonnet off her head and went to open the bathroom door with no success.

"No, No, No, No, No!" She yelled as she kept pulling the handle and shaking it. "This can't be happening!"

The sweat on her forehead was dripping into her eyes and making them sting. She rubbed one of her eyes with the back of her hand before going back to tug on the door. She was screaming for help, hoping someone would hear her and get someone from the check in counter.

After what seemed like an hour but was closer to ten minutes, she sat on the floor crying. Someone had to have heard her screaming for help. Right? Just then she heard the tub turn on and not just a trickle, it was pouring out of the faucet at full force. She stood up to turn it off but was perplexed when she looked down. The tub was not draining yet the stopper was still sitting on the sink.

The room was filling with steam, and the mirror had completely fogged up again. The bathroom was getting warmer, and the air was so thick it was getting hard to breathe.

That's when she felt it, an unmistakable presence behind her.

The air, already thick with steam and fear, suddenly turned icy, wrapping itself around her bare skin like a sheath. A shiver sliced down her spine, sharp and immediate, anchoring her to the spot. Every hair on her body stood on end.

Then came the breath.

It wasn't warm, human breath, it was cold, damp, and unnatural, brushing against the back of her neck in slow, deliberate waves. It lingered there, as if savoring her fear. Her breath hitched in her throat.

A moment later, she felt the strands of her hair being gently touched, as if invisible fingers were toying with them, curling them between cold digits. It was delicate. Almost affectionate. And somehow, that made it worse.

An impossibly cold, clammy hand pressed softly against the base of her neck. It moved with agonizing slowness, gliding down her shoulder, then her upper arm, its movements light, deliberate, and inescapably intimate. The skin it touched prickled with ice, like frostbite blooming beneath the surface. She could feel each finger, long and skeletal, dragging across her flesh.

Everything in her told her not to turn around. But she couldn't help it, she needed to see what was there. Slowly, cautiously, Jane began to turn. The mirror in front of her was completely fogged, the glass transformed into a murky, silver blur. It revealed nothing but distorted shapes and shadowy fog. Behind her, the steam coiled like smoke, cloaking the room in a pale mist that clung to the walls and hovered just above the floor.

It was like standing in a dream, or a nightmare, where the air was too still, too quiet, too watchful. She turned toward the bathroom door.

Nothing. No figure. No sign of movement. Just the same thick haze, humming pipes, and a silence that rang louder than any scream.

But sheknewsomething had touched her. That cold breath. That clammy hand. It wasn't imagined. It couldn't have been. Her body still trembled where it had been touched, her skin crawling with an invisible imprint.

Am I going mad?

She sat slowly on the edge of the tub, her towel clutched tightly around her. The porcelain beneath her felt slick and too warm. Her breath came in shallow bursts, her chest tight with confusion, fear, disbelief.

Was this what Madame Zodo had meant?

Tonight. Not someday. Tonight.

The words echoed in her mind like a curse.

Was this really it? Her final night alive?

Then came the push.

Sudden. Brutal. Invisible.

It felt like a gust of force, silent but impossibly strong, slamming into her.

She toppled into the tub.

She couldn't breathe. Her eyes opened but everything was warped as if she was looking through a fishbowl. Then it hit her, she was in the tub and she was drowning!

Panic ignited in her chest.

She tried to pull herself out, she braced her hands on the edges of the tub and pulled, but she couldn't move. She was being held down. Something was keeping her under. Hands she couldn't see were gripping her shoulders with iron force, pushing, anchoring, drowning her.

She thrashed wildly, limbs flailing, bubbles erupting from her mouth as she fought for breath that wouldn't come.

There was no one there. No onevisible.

She clawed at the air, at her own skin, trying to grasp what wasn't there, trying to fight back against the impossible.

Her lungs screamed.

Her chest convulsed.

The pressure mounted, a burning weight that wrapped around her like chains. Her vision narrowed. The water darkened. Her strength ebbed.

And then...Relief. This calmness came over her.

The invisible grip loosened. The weight lifted. The presence was gone.

With a violent gasp, she burst from the surface, flinging water into the air as her lungs expanded in a single, ragged, lifesaving breath. She choked, coughing, her entire body trembling from the shock. Soaked and shivering, she stumbled out of the tub, slipping on the slick tile, grabbing the sink to steady herself. She couldn't stay here. Shewouldn'tstay here.

She yanked the bathroom door open and sprinted into the room, her wet hair clinging to her face, her towel forgotten. Water trailing behind her.

She didn't bother with shoes. Or packing. Or dignity. She had to get out.

Now.

Chapter 3

Four days had passed since she had seen Jane Chapman in the hotel room, yet Madame Zodo couldn't stop thinking about her, that radiant woman in the black dress, cinched at the waist with a bold red belt and a smile that could've lit up even the darkest room. Jane had been vibrant, alive, full of curiosity and charm. But now, that smile haunted her.

Zodo sat alone in the quiet of her room, candlelight flickered throughout, her hands trembling as she held a cooling cup of tea she'd long forgotten to sip. The tarot deck lay untouched on the velvet table in front of her, as though even the cards feared what they might reveal.

Had she made it out of the hotel? Was she still alive? Had Jane listened to her warning?

Every time she tried to picture Jane in her mind, there was nothing. No images. No energy. Just a void, cold and silent. It was as if someone, or something, had cast a blanket of smoke over her memory, blotting out the light Jane once carried.

And then came the dreams.

Night after night, Zodo jolted awake, drenched in sweat, her heartbeat thundering in her ears. Always the same nightmare.

In the dreams the sequence was always the same, distorted, fragmented, but chillingly clear. It would begin with Jane and Betty, laughing softly, their hands resting lightly on the planchette of a Ouija board. Candlelight flickered around them. The air seemed calm, almost innocent. But even in the dream, Zodo could feel it, a heaviness lurking just beyond the glow.

As the girls whispered their questions into the shadows, the mood would shift. The warmth would vanish. The laughter would fade. And from the edge of the dream, a dark mist would begin to crawl in, slow and silent, as if it were watching.

The dark mist didn't speak. It didn't move. It simply stood behind them. A tall, shrouded silhouette, thick with shadow, darker than night itself. It radiated something ancient, something unnatural. Zodo couldn't see its face, except for the yellow glow of its eyes, the weight of its presence, and the way the candle flames trembled in response. She knew it was a Hollow One.

Then, always too quickly, the vision would change. Jane. In the bathtub. The water darkened with blood. Her head lolled back. Her eyes unblinking. Her body eerily still.

But just as quickly as Jane's face would be there, then these two new girls would take her place. It was blurry, undefined. They stood inside Room 1210, faces obscured by mist. Zodo couldn't see their features, couldn't place them in any time or context. Their clothes were wrong. They were not from her time period. They felt like echoes from a time that didn't exist yet.

And always, there was that name.

Zaron.

She always woke with it burning behind her eyes, like a brand she couldn't rub away. She'd hear it in the wind, would see it etched into her fogged mirrors, and worst of all, she would hear the tapping. Always the tapping. Soft, persistent:

Tap tap.

Zaron...

It was taunting her.

She was a woman gifted with foresight, vision, and power, but none of it mattered if the ones she tried to save wouldn't listen. And somehow, Zaron knew that. He was laughing at her, whispering through the cracks in her walls. The Hollow Ones knew they couldn't get to her, but they knew they could torment her by giving her images of people she could not save. She had to act. She needed answers. Who was Zaron and what did he want with the girls?

Zodo sat at her table, the tarot deck resting silently in front of her. She closed her eyes and inhaled deeply, her fingers brushing the worn edges of the cards.

"Show me why these visions won't stop," she whispered. "Who is Zaron? And why is he showing me these girls? Is he a Hollow One or a Demon?"

She shuffled slowly, deliberately, charging each motion with intent. As she pulled the first card, her hand trembled.

It was the Tower. Again, but this time... it had changed.

Two figures stood beneath the falling stones, but one had been scratched out, violently, as if someone had scratched the area with a blade. She had used the deck numerous times since she had left the hotel. The tower card had not been scratched any of those times. As her fingers brushed the card the memory of the hotel came to her.

She had just walked into the room with Betty. She could feel and see the presence of the spirit that stood in the corner. It was dark and misty, but she could slightly make out features that looked familiar, almost calming. When she tried to speak to the spirit in her mind it wouldn't say anything, but she didn't feel scared by the spirit, so she was sure at the time it was not a Hollow One.

As she settled in and began to read the cards for Jane, her mind told her something wasn't right. Every flip of the cards revealed only darkness. One by one, the cards whispered to her, no hope or future, only endings. Normally the visions of the persons future would flow freely, flashes of the persons path, echoes of moments to come but for Jane, there was nothing. The dark energy that stood in the corner seemed to laugh at Madame Zodo. As she focused harder on what she was feeling the blanket seemed to lift from her mind's eye. She now saw this spirit for what it was. It was most certainly a Hollow One, but this one seemed different. Stronger. She had never encountered a Hollow One like this before. She remembered reading about this one a long time ago, and hearing Madame Lynette speak of a stronger, more ancient one, but she never thought she would encounter one. Her hands were shaking, her mind was buzzing, she knew she needed to calm herself so that it couldn't feed on her fear. She closed her eyes, and grounded herself, controlling her breathing. When she opened her eyes, she looked at Jane. She remembered seeing the fear in Jane's eyes. Madame Zodo knew that no matter what she said to Jane, this Hollow One would consume her if Jane didn't leave the hotel room.

She remembered how she tried to warn her, but every time she spoke of the darkness in the room, the Hollow One stepped closer to Jane. She hoped if she scared Jane enough, that Jane would just leave the room with them. She remembered seeing the Hollow One standing inches from Jane and could feel this thing laughing at her.

As Betty had started ushering them out of the room, she

made one final decision. She unclasped her necklace and handed it to Jane. A talisman she had enchanted years ago. As long as she held onto the necklace, she wouldn't be able to be consumed by the Hollow One. She prayed that Jane would never let go of the necklace, because once the Hollow One chose you, they never let go.

Then out of nowhere the Hollow One was inside her mind, invading her consciousness. It had no true body, only the suggestion of one, formed from a dense fog that swirled around itself. The mist coiled and pulsed like something alive. In the heart of that churning darkness, two luminous yellow eyes cut through the void, cold, intelligent, and impossibly ancient. They didn't glow so much as burn. The creature's face was never still. Every time she tried to focus on it, the fog would shift, a suggestion of a face, the faint curve of a mouth, then it would shatter apart again, leaving only shifting shadows and the gleam of teeth. Those teeth were stark white and grotesquely sharp, dripping with dark thick blood.

The fog around it pulsed and expanded, seeping into the corners of her thoughts, making the air feel heavy. The Hollow One was not flesh. It was the embodiment of fear itself. A parasite born from terror, feeding on every scream, every racing heartbeat, and every cry.

What if Jane never made it out? What if she'd been consumed by that thing... that presence she'd felt in the room that day? Her heart ached remembering how awful that energy felt.

She clutched her arms to still their shaking as the tapping returned, louder this time, closer.

Tap tap.

It whispered so lightly, "Jacqueline."

She knew better than to let this creature scare her, it had no power here.

"Enough," she yelled, backing away from the table. "Enough of this. I am not afraid of you. You must leave this house."

She grabbed her double-edged dagger with the black handle, and drew a circle around herself and her altar. Then she sat at her altar, a narrow wooden space near the window lined with jars of herbs, oils, crystals, and many candles.

Tonight, she would find a way to protect the girls from her nightmares. She needed to find a way to let them know of the darkness in room 1210. If her nightmares were correct and they were premonitions of what was to come, they needed to know what they were facing, she needed to warn them.

She poured out her herbs of mug wort, wormwood, and rosemary, carefully forming a sigil on the altar. She lit each of the four candles, north, south, east, and west, until the air shimmered with sacred light. Then she poured oil on the fifth and final candle. Clutching her smoky quartz in her left hand, she lit the final wick and whispered:

"Candle burning precious light,

Bring to me this very night,

Wisdom bless my tongue, my lips,

Your guidance at my fingertips.

Let no shadow twist my sight,

Let the truth be cast in light.

Take this message through the flame,

To those who must outrun the name.

So mote it be."

With shaking hands, she picked up the Tower card and held it over the flame. As the edges blackened and curled, she whispered again and again, louder with every repetition:

"Let them see. Let them see. Let them see."

Smoke curled around her like fingers as she closed her eyes and meditated, casting her vision into the future. This time, the girls came into view, clearer than ever before. One blonde. One brunette. Both afraid. Both screaming.

Room 1210.

She poured her will into the space between worlds, begging the universe to let her message pass through, even if she would not live to see them hear it.

That night, she tried to sleep, she was exhausted, but her dreams were worse than ever.

She saw Jane again. Standing in Room 1210, shaking, whispering one word repeatedly as the shadows seemed to devour her:

"Zaron... Zaron... Zaron..."

Then came the two girls, backs pressed to the wall, eyes wild, their mouths open in a silent scream, chains dangling from their wrists.

Zodo woke before the end, and for the first time in years, she cried.

II

Part Two

Chapter 4

Summer of 2024

Brittany tapped the mic, "Is this thing on?"

Jules stared at the computer, "Yup, everything looks good."

Brittany: "Alright my banshee babes and geeky ghouls, we are back with another podcast episode."

Jules: "We got the privilege of investigating the very popular haunted house in Bucksport, Maine. The house of Jonathan Jenkins."

Brittany: "It was awesome, and spooky and you get to hear about this experience right from us."

Jules: "So, we pull up to the house, and this old gentleman comes out, limping his way down the stairs to our car."

Brittany: "It was very Willy Wonka-ish, when he comes out of the chocolate factory."

Jules: "As he greets us, he starts telling us that we need to be extra careful and that we need to make sure we cleanse ourselves before we go in."

Brittany: "The house was an old farmhouse, it was huge, cracked paint, cobwebs, and that musty smell that brings you back to your grandparent's homes, hashtag haunted house vibes."

Jules: "He told us we were more than welcome to walk

anywhere in the house we wanted, but that he would not be here. He said his daughter was taking him to her house for the night."

Brittany: "It was awesome, we had the whole place to ourselves and caught some amazing things. The moment we walked in lights started flickering, doors would shut on a level of the house you weren't on, knocks on the walls."

Jules: "Let's get into what happened from the start of the day, and the six hours we stayed there."

The girls went into their podcast episode talking about the orbs they caught, the shadows they swore were passing in front of windows, and the rocking chair in the living room that rocked on it own. The girls bantered back and forth, making jokes to keep the podcast light and just enjoying retelling their adventure.

Brittany: "Alright guys, thanks for listening in and enjoy the pictures we will post for you on our website."

Jules: "Stay creepy everyone and as always, make sure you follow the creepy thing into the woods. Bye guys!"

The girls giggled in unison as Jules hit the pause option on the computer screen. Brittany got up from the table and made her way to the kitchen, "Hey, I'm going to make a burrito. You want one Jules?"

"Absolutely girl, I will never say no to food."

Brittany and Jules had been friends for years, from going to middle school together, camp, high school, and then their paranormal journeys.

Brittany stands at 5'8", with porcelain skin and long, straight brunette hair that cascades down her back like a curtain of silk. She is the kind of girl who turns heads without even trying, blessed with striking light brown eyes that seem to glow in the right light, perfectly sculpted cheekbones, and full lips. Her figure is the kind that makes other girls do a double take, not out of envy, but awe. Brittany is the confident, magnetic one. She is always the first to walk into the room, fearless, no matter what might be lurking on the other side. If there was something waiting in the dark, she'd face it head on, no hesitation. She had been Jules' unofficial bodyguard for as long as either of them could remember, the one who always stepped between her and danger, even when the danger wasn't entirely human.

Jules, on the other hand, is the adorable girl next door. She is 5'3", with long, wavy blonde hair that bounces when she laughs. She is soft in the right places with natural curves. Her full cheeks, giving her a sweet charm that makes people instantly trust her. Jules is warmth and wit wrapped in a hoodie. She is also the one who cracks a joke about everything, sometimes to the point of being totally obnoxious, but most of the time, she is just downright hilarious. The kind of funny that sneaks up on you and has you laughing until your stomach hurts. She is the life of the group, the comic relief when things get tense. Yet she is also the biggest scaredy cat of the duo. If something creaks in the dark, she is already halfway to the car. Jules has no shame in shoving Brittany into a room first and hiding behind her like human armor.

These two girls are obsessed with Halloween and everything spooky. So, starting a paranormal investigation podcast was a no brainer. They were the perfect duo for it too. Both girls had always dreamed of traveling, but the fact that they could explore haunted places, dive into forgotten histories, and maybe even get paid for it someday? That was the ultimate win.

There was a fire in them every time they hit the road, a shared thrill in stepping into the unknown. From abandoned hospitals to remote graveyards, their passion pulsed in every investigation. What truly fueled them wasn't just the spooky stories, it was a chance to uncover the past, to prove that something does linger, that spirits might still walk among us, and that death isn't always the end.

Everywhere they went, people could tell they were the real deal. Their excitement was infectious, but more than that, it was clear how much they cared. They treated each location and each spirit with the utmost respect. For them, it was never about exploiting the supernatural for views or scares. It was about giving voice to the voiceless. Remembering the forgotten. And honoring those who still had something to say from beyond the veil.

A couple of years ago, the girls had traded the crowded back roads of Connecticut for the quiet wilderness of Maine. They now shared a cozy house tucked deep in the boondocks, where the nearest neighbor was over a mile away and the silence stretched on for miles. It was everything they'd hoped for. Peaceful, eerie, and just remote enough to feel like they were living inside a Stephen King novel. For two ghost chasing, thrill seeking podcasters, it was the perfect home base.

Jules and Brittany sat cross-legged on the soft carpet of Jules' dimly lit bedroom, their legs barely brushing, a sense of familiarity and comfort between them that needed no words. The faint crackle of incense danced through the air, its smoky tendrils curling like ghosts toward the ceiling. Frankincense, Jules' favorite. It always made the room feel like some sacred little hideaway. In the background, Fleetwood Mac played softly from a Bluetooth speaker, Stevie Nicks' voice weaving spells of its own.

Between them sat Jules' beloved tarot deck, worn at the edges from years of pulling cards for friends, family, and occasionally, strangers who needed answers more than she did.

"Okay," Brittany said, stretching her arms overhead before letting them flop down dramatically, "are we going to be massively popular with our podcast?"

Jules raised an eyebrow, a playful grin tugging at her lips as she began shuffling the cards. The soft rustle of card stock filled the air like a whisper. After a moment, she cut the deck and laid the top card down on the floor.

The Ace of Pentacles.

Brittany leaned in. "That's a good one, right?"

Jules beamed. "It's the best one for new beginnings and success. This is literally the universe giving us a gold coin. We're going to be amazing, Britt. Just you wait."

Brittany grinned. "I'll take it. Okay, next question. Am I finally going to find love? Like actual love, not some awkward Hinge disaster."

Wagging her eyebrows, she watched as Jules gathered the cards again and gave them another thoughtful shuffle.

"Let's see what fate says," Jules murmured. She flipped another card.

Two of Cups.

"Well, well," Jules said, holding it up like a treasure. "Look at that."

"Ooooh, what's it mean?" Brittany asked, leaning in, already excited.

"It means connection. Union. Maybe even soulmates," Jules said, winking. "It signifies a strong emotional bond, the beginning of something meaningful. You better get ready to be swept off your feet by prince charming."

Brittany fanned herself dramatically. "Finally! Maybe my love life won't be a horror movie subplot after all."

They both burst into laughter.

"One more," Brittany said, her voice softening. "Will we be best friends forever?"

Jules paused, resting her hand gently on the top of the deck. "I don't need a card for that one," she said with a crooked smile. "You're stuck with me, Britt. For life."

Brittany laughed. "Damn right I am."

Jules started to shuffle the cards again, but one slipped from her fingers and fluttered to the floor, landing face-up between them. The Tower.

Both girls froze.

The playful atmosphere dulled for a beat, the music fading into the background like it knew to quiet down.

They stared at the card, the jagged lightning bolt splitting the dark tower in two, people tumbling from its windows.

Jules was the first to move, scooping the card up quickly and stuffing it back into the middle of the deck with a forced laugh. "I'm so clumsy."

Brittany narrowed her eyes. "What does that one mean again?"

Jules hesitated, then gave a vague smile. "It symbolizes sudden change. Danger. Collapse. But it's not all bad. Sometimes things have to fall apart so better things can be built. It's a wake-up call."

"Well then," Brittany said with a smirk, trying to shake the chill crawling up her spine, "maybe it means all of your weird habits are finally going to come to an end."

Jules scoffed and grabbed a nearby throw pillow, lobbing it at Brittany. "Shut up, jerk."

"You know you love me," Brittany said, laughing.

"Pet peeves and all," Jules replied, sticking out her tongue. Their laughter returned, light and familiar. It chased the darkness out of the corners again.

Then Fleetwood Mac's Rhiannon started playing, and Jules gasped. "Oooh this one's my favorite!" she squealed, turning the volume up slightly. She rose to her feet and began spinning around the room, her arms moving in slow, perfect movements as if she were a makeshift witch casting spells.

Brittany laughed and pulled out her phone, immediately recording. "This is a memory I never want to forget," she said, smiling as the camera caught the glow on Jules' face.

"You better watch it," Jules teased, twirling, her voice playful. "Your phone is going to crack and then what will you do?"

"That would never happen because of you." Brittany replied firmly, capturing Jules in motion, a glowing soul, full of magic, light, and joy. Her laughter filled the room, her smile stretching wide and wild.

This was who she was. The girl who saw the best in everyone. The kind of person who could make even a haunted house feel like home.

"Come on, Britt," Jules said suddenly, reaching down and grabbing her friend's hand. "Dance with me."

With a roll of her eyes and a dramatic sigh, Brittany stood up, allowing herself to be twirled into Jules' arms. The two of them danced like they were spinning through their own little universe, the incense, the music, the tarot cards, and their laughter braiding together into something sacred. The girls fell to the floor laughing. "Oh my gosh my stomach hurts so bad." Brittany said holding herself.

"I know. Mine is killing me." Jules said still laughing.

Later that night Brittany sat in an over sized hoodie and leggings with little cartoon ghosts on them. Her fingers absentmindedly pulled at a loose thread while Jules sat behind her, braiding purple ribbon into her hair.

"Do you think ghosts sleep?" Brittany asked suddenly, staring up at the ceiling, where plastic stars still glowed faintly from the '90s.

Jules paused mid-braid, her brow furrowing in thought. "Probably not," she said finally. "Why else would they be up at 3 AM knocking stuff over and turning TV's on?"

They both burst into laughter, but as the giggles faded, a calm silence settled between them, the kind that only best friends know how to sit in.

"I think when I die," Jules said quietly, laying back and folding her arms behind her head, "I'd stay. Not in a creepy way. Just... close by. I'd want to make sure the people I love were okay. I'd turn their favorite songs on the radio or push their lucky coin into their pocket. You know, thoughtful ghost stuff."

Brittany lay down beside her and blinked up at the ceiling. "I'd want to be with you," she whispered.

Jules turned her head. "Always?"

"Always."

They pinky promised right then, fingers linked tightly between them, two girls with all the time in the world and boundless dreams.

"I wonder if ghosts can keep secrets," Brittany said.

Jules laughed, soft and sleepy. "Probably not, any ghost

shows we've watched, the ghosts seem to tell all."

"Well even in the afterlife you better keep all of mine." Brittany said chuckling.

"Always Britt." Jules said smiling.

Brittany turned her head to glance at Jules, her voice calm, laced with warmth.

"Do you remember the one and only time we fought?"

Jules blinked a few times, her lips curling into a grin. "Oh my god," she said, already laughing, "I seriously thought it was going to be the end of us. I remember crying into my stupid polka-dot pillow. All because of *Johnny freaking Lester.*"

"Ugh. Johnny Lester," Brittany groaned, covering her face with her hands. "What was wrong with us? We thought he was this hot ticket, like he was some kind of teen heartthrob sent straight from the gods."

"We were fourteen," Jules said, laughing harder now, "and apparently delusional. We were convinced we had found gold just because he wore a leather jacket and used Axe body spray."

"Thank god we realized fast that he was also flirting with Claire Barton." Jules said, wiping a tear of laughter from her eye.

"Ugh, Claire," Brittany said, glaring at the ceiling. "He told me he thought I was the most beautiful girl and then an hour later, told Claire she was the only girl for him. What a turd."

"A giant turd," Jules confirmed, nodding seriously. "Honestly, I think we should've thanked him. He brought us closer."

"Yeah," Brittany said, her voice quieting. She rolled onto her side and reached across the popcorn bag.

"I'm really glad we didn't let that break us up," she said softly. "That could've been one of those dumb friend ending moments, but... it wasn't."

Jules smiled, her eyes a little glassy now. "Of course it wasn't. Not even the great Johnny Lester could come between us."

Brittany chuckled. "Still, I'm sorry I got so mad. I really thought he was choosing me."

"I was just scared you'd beat me to kissing someone first," Jules teased, grinning. "I mean, that would've been criminal. You always win at everything."

"Yeah well, you win at being the best damn best friend on Earth," Brittany said with a wink.

Jules laughed. "Love you, chick."

"Love you more."

Jules lay there quietly beside Brittany, she looked over at Brittany who was sleeping hard, snoring softly. Jules smiled to herself, she was so thankful for her best friend. They had been through so much together and Jules didn't know if she would be who she is today if it hadn't been for their close friendship. They had grown up together and had a lifetime of memories. Jules remembered how Brittany had been there for her after her parents' tragedy and the moment that brought them even closer as friends.

***

Flashback: Summer 2004

Jules was woken up by her uncle Lenny softly shaking her. "Jules, I'm going to need you to get up, you're going to come home with me and Aunt Brenda tonight."

Jules rubbed her eyes, and her vision cleared. "Uncle Lenny? What are you doing here?"

He looked pale, his mouth opened, then closed again. He knelt down to her level before he finally spoke. "I have some bad news sweetheart. Your mom and dad were in a bad car accident. They didn't make it Jules."

Jules sat there confused, what he was saying didn't make sense. It couldn't be true. They were supposed to be home already, asleep in their bed. "Uncle Lenny, I think you're wrong. They're in their room."

Her uncle just bowed his head and shook his head slowly. "I'm so sorry sweetie. They didn't make it."

Jules wasn't sure she even understood what was going on. She just got up from bed and grabbed some clothes, stuffed them into a bag and took her uncles hand as they made their way out to the car. The whole ride to her uncle and aunts house she stared out the window completely numb. She figured this was all a misunderstanding and that her parents would come pick her up the next morning.

When they got to the house, her Aunt Brenda ran out of the house. She grabbed Jules and held her tight. "I am so sorry Jules." Her aunt held her tighter as she felt her aunts body shake lightly as if she was crying.

Jules didn't return the hug. She just walked into the house not fully aware this was happening.Her aunt had fixed up the couch for her, and she laid Jules down and covered her up. "I promise, we will clean out the extra room tomorrow so you can have your own room." She said gently, then kissed her on the forehead before walking down the hall. Jules watched her walk away, listening to her lightly sobbing.

Jules woke up the next morning expecting her parents to pull into the driveway. She stared out the window all day just hoping and waiting. She knew her parents' car would pull in any minute, her dad honking the horn, her mom getting out smiling and waving as she looked at Jules through the living room window.

Aunt Brenda broke through the day dream. "Jules, I cleaned out the spare bedroom and Uncle Lenny went and grabbed a bunch of your stuff from the house."

Jules looked at Aunt Brenda and felt confused and angry. "Why would you do that? Why would you take stuff from my room. My mom and dad will be back, and they will be pissed you went in their house without being asked."

Aunt Brenda didn't say a word. She just wiped her eye and slowly turned towards her room. Jules was so mad that they just assumed her parents were going to be gone forever. They were coming back for her, they had to, they were just stuck in traffic or lost.

Day after day Jules sat in front of the window watching the driveway and hoping. Her aunt and uncle tried to make her days fun, they bought her a small inflatable pool and a new bike, they tried to have movie nights and days at the zoo with her but every day she just stared out the window and every night she sat in bed hoping tomorrow would be the day. She didn't want to do anything. She didn't want to believe they were actually gone. She did not want to have fun without them.

Then came the first day of school as a fifth grader.She walked into school, and she felt like everyone was staring at her. She hated this feeling. She could hear the whispers behind her back that she was an orphan now.

But then she heard her name, "Jules!"

She looked up to see Brittany walking towards her, smiling wide. "I missed you. So glad the summers over and I'm back from camp." Brittany said cheerfully.

Jules just gave her a small smile and kept on moving towards her class. "I know you don't want to talk about it, my parents told me when I got home. I don't want you to feel like everyone is only talking about that, so I didn't want to bring it up, but if you wanna talk... I am always here." Brittany said.

Jules stopped for a second and looked at her and smiled. "I know Britt, Thank you. Right now I just want to go to class and have a normal day."

Brittany walked beside her, her arm entwined in Jules, both of them quiet, just walking. It was exactly what Jules needed. Just peace and quiet and her normal structure of school.Everyday Brittany just sat with her, quietly hanging out with Jules. No pressure, no prying. She didn't try to fix Jules. She was just there.

One day at lunch Brittany came over to the table. Jules sat there, tears sliding down her cheeks. Brittany knew a hug or speaking would be too much for Jules, so she took out her pudding cup and sat it on the table next to Jules. Jules looked over at Brittany with a small smile, grabbed the cup and peeled the foil top and slowly ate it. It tasted like childhood, and it was comforting.

Brittany gave up her pudding cup every day to Jules just to see her smile. Jules had never felt so loved by someone since her parents, and that small gesture stitched something in Jules back together she never thought could be fixed.

***

Back to the present

Jules watched Brittany as she lightly snored in her sleep. She would never forget how much Brittany meant to her and what she did for her. "I never say it enough," Jules whispered. "But I wouldn't have survived without you."

She closed her eyes, feeling at peace, Brittany had given her more than just pudding cups and quiet comfort. Brittany had shown her unconditional love just by being there when most people had kept their distance.She always missed her parents but knew she had won the friendship jackpot by getting to be Brittany's best friend. And she would make sure Brittany never forgot how thankful she was to have her in her life. Brittany would never feel alone ever.

Chapter 5

Ding.

Brittany was woken up by her phone going off. She rubbed at her eyes and stared at the screen groggily. The time said 8 a.m. She groaned as she tapped the screen.

The message was from one of her Facebook group friends, "You have to investigate Devil's Hopyard. Trust me, this place was awesome."

Brittany went into the kitchen to show Jules the message. The smell of coffee already permeated the air. "Jules, we've got a new spot to look at." She handed her the phone.

As soon as Jules saw the name, her heart jumped. Devil's Hopyard was one of their favorite places growing up. They'd hiked its trails countless times, had lazy summer picnics by the falls, and camped out as kids. It wasn't just another haunted location. It was personal.

"Oh my gosh Brittany, this is going to be awesome! We love it there."

"I know, right? Some of our best memories are of being there. I figured since we already took the week off from work we should go, plus I may have already booked a site for tonight."

Jules squealed. "Sweet, and I thought we were just going to veg out on the couch the whole time."

Without hesitation, they both ran to their rooms and packed their gear, shoving clothes and ghost gear in their bags quicker than they had ever packed before. Then they hopped in the car, and made the familiar drive back to East Haddam, Connecticut. Back to the place where adventure had once meant nothing more than a trail and a waterfall... and now maybe, something much more.

The drive from Maine to Connecticut was filled with red bull, random playlists, and excited chatter.

"Can you believe we are actually going back to Connecticut, but not just anywhere in Connecticut, Devils Hopyard!" Jules said, practically squealing with excitement.

"I know right! This is going to be awesome, we haven't camped there in years."

"The history of this place is the best Brittany. Listen to this. Devil's Hopyard actually got its name from a man who once lived there a long time ago. He was a hop farmer who also brewed his own beer nearby. His last name was Dibble."

"So basically, this place got its name because people played the telephone game." Brittany said chuckling.

"Exactly. It went from Dibble's Hopyard to Devils Hopyard. Then came the lore that the name originated from the puritans who believed whole heartedly that the Devil existed and that he would come down to the Hopyard and sit at the top of Chapman Falls and watch the witches of the time cast spells in Chapman's pool."

"And of course we all know how much satanic cults love anything with the name Devil in it." Brittany said sarcastically.

"You know it, people would come here and do rituals, sacrifice animals, and play with Ouija boards and other divination tools, trying to contact the Devil himself, and BAM! You now have a place full of hauntings because people conjured them to the area. Nobody knows for certain if the Devil really did come down and hang out, but you can bet on your life something definitely lurks in the woods now."

"Ooh how spooky," Brittany said. "Guess we will find out for certain tonight."

As they crossed into Connecticut, the familiar roads triggered a rush of memories for both of them. The trees grew thicker as they approached the entrance to Devils Hopyard State Park. The towering limbs of the trees casting long shadows across the narrow road. It was just how they remembered it and yet, the silence seemed deeper, more watchful.

They parked at the campsite they would be staying at for the night. The smell of moss, pine, and earth wrapping around them like a familiar blanket.

"This is wild." Jules said, stretching and straightening out her shirt. "It's like stepping back into a memory."

Brittany smiled, slinging her backpack over her shoulder. "A memory with a paranormal twist."

They set up their tent and then walked over to Chapman Falls. As they got closer, the sound of rushing water from the falls and the feel of the mist in the air filled their senses. They walked over to the bridge that looked down on Chapman falls. Jules and Brittany stood with their arms resting on the bridge's ledge. They turned their mics on, and Jules hit the recording button on her phone.

Podcast Recording - 4

(Recording begins. Static. Then the familiar hum of a Red Bull being cracked open.)

Brittany chuckled and started it off. "Hello fellow spooky ghouls and gals!"

"We are the Banshee Seekers" (They stated in unison).

"I'm Jules"

"And I'm Brittany, and we are coming to you live from deep inside Connecticut's favorite demon infested picnic area: Devil's Hopyard!"

Jules snorted. "Demon infested picnic area? That's the energy we're starting with? Oh, I am definitely going to need more than one drink and now possibly a hot dog."

"Of course you want a hot dog."

Brittany and Jules broke out into laughter.

Brittany took a deep breath to calm the giggles before speaking again. "My energy is from being exhausted. We danced all night to Stevie Nicks and then you made me listen to EVP recordings for hours and then I was woken up early by a friend who said we had to investigate here."

"And it was worth it. They definitely said your name in that EVP." Jules said excitedly.

"They said 'burrito.'"

"Which coincidentally is what you were eating. Spirits know your snack of choice, Brittany."

They were both lost in laughter once again.

"OK." Jules said, wiping her eyes. "Let's get back on topic. So we are standing at the top of Chapman Falls. Gorgeous evening, the suns fading and giving us a beautiful sunset, the water is crashing down like something out of a painting... and this is the spot where the Devil himself supposedly came down and just...sat. Right on top of these falls.

"Like a grumpy little demon tourist."

"Exactly! And the story goes, he dipped his tail in the water, got mad that it got wet, and threw a full-on tantrum. Stomped his hooves in the pool at the bottom of the falls, and that's how those scorched looking marks got left in the rocks that look like his footprints."

"Ooh." Brittany said holding her pointer finger in the air. "Fun fact. It might not have been the Devil at all. The area used to be called Dibble's Hopyard, after this guy whose last name was Dibble and he grew hops nearby for beer. Total normal farmer. But over time, you know how people are... someone misheard it, passed it along, and suddenly 'Dibble' became 'Devil'. Like a spooky game of telephone."

"I love that."

"Right? Re brand your farm as a satanic landmark, and suddenly everyone's interested."

"Yes! But back to the spooky. There's also this legend of the lady in white. People say she walks along the river near the falls, looking for something she will never find."

Brittany interjected and spoke in a spooky voice. "But no one knows what. Not a name, not a face. Just... searching."

"Which is honestly so sad. Imagine wandering forever but not ever being able to find it. It's like me trying to find my car keys. I walk into the kitchen to look for them and then forget why I'm in the kitchen."

Brittany rolled her eyes and said sarcastically. "Yeah, just like that, Jules. Exactly like that."

Jules laughed. "Okay fine, maybe not eternal ghost sorrow, but still same concept."

"We are going to head down the path to the bottom of the falls. The sound of the water, the mist, the mossy rocks, it's got that perfect Instagram hiking girl vibe."

"Except a lot of people report feeling weird here. Like, in a trance almost. Just staring at the water like it is pulling them in."

"Or maybe they're just high on reefer." Brittany said with a mischievous lift of her eyebrows.

"Brittany!" Jules said laughing.

"I'm just saying. People in Connecticut be lighting up on trails."

Just then Jules put her hand up and froze. "Did you hear that? It sounded like someone crying." Jules whispered.

"It has to be the water playing tricks Jules."

"Maybe. But there are rumors of people doing seances here, trying to summon demons with Ouija boards. And not the friendly demons either. Maybe there's a chance I really am hearing something."

And then Jules heard it again. But this time, it wasn't just in the general area. It felt like she was crying right into her ear.

"OK, That's it." Jules said, her voice cracking. "We're leaving!" She hit the stop button on the recording.

As they turned to leave, they saw her. The lady in white. A faint, misty figure at the edge of the falls. She was just standing there. She looked so sad, her head slumped a little, her shoulders leaned in, it looked as if she was crying. Then the air got heavy, it felt like they couldn't breathe, and Brittany felt this intense sadness out of nowhere.

And then the lady vanished quickly as if she had never been there. But the footprints did not. The girls watched wet, bare footprints appear in the dirt. Like someone was walking right towards them.

"Yeah, not a huge fan of phantom footprints coming towards us." Jules said with a shaky voice.

"Yeah, me neither, let's go back to the safety of our campsite."

They booked it back to the tent, running as fast as they could.

Brittany looked over her shoulder but didn't see anything following them. "Come on Jules, we are almost there."

Jules could feel herself slowing down, her chest was burning, and she could barely breath. She started to slow down a little and was about to just start walking when she heard a twig snap in the woods next to her. She slowed down a little more to try and see what made the noise but then twigs started snapping faster as if something was running after her. "Oh, hell no, I'm not getting dragged into the creepy forest by a sad lady." Jules pushed herself as much as she could, pushing past Brittany and seeing the road for the campsite right in front of them.

Their shoes crunched on the rocky path of the campground, both of them out of breath. When they finally caught their breath, they slowly made their walk to campsite ten. "You would pick the campsite that is farthest away." Jules said chuckling.

"Makes it a little bit spookier, at the time that sounded perfect. Not so much now that my legs feel like Jello."

The girls giggled now that they had got far enough away. Then they started buzzing with excitement. "We saw a real ghost. Not a light. Not a trick of the night. An actual apparition." Jules stated excitedly.

"This one...this one we will never forget." Brittany said.

The girls walked into their campsite lost in deep thought over the white lady and what may happen throughout the night.

"You don't think anything else will happen tonight, do you?" Jules asked nervously.

"Honestly, I really hope not. I don't mind seeing or hearing things, but I don't want to wake up to anything. That to me is more terrifying than anything."

Darkness crept over the campsite, and it was so quiet that

the sound seemed to echo louder than normal. As Jules' shoes crunched on the dirt her hands started to shake as her mind went crazy thinking about spending the night in the dark with only a tent to keep them safe. Her imagination was running wild and making her even more scared. As Jules looked at the tent, she swore she saw a shadow dart in front of it.

"Brittany, did you see anything in front of the tent?"

"No, why. What did you see?" Brittany asked nervously.

"I thought I saw a shadow but at this point I know I am probably just freaking myself out. My imagination is getting the better of me."

"I'm sure you're right. We will make a campfire and eat some tasty sticky s'mores until we pass out." Brittany said trying to lighten the mood.

Brittany crouched in front of the fire pit, lighting up the toilet paper rolls filled with lint they had brought as their makeshift fire starters. Jules could hear the crackle of the lint starting to ignite. She loved that sound and started to relax a little and take her mind off of what they had seen earlier. Jules went back to the car, popped the trunk open and grabbed the two camping chairs. As she slung the chair bags over her shoulder she froze.

Jules

It was a whisper, soft, unmistakable. Her hair rose on her arms and her heart started to quicken. She looked around but all she saw was darkness all around her. Nothing moved, there was no wind. No animal noises, nothing. Just complete darkness and silence. Her feet moved a little faster as she made her way back to where Brittany was at the fire pit.

"Hey Britt, do you think it's weird that it's so quiet here? There are not even animal noises."

"Honestly, I wasn't even paying attention." Brittany looked up and towards the forest in front of her. Her head swiveled left and then right listening to the eerie silence. "You're right. It's too quiet, as if someone muted the sound."

"I'm just going to throw some music on, I need to bring this place to life." Jules grabbed her phone and clicked on her camping playlist she had made. Green Day came from her phone's speaker. She set the phone down on the picnic table and grabbed the chairs to set them up near the now crackling fire that Brittany had created.

Jules sat down, her eyes getting lost in the flames. Brittany sat next to her, poking at the fire. It almost seemed as if they were in a dome cut off from the rest of the world. There were no other campers near them, there didn't seem to be any animals awake making noise. It was just the crackle of the fire and the low volume of punk music from Jules' phone.

Brittany looked out at the forest, dark and ominous. She swore she saw movement in between the trees. Her eyes fixated on the spot for a moment, but then nothing. She shook her head and blinked a couple of times. She knew she was letting her imagination get the better of her. She went back to poking the fire, losing herself in the crackle and heat.

Brittany

Brittany's head shot up, she knew she heard the whisper. In between the trees she could see misty fog, but as quickly as she saw the fog it seemed to dissipate. "Jules, do you see anything in the trees? Or hear anything?"

Jules looked into the forest but only saw darkness. "No, did you?"

Brittany didn't answer, she just stared into the woods, waiting.

Crackkk

A twig cracked behind them. Both girls jumped up and spun around, staring into the forest behind them. Nothing. Just darkness.

"We are completely freaking ourselves out Brittany. It was probably just a squirrel."

"Why don't we go check it out? We do always say if you see something creepy in the woods, follow it."

"That's just a funny quip to say at the ending, you don't actually do that. That's how people die in horror movies."

"Yeah, you're right. It's more likely a squirrel or raccoon, not something coming for us."

"Exactly. We have no reason to be scared over here. Plus, it's s'mores time."

The girls grabbed the marshmallows and stabbed them onto their sticks. They giggled and joked about being scaredy cats and talked about the cool experiences they had from other investigations and slowly the fear of the darkness eased. Soon the only sounds were of the girls laughing as they picked on each other and the sound of music floating through the air.

"I'm pooped," Jules said in a yawn "I'm going to bed."

"I'm right there with you, this has been quite the day and mentally I'm drained." Brittany stretched her arms out wide, smacking Jules playfully.

Jules laughed and slapped her playfully back before jumping up and running towards the tent. Brittany tossed dirt on the fire watching as the fire died and the light darkened around her. The hair on her neck stood straight up and she got a tingle that ran down her spine. It felt as if someone was standing behind her, watching. She spun around. Nothing, just darkness.

"That is it, I am going to bed, I am freaking myself out." She muttered to herself as she quickly made her way into the tent.

They both laid there snuggled in their sleeping bags, the only sound came from the battery powered fans. They slowly drifted off into sleep, but the girls didn't feel alone that night, yet neither of the girls would say that out loud, because they both knew, the moment they acknowledged whatever this was, it was not going to let them sleep.

Jules

Jules shot up, she knew she heard her name. She rubbed her eyes and looked around the dark tent. Nothing was in there with them, and other than the fans it was silent. She looked over at Brittany who was sleeping like a rock. She grabbed her phone to check the time and was annoyed that it was 3:10am and she was awake.

Crackkkk

Jules' heart started racing as she heard the crack of a stick coming from outside the tent. Her eyes scanned the walls of the tent but couldn't see any movements coming from outside.

Then came the sound of footsteps all around. It seemed to be encircling the tent. "Brittany!" Jules whispered and then shook her. "Brittany!"

"What?" Brittany groaned as she rolled over hoping Jules would let her sleep longer.

"There's someone walking around our tent." Jules whispered with a shaky voice.

Brittany opened her eyes slightly. Then she heard it. The shuffle of footsteps walking around the tent. Brittany shot up and stared at Jules as she mouthed the words "What the fuck."

"I don't know." Jules mouthed back.

Brittany grabbed Jules' hand as they listened to the footsteps encircle the tent. Whatever it was circled the tent three times.

Then nothing.

Complete silence, even the fans stopped working.

The girls looked at each other, fear in their eyes. Their hands were shaking as they held each other tighter.

Then they heard another sound.

Weeping.

"The white lady" Jules mouthed.

The weeping seemed to get closer to the tent but once it seemed to be right outside the tent it stopped. Then they heard what sounded like someone had turned on a faucet full blast. It didn't make sense to the girls because there was no water near the campsite.

"What the fuck is going on?" Brittany whispered.

Jules just shook her head. She wasn't sure she wanted to know.

Crackkkkk.

Another twig snapped near the front of the tent.

"That zipper better stay put." Brittany whispered, her voice trembling.

The fans powered back on, and Green Day blared loudly from Jules' phone. Both girls screamed as Jules rummaged through her small pile of clothes looking for the phone. She flipped her pillow out of the way frantically.

"Where is my phone?" She muttered loudly to herself.

Jules jumped out of the sleeping bag and threw the sleeping bag out of the way. The bright light of the phone lit up the tent, and she slammed her finger on the pause icon.

The tent went completely silent. No music. No fans. Just the girls breathing heavily. After a couple of seconds of hearing nothing, Jules grabbed her sleeping bag and put it back in place and slid inside. The girls didn't talk, they just listened. And listened.

Silence. Dead silence.

No crickets. No animals. No more weeping. No twigs breaking. No fans.

The girls laid there, hands intertwined in each other's, just breathing heavily and praying for morning to come.

Chapter 6

The morning after their trip to Devil's Hopyard, the girls were back at Brittany's moms' house. The energy from the night before had faded into a kind of dreamy buzz, the kind that always followed an investigation. Part adrenaline, part exhaustion. Neither girl talked about what they had heard in the tent or the hoof prints that were seen encircled outside the tent that morning. Neither girl seemed to want to believe what may have visited them in the night. Yet as scared as they were last night, they also knew that they were proving to themselves that more than just the living walked the earth and it made them more determined to keep looking and prove to others that when you died, that was not the end.

The late afternoon sun filtered lazily through the living room windows, casting golden streaks across the couch where Jules was sprawled, phone in hand, endlessly scrolling.

"I swear," she groaned, "finding a haunted place that a million people haven't already investigated is getting harder and harder."

Brittany, perched on the arm of the couch, sipping her second Red Bull of the day, nodded in agreement. "It really is. And everyone just cuts and pastes the same history repeatedly. Toss in some half-baked EVP clips and a few sarcastic jokes.

It's all so... overdone."

Jules flicked her thumb across the screen. "Reddit's literally a dumpster fire, but hopefully it will cough up gold."

Jules saw a post that caught her attention. "Dude," Jules said excitedly. "Listen to this creepy ass rhyme someone wrote.

'The Hollow One's creep, the Hollow One's crawl,
They crawl through the cracks of the darkest hall.
They feed on your fear. they whisper your name.
They twist what you see, they play their sick game.
He takes your voice, he steals your cries,
He paints your dreams with crawling lies.
Round and round your mind they spin,
Open the door and they crawl right in.'

Is that not terrifyingly awesome?"

"Oh man, that would make an awesome rhyme for a creepy horror movie. I would totally go see that."

"Same, they need to up their game and make a truly scary movie that makes you feel as if it could really happen to you."

"Absolutely," Brittany exclaimed. "I want to feel like the monster could actually come for me next."

They both chuckled and Jules went back to scrolling through her phone hoping to find their next scary spot.

She scrolled past stories about abandoned hospitals, haunted tunnels, and the usual over hyped tourist traps. Nothing stood out, until a post title caught her eye.

The title read: *Room 1210 at the Davidson House – Don't go alone*

Her heart skipped. "Anonymous? That's weird." She muttered, tapping the post open. The writing was frantic and raw. It didn't feel performative.

She read the rest of the post excitedly to herself:

Okay, I don't usually post stuff like this, and I'm writing this anonymously because I do not want this tied to my main page. But I stayed at the Davidson House this past weekend, room 1210. DO NOT GO IN THERE!

From the second I walked into the hotel, I felt weird. Not just creeped out...watched. The lobby was beautiful, and everyone was super polite, but something felt off. It was nothing compared to when I got into room 1210. The moment the door shut behind me, the air got heavy, and thick. I know that sounds dramatic, but I've never felt anything like it. It was like walking into a sealed tomb. I tried to brush it off as anxiety. Then the water in the tub turned on by itself. Full blast! I shut it off and seconds later the A/C started clicking on and off randomly. I told myself it's an old hotel so the electronics and plumbing in the room must be wonky. I noticed there was no towels in the bathroom so I called down to the front desk, and they stated someone would be up shortly with them and apologized. I laid down on the bed, exhausted from the drive. I threw some light music on and just wanted to relax. Then the mattress shifted. There was pressure on my legs, like someone was crawling on top of me. I tried to move and couldn't. Something was holding me down. I couldn't breathe, my heart was pounding like it would literally burst out of my chest. I couldn't talk or scream. It was as if I was frozen. Then something knocked on the door. I heard a lady outside, "housekeeping, I have your towels." The knock saved me!!!! The second she talked, the pressure lifted. I could move again. I got up, didn't say a word, just grabbed my stuff and ran out of the room. I didn't even check out at the desk. I got into my car and drove the five hours back home. The whole hotel is definitely haunted but room 1210 is the worst! If you read this and still want to go, do not go alone!

Jules stared at the screen for a long moment, then looked up, her eyes wide and gleaming. She shoved the phone into Brittany's face. "We are totally going!"

Brittany grabbed the phone and read the post. Then leaped from the couch. "Finally! A cool place. Oh my god, we've been waiting for something like this for months."

They spent the next hour cross-referencing business listings, obscure booking sites, and a local registry of B&Bs. Most hotels were small, modern, and boring. The only thing on this place is their website and reviews stating that the people who stayed here absolutely loved their stay and the employees were phenomenal, nothing haunted or creepy at all. They also tried to figure out who may have posted the story hoping they could message this person and find out more details. The person who had made the post had made an account for this one post. They hoped whoever had made this account would randomly check the messages and get back to them.

Brittany googled the hotel, looking up pictures of where they would be staying. "Shut up! This place is gorgeous. The velvet chairs, Gothic vibes in the rooms, the chandeliers. I want to move in." Brittany said in a very excited voice.

Jules giggled with excitement. "I know, I'm so excited! And... booked. Davidson House, here we come!"

"When are we going?" Brittany said excitedly.

"Tomorrow, I figured we should make the most of our short trip back to Connecticut."

"Heck yeah," Brittany shouted. "This is going to be the best podcast episode yet, I can feel it."

Chapter 7

From a distance, the hotel looked like a forgotten dream. Jules stared at the towering fifteen stories high hotel, its whitewashed facade gleamed against the fading light, framed by ivy wrapped pillars. Brittany stared at the statues that lined the front path, they were like silent gargoyles from hunchback of Notre Dame, and the grand porch invited you in with a strange, regal allure.

But the closer the girls got, the more that beauty began to fracture.

Jules noticed the paint peeling. Cracks snaked along the surface, telling stories the walls would never dare speak aloud. Brittany's fingers glided along the floral designs of the massive wooden doors. Her hand fell to the cold metal handle and as she opened the door it let out a long, haunted creak. The kind of sound that doesn't just echo... it lingers.

Inside, Jules stared at the lobby. She noticed the carpet beneath your feet. It had swirling colors of grays, blues, and reds, soft but strangely disorienting, like it's pulling you in. Only when you stare do you notice the faint, hidden images of birds woven into the design, so subtle you would miss them unless you were really looking.

Brittany looked to the left, a sitting area with four massive chairs that looked like thrones. Each one gilded in gold, with crimson velvet cushions so plush they seem to whisper forgotten secrets. A small room is to the left of the chairs, two steps down into the room that lead to a bar with a couple of tables. The girls made their way to the check-in desk on the other side of the large lobby on the right. Jules noticed the desk gleamed like it was just polished, a slab of dark mahogany. Jules nudged Brittany and pointed to the wall of antique mail slots from the 1900's that remained untouched, each numbered box still holding an old skeleton key. "I love that they kept the old mailboxes!"

The staff greeted them with wide, polite smiles, but Brittany noticed there was a robotic, practiced rhythm in their welcome, as if someone told them how to act human but forgot to mention warmth, their hospitality wrapped in a waxy mask.

As Brittany and Jules receive their key cards, they made their way toward the elevators though calling them that felt almost wrong.

"Wow Jules, Look at this elevator." Brittany said excitedly. She had never seen an elevator like this before. It stood like something out of an old film. Tall, moody, and dressed in black. The walls surrounding it were sleek and glossy. A pair of antique wall sconces flickered with warm, golden light, casting soft halos that barely reached the corners. The metal elevator door itself was a piece of art. She noticed the floral patterns were like the doors outside.

"This feels like we're about to summon Dracula," Jules whispered, only half joking.

The air here felt still, Jules thought, like it hadn't moved in decades. Even the glowing red button beside the door looked oddly ominous. When the doors finally creaked open with a slow, metallic groan, it was as if they had stepped into a capsule of the past.

Brittany laughed, twirling inside as her reflection multiplied around her. "I feel like royalty," she said, voice echoing slightly.

Jules smirked, bowing with exaggerated flourish.

"After you, Queen Brittany," she said, swinging an arm toward the entrance.

The girls stepped into the elevator, the worn metal doors groaning as they slid shut behind them. Inside, Brittany smelled the faint odor of old perfume and dust, like a haunted dressing room. Jules twirled as she stared at waist length mirrors that wrapped the walls. Brittany loved the sound of the swing music, like something from a dusty phonograph in the 1880's. Red velvet carpet lined the floor like a royal carpet rolled out just for them.

A soft chime echoed as the car began its slow ascent. As beautiful as everything looked, something about it made the girls feel just a little... off.

Each time the elevator passed a floor, they heard the dullding, echoing unnaturally in the cramped space. As it reached the twelfth floor, it chimed again, and the doors began to part with a mechanical shudder. But instead of opening fully, they jerked to a stop about a foot apart. Through the narrow gap, only darkness waited for the girls.

Jules and Brittany froze, exchanging a glance that saidthis isn't normal. Before either could react, the doors slammed shut again with a startlingclank. The elevator continued to ascend, but now the music was slowing, distorting, stretching into something warped and unsettling, like a record player winding down.

The overhead lights flickered ominously.

"Okay, I amnota huge fan of this," Jules said, her voice trembling despite the effort to sound calm.

"It's fine," Brittany replied, trying to stay upbeat. "At least we're not plummeting to our deaths, right? It'll open on the next floor. Old buildings do weird things."

The elevator chimed again. The panel above them claimed they'd reached the fourteenth floor, but they both knew better. In places like this, there was never a labeled thirteenth floor just a skip in the numbers. This wasit.

The doors glided open silently. The flickering stopped. The lights returned to their full glow. The music snapped back to its cheerful, elevator tune, as if nothing had happened at all.

"See?" Brittany said, stepping out. "Just an old elevator being moody."

Jules didn't move. Her eyes were fixed on the number above the door.

"Yeah," she muttered. "Except it dropped us off on thethirt eenthfloor."

Brittany turned to press the button for floor twelve, but before she could, Jules bolted out of the elevator.

"Nope. I'll take the stairs," she said. "I've seen this movie before, and I'm not dying in an elevator."

Brittany laughed, shaking her head as the doors started to close again. "Scaredy cat," she called out with a smirk.

Brittany walked out of the elevator and turned to watch the doors shut. Just before the elevator doors fully shut, the lights flickered once more and she could have sworn she saw a dark shadow, and this time, Brittany wasn't smiling.

They made their way to the door labeled STAIRS and made the quick decent to a big white door labeled 12. They opened the door to their floor revealing a long hallway cloaked in utter silence. The lighting here was dimmer than in the lobby, as if the bulbs were dipped in sepia.

Everything feels a little... off. The air is colder. The silence thicker.

Jules noticed the carpet had the same swirling pattern from below, but up here, the colors seem darker, more muted. The birds woven into the fabric were easier to see. Wings stretched wide, beaks open mid-screech, frozen in silent warning. It made Jules feel uneasy.

Brittany and Jules stepped out, their boots muffled against the thick floor. The hallway stretched endlessly in both directions, lined with white wooden doors spaced perfectly apart. Faint golden numbers were etched onto the surface of each one, almost glowing.

When they finally found Room 1210, they paused. It looked like every other door on the floor. White, pristine, polished. But the air around it felt... wrong. Stale, maybe. Or charged. Jules squinted at the door handle. It was slightly tarnished, like it had been touched too many times by hands that never truly left. Brittany lifted the key card, hesitated, then slid it through.

Click.

The door creaked open-slowly, like it had been waiting years to be opened again. Jules flipped the light switch on and the girls let out a synchronized squeal.

"Oh my God, look at this place!" Jules shrieked, practically skipping inside.

Brittany followed, eyes wide, smiling. "Is this real life?! I feel like we broke into a vampire's penthouse."

They darted around the room like kids in a haunted candy

store, pointing out the large king size beds with the plush off white comforter, the velvet drapes, the golden chandeliers crystals looked like they were dripping with luxury. The entire room glowed with a haunted kind of elegance. Everything was antique, but somehow... fresh. As if the past never quite let go. On the far wall Jules noticed a floor to ceiling bookcase. It looked like it had been there for centuries, dark walnut wood, carved trim, and rows of aging spines.

"Oh yes," Jules said excitedly. "Please tell me this is full of forbidden knowledge and hot vampire poetry."

They scanned the titles, quickly realizing someone had a twisted sense of humor. "How to Host a Party with Thirteen Ghosts," Brittany read, laughing. "Do they RSVP from beyond?"

Jules giggled, picking up another. "Seances for Dummies. There's even a sticky note on the front that says, 'don't feed the spirits after midnight.'"

"Classic," Brittany said, chuckling.

But then, Jules paused. Her hand hovered over a spine, slightly thicker than the others. Its title was burned into the leather cover, the letters sharp and deep.

The Night Brittany Would Never Forget

Their laughter stopped. A beat of silence passed between them.

"Okay, that's... weird," Jules murmured, slowly pulling it from the shelf.

Brittany blinked at the book. Her name wasn't exactly rare, but something about the way it was written, like a warning, sent a chill trailing down her neck. Like the title was made for her. She took the book, flipping it open. Blank. Every page, empty. Brittany exhaled with a nervous chuckle. "Okay,

I mean, it's clearly just a coincidence. There's a million Brittany's in the world."

Jules nodded, but her smile didn't quite reach her eyes. "Yeah. Totally. Just... bad timing, right?"

They set the book aside and moved to the plush red couch that sat beneath the wide window. The cushions were so soft it felt like sitting on a cloud that had once belonged to royalty. On the coffee table before them, they laid out their ghost hunting gear. An EMF detector, a spirit box, flashlights, and their voice recorder.

Just beyond the couch, a mini fridge hummed faintly beside a small coffee bar, complete with a gleaming new machine that looked starkly out of place next to the lace doilies and candelabra. The room was a strange fusion of past and present, as if the modern amenities had been politely tucked into place, careful not to disturb the ghosts who still called it home.

"I swear, it's like they're trying to make ghosts feel comfortable," Jules whispered, eyeing the coffee pot. "Like... 'Here's a cappuccino for your eternal suffering."

Brittany snorted. "I'd haunt this place too if they had espresso."

They both laughed, the sound bouncing off the high ceiling and into the stillness beyond. But outside, the wind had picked up. The hour was growing late, and while the girls were still giddy and giggling on the velvet couch, the room itself... was listening.

Brittany knelt beside the tripod, carefully adjusting the camera to face the couch. "Alright, let's catch absolutely nothing in stunning 4K," she joked, her voice light as she hit record and the little red light blinked to life.

Behind her, Jules was already skipping around the beds,

placing the cat balls near the pillows that lit up if anything touched them.

"You never know," she said, placing one gently in the center. "Maybe there's a classy Victorian spirit, or a raver who likes a good glow orb." They both laughed.

Next, they swept the room with the EMF detector, moving slowly, deliberately. Brittany passed it along the walls, the outlets, even over the mini fridge and the strange vintage style lamp beside the bed. No spikes. Not even a flicker.

"Well," Jules said, raising an eyebrow, "at least we won't have to debunk anything. Yet."

"Yet," Brittany echoed with a grin.

Jules placed the REMPOD near the door. This was her favorite piece of equipment. It uses lights and sounds to alert you if there is anything in its path due to temperature changes. "Okay," she said, standing back. "If anything walks by, we'll know."

On the coffee table, Brittany set down a small flashlight. One of the ones that spirits were said to be able to manipulate by loosening the end just slightly. She twisted it, then laid it down gently. "Alright, if someone wants to talk tonight," she said softly, "this is yours."

Brittany then unpacked their recorder and microphones. She clipped hers to her hoodie and handed Jules the other, her excitement bubbling up again. "Honestly, even if we don't catch anything, this room is incredible. I feel like we're staying in the lap of haunted luxury."

Jules chuckled, clipping on her mic. "I know, right? It's almost too pretty. But let's be real, there's literally nothing online about this place. No deaths. No murders. No tragic brides. Just that one weird Reddit post."

"Which, let's be honest, was probably written by someone who got high and saw their own reflection," Brittany added, laughing as she reached for her Red Bull. "But with how old this place is, someone had to have… stayed after checkout."

They settled into the plush couch, their gear gleaming under the low chandelier light. Jules opened her recording app and tapped the big red button.

"Alright, banshee babes and ghost geeks," she said into the mic, her voice full of energy, "we are coming to you live from Room 1210 at the Davidson House, possibly the fanciest room we've ever investigated."

Brittany jumped in. "And we've got our gear, our guts, and our caffeine. Let's see who's lurking in the walls tonight."

Brittany leaned in, eyes darting around the room. "And let us tell you, this place is drop dead gorgeous. Like… ballgown and bloodstains gorgeous."

"No, seriously. There are birds in the carpet. Not like, actual birds. They're hard to see as if they're hiding. Just watching and judging you."

They laughed, the sound bright and out of place in the heavy stillness of the room. But beneath their playful tone, something coiled in the silence. The chandelier above gave a slight creak.

Brittany paused. "Did you hear that?"

Jules held up a hand. They waited. Nothing. "I'm sure it was just the building settling," she whispered though she couldn't shake the sudden chill down her spine.

Brittany wasn't convinced but smiled anyway. "That's what they always say… right before the haunting starts."

They kept recording. Bantering, joking, narrating the eerie elegance of the hotel. But the longer they talked, the heavier the air felt. The room didn't just listen. It seemed to lean in.

Ten minutes passed in laughter, banter, and hopeful prodding at the spirit world.

Then, *click*. The flashlight flickered on. They both froze.

Jules leaned forward, eyes wide. "Thank you! Whoever just turned on the flashlight, we really appreciate it."

Brittany sat straighter, her voice breathless. "Oh my god, it actually worked."

The REMPOD lit up and chimed. They both gasped.

"This is so exciting," Brittany whispered, grinning wildly. "We're getting real activity."

Jules leaned in. "Can you tell us your name? Or how long you've been here?" She tapped the recorder and let it run for a few seconds before hitting playback.

Nothing.

Just static.

Brittany tilted her head. "Guess this one's shy."

Jules tried again. "If you want to speak with us and answer some questions, can you turn the flashlight on again?"

A beat of silence.

Click.

The flashlight lit up.

Brittany's eyes sparkled. "Oh wow. This is insane."

Jules kept her voice calm, respectful. "Thank you so much for answering. Brittany maybe we should turn the spirit box on and see if whoever is here will have an easier time using that."

Brittany agreed and switched the box on. The sound of static filled the room. Just as quick as they turned it on, they heard a very clear "Hi".

The girls stared at each other in disbelief. "Oh My God! Jules, please tell me you heard that?" Brittany shrieked.

"Yes! That was definitely a hi, can you tell us your name?"

The spirit box rushed from one AM station to the next, but no words popped out. After a couple of minutes, they asked the question again. Just white noise.

"Can you tell me if you're the only one here." Brittany asked as she watched the box intently.

Then came a weird sound, it almost sounded like someone screaming but both girls shrugged it off. "There's no way that was a spirit. It must have just been a weird glitch from the box." Jules said a little shakily.

Then the noise paused, complete silence. Both the girls stared intently at the box. After a couple of seconds Brittany went to grab the box assuming it had died. They both jumped when the box came to life once again just as Brittany went to touch it.

"Is this spirit playing with us right now?" Brittany said chuckling.

"Ooooh, maybe we have a trickster spirit with us." Jules said as she clapped her hands together and chuckled.

Then three words came out clear as day, one right after the other.

Tower....Jane....Zodo.

"I'm so confused by that sentence." Brittany said.

"Maybe it wasn't a sentence but three separate words?" Jules said questioningly.

"Even if that's the case, those make no sense. Is Jane locked in a tower by Zodo?"

"Well, that can't be right," stated Jules. "We don't even have towers near here."

Then the spirit box sputtered out the three words again but

with longer pauses.

Tower............Jane..............Zodo

"These have to be three random words. They're not meant to make sense in a sentence but together they matter." Jules stated.

The flashlight turned on next to Brittany. "Oh my god Jules! I think that was her confirming. This must be Jane." Brittany exclaimed.

"Is your name Jane? If it is, turn the flashlight off." Jules said.

Click. The flashlight turned off quickly.

"Hi Jane!" Brittany said excitedly.

Then the spirit box spit out one more word.

RUN.

The word was clear as day. Both girls stared at each other in disbelief. Had they just heard what they thought they heard. Brittany quickly turned off the spirit box and twisted the flashlight off.

"I don't know how I feel about this Jules," Brittany said shakily. "What if she really is telling us to run. What if that Reddit post was right and something bad is here."

"I feel like we would have seen something or felt something that made us believe that intently by now, right?" Jules asked worriedly.

"I don't know Jules. I know I don't want to get held down on the bed though."

As Jules went to reply she looked over at the bookcase. She could have sworn she saw a book move. Just as she went to reply again, she heard a creak echo from near the bookcase and saw the book move again. "Brittany, I swear I keep seeing a book shift in the bookcase."

Brittany slowly turned her head towards the bookcase. Just as she got a good glimpse of the bookcase one of the books seemed to be pulled from its spot and then hit the floor.

"What the fuck!" Brittany shouted.

They both jumped up from the couch not knowing how to feel about what they just witnessed. As scared as they were the girls were also curious as to what book fell and why. Brittany took a hesitant step forward, every hair on her body standing on end and she bent down and picked it up. The color drained from her face.

"Which book is it?" Jules asked worryingly.

Brittany turned the book around. *The night Brittany will never forget* etched into the leather.

Jules swallows hard, the room feeling smaller, heavier. She took the book from Brittany. As scared as she was, she opened the book praying it was still blank like before. As she flipped the pages she breathed a sigh of relief. "Still blank."

And then a card slipped out from between the pages and fluttered to the ground. It landed face up and the girls stood in disbelief at the card staring them in the face.

The Tower.

They saw the card with lightning splitting the sky. Two figures fall from a crumbling structure, their faces twisted in horror.

"That's the card that Jane said from the spirit box," Jules states shakily. "And oddly enough a card we have seen before when doing readings."

"Alright, I don't feel right staying in here Jules. None of this seems safe and I know what that card can mean."

"I think you may be right, let's get out of here."

Jules grabbed her phone to see the time, but her phone was

dead. "What?" she said, tapping her phone repeatedly. "It was at ninety percent when we started." She showed Brittany her screen.

"Maybe Jane drained your power when she was trying to talk to us."

Jules looked at her with this terrified feeling in her gut. "I hope that's what it was."

The girls opened the door and stepped into the hallway. The door clicking shut behind them.

And the moment it did...buzz. Jules' phone vibrated in her hand and lit up. They both froze. She looked down. The screen glowed bright, as if nothing had happened and the battery percentage still said ninety percent.

"What is going on?" Jules asked, her voice barely above a whisper.

Brittany was shaking. "I'm not sure... but this is weird."

The hallway outside Room 1210 was unsettlingly quiet. No voices. No footsteps. Just the soft hum of electricity somewhere far off, like the hotel itself was sleeping, or pretending to.

Brittany crossed her arms tightly across her chest as they started walking. "Tell me again why this place has no history of being haunted?"

Jules tried to laugh, but it came out thin. "Because the ghosts here are apparently great at keeping secrets, unlike what I thought."

They wandered down the long, dim hallway, their footsteps muffled by the ornate carpet. The wallpaper lining the walls was a pale gold floral pattern like inside the elevator, but older looking, faded, peeling way.

Occasionally, a wall sconce would flicker slightly as they

passed beneath it, but neither of them commented on it.

As they turned the corner at the end of the hall, they found a grand staircase, the kind that spiraled with dramatic flair, framed by intricate iron banisters and a crimson runner that flowed down the steps like a royal rug. It was beautiful... and wrong. The kind of staircase you only see in ghost stories and nightmares.

"Do we take the stairs or..." Brittany trailed off, eyes landing on the elevator.

"Definitely the stairs." Jules said.

As they reached the fifth floor, they heard something that made both of them pause. Music. Faint and crackling, like it was coming from an old phonograph down the hallway. A slow, eerie piano melody.

Brittany glanced at Jules. "Is that... real?"

Jules shook her head. "I don't know."

They stepped carefully onto the fifth floor landing and followed the sound. It led them past two rooms, then three... but as they approached a faded wooden door marked "Ballroom," the music stopped. Dead silence. The door stood slightly ajar, its frosted glass etched with elegant swirls and a worn image of a chandelier. Jules pushed it open slowly.

Inside was a massive ballroom, bathed in a grayish blue glow from tall windows lining one side. Dust floated like snow in the air. The wooden floor was polished but cracked in places. At the far end, an old piano sat beneath a sheet, the edges of it barely visible.

"Nope," Brittany whispered. "No ghost pianos tonight."

But Jules had already stepped inside. "We're here. Might as well check it out. Let's take our mind off the room and investigate a different area."

As they moved deeper into the room, their footsteps echoed unnaturally, too loud, too hollow. Brittany's eyes scanned the corners, and for a moment, she thought she saw movement in the far mirror lined wall. A flicker. A figure. But when she looked again, it was gone. Then the piano seemed to play one note. Just one key but it was enough to scare her.

"Let's go," she said insistently, gently tugging Jules back toward the hall. "I've seen enough abandoned ballrooms for one lifetime."

They exited quickly and continued down the stairwell towards the second floor. When they opened the door they saw signs that were all in delicate calligraphy, etched into dark cherry wood placards. The hallway was L shaped. There were several doors and then a sign at the end of the small hallway with the words LOBBY. They started walking down the hallway and came across an old framed photo on the wall. It showed a woman. Elegant. Pale. Sharp cheekbones. Her eyes light brown. Hair pinned perfectly into place. She was wearing a black swing dress. Brittany stopped. Cold creeping down her spine. Jules leaned closer. Something about this photo felt off.

Jules eyes gazed down to the placard at the bottom of the frame. The name, written in perfect delicate cursive,

Jane Chapman

Jules didn't speak. She couldn't. Brittany's breath caught in her throat. They stood in silence, both staring at a woman who had, until now, only been a whispered name through a spirit box. Their eyes met. They didn't have to say anything. The realization had landed heavy on both of them. This was probably the Jane from the box in their room.

A soft creak echoed from the hallway. They both looked towards the sound. There standing at the end of the hall was the woman from the photo. Same dress, same face. Standing still, Watching. Her expression was unreadable.

Brittany and Jules froze, neither of them daring to move or even blink. The air felt like ice. The woman's dress shifted slightly as if brushed by wind, though the hall was still. Then, without a sound, she turned and walked around the corner. Not rushed. Not frantic. Just... gone.

The girls exchanged a single panicked look before rushing toward the corner, their footsteps fast but hushed against the thick carpet. They reached the bend in the hallway within seconds but there was no one there. Just a long, empty corridor stretching into stillness.

"No way in hell she moved that fast," Brittany whispered, her voice shaking.

"Absolutely not," Jules said, eyes scanning the hallway. "Why would she be running? And even if she went into a room, we would have heard the door click."

Brittany's face was pale. "I'm done. Let's get out of this area."

"Lobby?" Jules asked.

"Lobby." Brittany confirmed.

They moved quickly but cautiously, heading to the end of the hallway. The hallway gave way to an unexpected opening, and suddenly, they found themselves looking out over a grand lobby. A balcony stretched before them, a railing worn but elegant and four steps that led to the main floor where the gorgeous throne chairs were. Once they hit the lobby floor the weight that had been pressing on their chests began to lift. The chill they had been carrying since Room 1210 faded. The contrast when they got to the lobby was staggering. It was warm and alive.

Even at ten at night, the grand room buzzed with life. The clink of glasses and the hum of conversation spilled from the bar. Two staff members behind the check in counter were laughing at something on a computer screen. A bellhop strolled past them with a cart, offering a casual smile.

It felt.... Real. They sank into the gold trimmed, red velvet throne chairs in the sitting area, each exhaling deeply for the first time in what felt like hours.

"I mean... electronics short out all the time." Jules said more to herself than anyone else.

Brittany nodded quickly. "Maybe the book fell because of bad shelving or unlevel floorboards."

"And the spirit box. Maybe we just heard what we wanted to hear." Jules added.

"And clearly we didn't actually see Jane. It could have been a shadow, our brains trying to make a shape out of nothing." Brittany added.

They both sat there for a long moment, building their wall of logic, stacking it high and firm against the growing, unexplainable chill that had followed them from room 1210.

By the time they had finished trying to poke holes in every piece of evidence they'd gathered, they both glanced at each other knowing what they had seen was more than a shadow, and books don't just fall from a bookcase.

"Maybe we should ask the front desk staff?" Brittany said. "They must know something."

Jules smiled. "Perfect! They must know who Jane is."

They walked over to the front desk where a young man, probably in his early 20s stood before them looking quite bored. The woman who had stood with him now gone.

"Hi," Brittany said with a polite smile "we had a question

about our room and who may have stayed there a long time ago."

He looked up at her, arching an eyebrow and smirked. "You know we can't give details about people who have stayed here prior. It's hotel policy."

Jules piped up then, "But this would have been *way* back. She would have stayed in room 1210."

As the last words came out of her mouth the man looked at her, his smirk vanished, and his eyes widened. "What about room 1210? Did.....Did you see something?"

Both girls glanced at each other cautiously and then back at him. "Why... should we have?" Brittany asked.

The man looked down at his computer, back at them, and then back down at his computer, his hands hovering over the keyboard. "I mean, uhhh, no. There's been rumors but that room has been closed for over 60 years."

"60 years!" Jules blurted. "Why?"

The boy shushed them. "I'm not supposed to get into the history of the room. My manager would flip."

"OK well we definitely saw something and had activity. We would like to know what we are getting into so if you could kindly explain why we have an extra roommate in our room, that would be awesome." Brittany said abruptly.

"OK, OK. But you can't say anything to my manager."

"We won't say anything. Scouts honor." Brittany said as she held up the hand gesture from Star Trek.

He lifted one eyebrow at her, shook his head, and gestured for them to come to the edge of the desk away from any guests who might need help. "In the 1950s there was a girl who stayed here all the time. Wealthy family. They would rent the room out for weeks out of the year for her. One night it is said that she had a couple people visit her at her room, one of them being a supposed psychic. The next morning when the cleaning staff went in to clean the room, they found her dead in the bathtub."

Jules swallowed hard. Brittany's face was unreadable.

He continued. "Her friend had been questioned, and she stated the psychic had come to the room and told Jane she would be in danger and needed to leave immediately. Of course, the police didn't believe that and ruled the case a suicide. Everyone had been really distraught about Jane passing away and a picture of her was placed near the lobby to keep her memory alive. Her parents were devastated by the news of their child's suicide and asked that this not get out to the press or anywhere else. They didn't want her to be remembered this way."

"So, you guys closed the room after she died?" Brittany asked.

"Not right away. We had the room cleaned and for a couple weeks it was closed but then the owner wanted the room to be used as normal. Many people came to us complaining that the water would run on its own, noises would keep them awake, and they would hear books fall but when they went to look nothing had been moved. After many complaints the owner closed the room."

"Until a month ago." Jules said.

"Yup," He nodded. "New management came in, stated that the room sounded cool and that some people would enjoy a room like that. Granted we are not supposed to tell anyone about the history of the room. We opened the room back up and then you guys called and asked specifically for the room. I thought it was very weird since there were no stories of this room online."

"Well, we have a podcast and figured this sounded perfect. No one had ever covered this hotel before, and we had seen a quick post about room 1210."

"Ahh, that makes more sense now. I'm sure there are stories circulating about people who got scared in the room a long time ago. Well, I hope you guys enjoy the room and get what you need for your podcast. Our staff has to dust the room and vacuum periodically and they've never stated they felt anything bad. You guys should be fine."

"Thank you again for telling us the story. This will help our investigation." Jules stated enthusiastically.

"Anytime, if you have any more questions, I can try to be of help. Just come on down, I'll be here until 7am."

"Thank you," Brittany leaned in to read his name tag "Brad. You have been very helpful."

"Well," Brittany said, glancing at the antique clock behind the front desk. Its minute hand ticked with a slow, eerie rhythm, "we've got some time to kill before the witching hour." She turned to Jules, wiggling her eyebrows mischievously. "Why don't we walk around the hotel a bit? Snap some pictures of the lobby, maybe hit up the bar? You know... classic ghost hunters pretending to be tourists."

Jules grinned. "That sounds perfect. I could seriously use a drink. Nothing like alcohol to keep the ghosts at bay."

They had just turned to leave the front desk when Brad called out after them.

"Hey, if you two are looking for a way to kill some time," he said, leaning casually against the counter, "How about I buy you a drink? You could interview me for your podcast. I know a lot about the hotel's history. I could even let you record it if you want."

Jules's eyes lit up, and she looked at Brittany with an excited grin. "That would be amazing!" she said, practically bouncing on her toes. "Getting real history from someone who works here? That would make our episode really come to life."

Brittany nodded. "Seriously, you'd be doing us a huge favor."

"Great," Brad said. "Let me just let the other girl know I'm going on break. I'll meet you both at the host stand in a few."

They watched as Brad disappeared through a narrow door labeled Employees Only, the latch clicking shut behind him.

"This is going to be awesome," Brittany whispered.

"I know, our first interview," Jules squeaked. The two girls clapped and let out giddy laughs like teenagers before prom.

The bar was dimly lit, all dark wood and red velvet, like something out of an old noir film. A glowing chandelier hung overhead, casting long shadows across the walls. They were seated at a four-top near the back of the lounge, Brad joining them just moments later. The host handed out menus and promised their server would be right over.

"Okay, Brad," Jules said laughing nervously, "bear with us, we've never actually interviewed someone before."

Brad leaned back in his chair with a calm smile. "I'm honored. Really. I hope I do your podcast justice."

"Oh, trust me," Brittany said with a smirk, "anything's better than just listening to the two of us cackling as we try to discuss a paranormal topic."

Their server arrived with waters and took their drink orders, three house lagers. Brittany started setting up the mics while Jules's hands trembled slightly as she fiddled with the recording equipment, clearly trying to mask her nerves.

"Sorry," she muttered. "I tend to stutter when I get nervous.

Please don't laugh."

Brad chuckled. "Scout's honor," he said, then flashed the Vulcan salute. "And Trekkie solidarity."

Brittany burst out laughing. "Okay, you officially passed the vibe check. No picking on us just because we're nerds."

"Never," Brad said with a wink.

When their beers arrived, Brittany noticed the way the server lingered just a second too long near Brad before walking off.

"Ooooh," she teased, nudging him with her elbow. "Looks like someone's got a fan."

Brad's cheeks flushed just slightly. "Nah, I don't think so."

"Stop, Brittany," Jules said, laughing. "You're going to scare the poor guy off before we even hit record."

Jules took a long sip of her beer. "Okay. Liquid courage? Check. Let's do this."

The girls began their questions with enthusiasm, asking Brad about the hotel's construction, its original owners, and why it had been such a hot spot in its heyday. Brad's answers flowed smoothly, he never stuttered or searched for answers, it was like he had rehearsed this exact talk a million times.

They moved on to lighter banter, sharing stories from their past episodes. They told him about their visit to Devil's Hopyard, about getting scared half to death by a squirrel, and how that moment still lived rent-free in their nightmares.

Brad chuckled. "Okay, my turn to ask you two a question." he said, resting his arms on the table.

"Ooh, OK, bring it on." Brittany said.

"What made you two decide to start a podcast?"

Brittany looked at Jules, and they exchanged a warm, knowing glance, like they were seeing a shared memory flowing between them.

"You tell him Jules," Brittany said. "You always tell it better."

Jules smiled, her expression softening. "Okay... Well, it started one night when we went to a haunted house tour. It was supposed to be a group event, but when we showed up, it was just us."

"The guide said we lucked out," Brittany chimed in, "called it a 'private tour', chuckled as she said we had got a massive deal on tickets."

"We laughed the whole time," Jules continued. "The mansion was massive and stunning. The guy who built it put so much detail into everything, even the door hinges looked like they belonged in a museum. As we walked through, little things started to happen. Doors creaking shut behind us. A child's laugh echoing in an empty hall. A ball rolling across the floor out of nowhere. We were hooked."

Brittany leaned in. "We were like little kids on Christmas morning."

"We told the tour guide that we had always loved haunted history." Jules chimed back in. "We both used to watch all the popular ghost shows on TV, read a lot of horror books, and knew we always wanted to do something along these lines. The tour guide said she could tell we were passionate. We told her we wanted to prove there was life after death. That you didn't just live, and then take a dirt nap forever."

Brittany chimed in, "She told us we should start a podcast and share haunted history in our own voices. We took it as a sign."

"Because we were the only two on the tour, she even let us record our first episode right there in the mansion," Jules said, her voice dreamy. "It felt like fate."

"And that episode?" Brittany said with a grin, "It blew up. We posted it a week later, and people loved it. They liked our mix of history and banter, the fact that we didn't try to be overly serious. We loved it so much we never wanted to stop."

"This is only our fifth episode," Jules added, "but the support has been incredible. We know we're on the right path, and we have proven time and again with our investigations that there is something after death."

Brad took a sip of his beer and smiled. "Honestly, I was captivated just by you two retelling why you started. I'm really happy for you guys and I'm glad I got to be your first interview."

The girls beamed, cheeks flushed with pride and beer. Time had slipped past them quickly. The clock above the bar now read 12:03.

"Well," Brittany said, glancing at Jules, "I think we wasted enough time."

Jules stood, brushing off her jeans. "Guess that means it's time for us to go back up."

They packed up their gear, thanked Brad again, and headed toward the elevator, a new confidence blooming in their chests. They had their first interview. The story of the hotel was being told.

And now, they weren't so scared to show people what may be lurking in Room 1210.

Chapter 8

They turned around and walked to the stairs, buzzing now with adrenaline and a strange excitement. If Jane was really haunting the room, it didn't feel malevolent anymore. Maybe it wasn't something to fear, maybe it was something to connect with.

At the stairwell, they paused and looked up at the stairs that never ended. Brittany groaned. "Are we really going to walk up twelve flights of stairs?"

"We could.. try the elevator again." Jules offered.

Brittany looked at her. "You sure?"

Jules nodded. "We have watched people coming and going from them all night. Nothing's happened. I think we're just being paranoid."

They turned, closed the heavy stairwell door behind them, and walked to the main elevator. The up arrow button glowed softly under Brittany's finger as she pressed it. And they waited. A soft ding echoed throughout the area. The doors slid open with a smooth hiss.

"See?" Jules smiled. "Totally normal."

They stepped inside. Neither noticed the mirrored panel above them slowly fog over...like breath from something unseen. They shared a look, just to make sure the other was still okay.

"I still can't believe how stunning this place is." Brittany said, her voice soft now, as though the air around them had suddenly thickened.

"I know," Jules replied, glancing around the elevator. "It's like we're inside a music box."

The elevator started moving. Slow and smooth, but then something changed. A quiet tap, like fingernails against glass, sounded behind them.

Brittany turned quickly. Nothing. Just her own reflection staring back at her in the mirrored wall. The music crackled once, then continued. Another tap. This time to the left.

Jules turned. "Did you...?"

Brittany nodded. "Yeah."

They looked at each other in the mirrored wall. Or rather... they thought they did. Brittany's reflection was just a second to slow.

Jules froze. "Did you see that?"

"I... no. I don't know. I don't want to let it know I saw." Brittany's voice faltered as her eyes locked in on the glass.

The mirrored panel behind Jules had begun to fog up, slowly, steadily, like someone was exhaling just inches from the other side.

The lights flickered. The music started to sound off, as if it was in slow motion.

Jules slammed her hand on the door open button, nothing happened.

Brittany was breathing faster now, staring at the mirrors, watching as her reflection would slowly tilt her head one way and then the other just slightly off from her real movements.

Subtle, but wrong.

"Come on, come on, come on." Jules muttered, hitting the button repeatedly. She looked over at Brittany who looked like a stone figure, just staring into the mirrors, in a trance.

"Brittany, stop staring at the reflection."

"I can't." Brittany said with a shaky voice. "It won't let me turn away."

Ding.

The twelfth floor. The music went back to normal, the lights came back full force and were almost too bright. The doors opened smoothly, as if nothing had happened. The trance that held Brittany in place had let go. They didn't speak. They just stepped out, slowly, cautiously.

Only when the doors slid shut did Brittany finally whisper: "That wasn't us freaking ourselves out was it?"

"No, that was something else."

Chapter 9

Back in the safety of the room the girls sat on the couch not knowing what just happened or why it was happening outside of the room. Was Jane trying to tell them something, or was there something more malevolent in this hotel that no one knew about?

Jules reached into her backpack and pulled out a small Bluetooth speaker. "Let's throw on something upbeat. Just... vibe it out. Good energy only!"

Brittany grinned and flopped on the couch. "I'm down for that. I'm sure Jane loves a good beat."

Jules laughed. "You think she's into pop?" She hit play and the hum of Taylor Swift filled the room, making it come alive.

Brittany hopped off the couch and the girls moved around the space, laughing and dancing, and shaking off the nervous energy.

It felt better, lighter. But behind the laughter and music the room still watched. It was listening. And in the bathroom mirror, a faint hand print began to form, slowly, from the inside.

Taylor Swift's "22" blared from Jules' phone, bounding off the velvet curtains and gold trim of the room.

They sang the song in unison, smiling and dancing. Brittany

grabbed two drinks from the mini fridge and popped one open. She handed the other to Jules with a small curtsy and a laugh.

Jules smirked, gave a slight curtsy back, and raised the can. "To ghost parties and emotional damage."

They clinked their cans together and took a long sip as the music rolled on. For a few more minutes, they weren't paranormal investigators. They were just two best friends having the time of their lives in the most gorgeous room they'd ever seen. Twirling around in socked feet, tossing pillows at each other, and dropping into ridiculous British accents mid lyric, "we're not like regular girls, were haunted girls!"

Eventually the whirlwind of dancing gave way to breathless laughter, and they collapsed onto the couch.

"I swear, if our friends could see us now..." Jules started.

"They'd be jealous." Brittany grinned. "We're literally sipping Red Bull in a Gothic castle suite singing Taylor Swift with invisible guests."

They erupted into another fit of laughter. Then the tea started spilling about exes, chaotic friends, failed hinge dates, and the boy back home who ghosted Brittany and stole her waffle iron. They leaned in close, voice pitches rising and falling, hands flying mid story. For a while it was just a friendship and drinks and the safe buzz of being together.

Then they heard a sound from near the bookcase. It sounded as if a books pages were being flipped quickly.

Pffffffffffff.

Brittany looked over to see the book with her name on it. The pages flipping frantically, and she looked more intently. Words seemed to appear on the pages. Brittany jumped up from the couch to grab the book. "Jules! There's writing in the book!" She shouted.

"What? How is that even possible?" Jules asked, alarm flashing in her eyes.

"I don't know but see for yourself." Brittany said as she plopped down beside Jules. She handed Jules the book. Her fingers flipped the pages quickly as her hands shook. "This is not possible, we've looked at this book numerous times and it has been blank every time." Jules exclaimed.

Brittany looked at her, a terrified expression on her face. "I know Jules, I don't know about this."

Jules flipped the page and started reading, the words were written in what looked like perfect cursive with a feather pen. Her finger slid down the words as she read quickly. Her eyes zig zagging over the words, her eyes widening with every movement. "Brittany," she said shakily. "This is about the night Jane died."

"It can't be!" Brittany blurted.

"See for yourself." Jules said and held out the book to her.

Brittany grabbed the book and started reading. The words on the pages had Brittany's face paling. Her eyebrows furrowed and her hands shook as she read the words written on the pages.

"*Jane's friend Betty and Madame Zodo stood at the door. As Zodo walked in she warned of a presence in the room.*"

Brittany's fingers trembled as she read about the tarot reading. Her eyes paused on the Tower card. Shocked at what had fallen out of this book just over an hour ago. It then went on to explain Madame Zodo's final words.

"*Be safe my child. The energy in here has darkened further. Do not trust this shadow figure, he is not a lingering soul. You should leave.*"

Brittany's face paled. She couldn't read anymore. She

handed Jules the book. Jules took the book and read from it aloud, her voice shaky.

"I felt the breath on me first. Then the hand. It's movements light, intimate. It prickled like frostbite. Then came the push. The invisible grip. I felt my lungs tighten, felt my body convulse. Then nothing. The invisible hands released me, and I gasped for air. I grabbed my dress and left the bathroom, knowing I needed to get out. But I never did, did I?"

Both girls sat there, shocked. Silent. Brittany looked at Jules who had tears streaming down her face. "She never got out Brittany. Whatever is in here kept her here and still is," she said in a shaky voice "We have to help her."

"Oh no!" Brittany exclaimed. "We have to leave. She is warning us, not asking for help Jules."

"But Brittany....She is trapped here. She died here. She thought she made it but at the last moment, but she didn't. We can't let her keep reliving this."

Brittany shook her head. "This is way more than we even know how to do. We don't know how to help spirits cross over. We are not sensitives. We wouldn't even know the first thing about breaking her out of here."

"Well, we have to try! She came to us for a reason."

"And how do we know it's really her?" Brittany snapped. "What if it's something *pretending* to be Jane? A demon? A mimic? Whatever this is, it knows things. Brad basically told us everything this book just said."

Jules paused, her expression torn.

"Demons listen very well and can fix in your mind whatever they want you to think. I don't care, we need to go. We will bring someone back who knows how to keep us safe." Brittany stated adamantly.

"You're right. I know you're right. Let's go find someone who can help."

Just then a soft knock echoed through the room and both girls froze. Their eyes met, wide, panicked, searching the other for courage neither of them felt.

The knock came again. Louder. Slower.

Tap tap.

"Should we open it?" Jules whispered, her voice barely audible. "Or... do you think it's something we don't want to see?"

Brittany didn't answer. She stood completely still, her body rigid, her breath held tight in her throat. The shadows in the corners of the room seemed to grow darker, deeper and heavier.

Jules looked at her friend, really looked at her. Brittany's eyes were glazed, distant. She looked like someone watching a memory she couldn't escape.

"Britt," Jules said softly, "hey... snap out of it."

Nothing.

Jules' heart was pounding as she crept toward the door. Her hand hovered over the knob as if it might burn her. With one final glance at Brittany, she slowly turned it.

The door creaked open, and standing there was Brad, out of breath, eyes bright with excitement.

"Brad?" Jules gasped, flooded with relief. "What are you doing here?"

He grinned, holding something wrapped in an old cloth. "I found something. You two are going to love this. Perfect for your podcast. I mean, like, next level cool."

Curious, Jules pulled back the cloth. Inside was a leather-bound book, its cover cracked with age, its spine thick with dust. Scrawled faintly across the inside in curling ink was a name:

Madame Zodo.

Jules's mouth fell open. "No way. Brittany's going to lose her mind when she sees this."

As Brad stepped into the room, Brittany finally stirred. Her head turned toward him slowly, eyes narrowing, the trance dissolving like mist. Her arms dropped to her sides, and a strange, unreadable look passed across her face.

"Hey, Brittany," Brad said cheerfully. "I found something I think you're really going to want to see. Might even give our Jane story the twist we have been waiting for."

Brittany's expression shifted into confusion. "I thought..." she began quietly, "I thought we weren't supposed to talk about Jane. Her parents never wanted her story out there."

Brad shrugged. "They're dead now. So, it doesn't really matter anymore."

Jules gasped, unsure how to respond, then quickly took the book from him, her fingers flipping through the brittle pages with excitement. "This is amazing," she said, her voice full of wonder. "This could add so much to the podcast. This is, like, real witch stuff Brittany."

As she scanned the pages, Brittany moved closer, hesitant. Her fingers brushed the edges of the worn paper, and a strange vibration buzzed through her hand, sharp and cold. She pulled back immediately. "Jules... I don't know. Something feels wrong about this."

Jules laughed lightly. "Seriously? You're the one always trying to convince me to go deeper into the creepy stuff. And now you're getting cold feet?" She turned the page to one marked *Communication Across Time*, a spell, scrawled in a mixture of English and Latin. Symbols surrounded it. Candles. Incantations. Diagrams.

Brittany reached out and touched the page and froze. Images flashed through her mind, a burning card, candles flickering in a circle, an altar drenched in herbs. Words whispered in a voice she didn't know but somehow recognized. Her heart pounded in her ears.

"Don't turn that page, Jules," she said suddenly. Her voice shook.

Jules looked up, startled. "What? Why?"

Brittany's hand hovered above the parchment. "I've seen this before. I don't know where. I don't know when. It feels like... déjà vu. Like we were meant to see this."

"Brittany," Jules said gently, "we've never talked about witches. We do haunted hotels, not spells and magic. Maybe it reminds you of a movie or something?"

Brittany shook her head slowly. "No... this feels different. Like a warning. Like we're standing at the edge of something we don't understand."

Jules raised an eyebrow, still grinning. "Come on. You're freaking yourself out. It's just a book."

But Brittany refused to touch it again. She stood back, arms crossed, eyes fixed on the text like it might come alive and bite her. Something about the words clawed at the edge of her memory, like a voice calling out from a dream.

And then she looked at Brad. He was just standing there. Staring at her.Smiling. "Pretty cool, right?" he said, breaking the silence. "I'm glad I found it for you. Madame Zodo was the psychic who came here that night. To see Jane."

Jules squealed. "Oh my god, this is going to blow our listeners' minds! Can we take pictures?"

Brad nodded. "Yeah, go for it. I have to head back down to the desk, though. Other girl left for the night, so it's just me."

Jules walked him to the door and he stepped out into the hallway, "I hope you guys have a good night, I probably won't see you in the morning. I'll be gone by then."

Jules waved and shut the door behind him. She spun around, staring at the book. "Seriously, Britt. This is the coolest thing we've ever found."

But Brittany wasn't smiling. She stood in silence, staring at the page Jules had left open.

"Something's wrong with this book," she whispered. "I don't know why. But I feel it. I feel it in my bones. I get these flashes like we've seen it before. Heard those words. Lived them. Something. I can't put my finger on it."

Jules tilted her head, unconvinced. "Maybe you're just tired. We have been through a lot in these past few days."

"No..." Brittany shook her head again. "This isn't tired. This feels like a warning. I don't think we're supposed to have this book. Or maybe it's a warning for a different reason." She backed away slowly, hands trembling at her sides. And for the first time since they started their podcast, Brittany didn't want to press forward. She wanted to run.

Brittany stared at the words, her breath catching in her throat. They were familiar. Not from memory, from something deeper. A sensation. A whisper she'd never truly heard but somehow already knew. "Jules," she said, voice barely above a whisper, "I've... I've dreamed these words. I know it."

Jules looked up from her phone, pausing mid-snap. "What are you talking about?"

"I've heard this before, I know this spell. I can feel it." She reached for the page, her fingers trembling as they hovered just above the ink. Her skin tingled. Her chest felt heavy.

She stared at the words as they seemed to burn into the page:

"Candle burning precious light,
Bring to me this very night,
Wisdom bless my tongue, my lips,
Your guidance at my fingertips.
Let no shadow twist my sight,
Let the truth be cast in light.
Take this message through the flame,
To those who must outrun the name.
So mote it be."

And then she remembered the name from her dream, *Zaron*. It just kind of sat there going over and over, whispering in her brain, but she didn't know why she knew this name. She didn't know why that name sounded so familiar, but she knew she had dreamt about this name many times for a reason. She could still recall seeing this lady sitting at a table, casting this spell and then hearing the name Zaron being whispered softly like wind going through the room.

"Jules, we need to leave this room. My dream doesn't end well, and I don't want this to ever come true."

"I'm so confused Brittany, you've never talked about a dream like this or ever brought up this witch spell. Why not?"

"Because" Brittany said shaking. "This dream scares me to death. I wake up absolutely terrified and covered in sweat. This dream haunts me, and I think I know how Jane died. I see her in my dream, she is laying in the bathtub, and she's not moving and then my dream moves to the lady reciting this spell and I see this dark shadow but he makes you feel extremely scared and then he laughs like he is enjoying every moment of your fear."

"Oh my gosh Britt, that sounds horrible. I'm so sorry. I wonder if the lady you dream about is Madame Zodo?"

"I don't know, but I really do not want to ever find out because then the rest of the dream is true and I'm not just dreaming, it would mean that I can actually see the past and the future."

"Alright, grab the book and let's go." Said Jules.

They stood up grabbing their equipment and stuffing it quickly in their bags. The lights started flickering and they could have sworn they heard something laugh.

"Quicker Jules, I don't care if we forget shit, we will buy new stuff. Let's just get the fuck out!"

"OK, I think I have everything." Jules grabbed her bag and flung it over her shoulder, but as she ran for the door something shiny caught her eye on the bathroom floor. She froze and stared at the object. This strong curiosity came over her, made her feel as if she had to know what was on the floor. As she got closer to the bathroom, whatever was on the floor felt even farther away, almost like it was a mirage. Without realizing how far she had gone into the bathroom she finally got to what was on the floor. It was a tube of lipstick. A beautiful silvery tube, almost like a bullet. As she went to pick it up, she heard the door close behind her.

Chapter 10

Jules turned slowly, dread filling in her chest. She prayed she had not just heard the door shut behind her. Then she heard the familiar sound from the bathtub.

Shhhhh-clunk.

Water. That was definitely running water. Jules was frozen in place, Jane's final moments in the leather book running through her mind.

"Is that... the tub." Brittany whispered. "Please tell me you didn't decide to do one more experiment before we leave."

Jules barely found her voice, "Brittany, something's wrong. I didn't turn the water on, IT did it."

Brittany could hear the water still running from outside the door. She tried to open the door but it wouldn't budge. "Jules, this isn't funny. Open up the door."

"What do you mean?" Jules said terrified.

"Jules, you must have locked the door. Open it up."

Jules went to the door but it wouldn't budge. The doorknob would turn but it was as if someone had glued the door shut. "Brittany it won't open! Brittany, get me out of here!" She said panicking.

"OK, don't worry. It has to open." She pulled as hard as she could. She went to her purse and grabbed a credit card and slid the card between the door and latch and could feel the latch move. "OK I have the latch pushed back, now open the door."

Jules pushed as hard as she could, but the door would not budge. "Brittany," Jules choked out, panic flooding her voice "what's going on? I'm not going to die like Jane, am I?"

"God Jules, No!" Brittany snapped, refusing to let fear win. "We are going to get you out."

Brittany bolted to the phone and called down to Brad. "Hello, front desk, Brad speaking, how can I-"

"Brad" Brittany said in a worried tone "Jules is stuck in the bathroom and we can't open the door."

"This isn't a prank, right? Since I did just tell you the story." Brad questioned.

"No Brad! She's really stuck! We need help, now!"

"OK, sorry. I will have someone come up right away to help get the door unstuck." Brad said sharply.

"Please hurry. Something doesn't feel right." Brittany quickly hung up and went back to the door. "Jules, talk to me. Are you OK?" Brittany could hear a soft cry come from the other side of the door.

"I just found this on the sink Brittany. Just know... I love you." She then slid something underneath the door to Brittany. Brittany picked up the object she had slid to her. It was a card. As she flipped it over, what stared back at her made her nauseous. Looking back at her was the Tower card. Only now, one of the people falling from the tower in the card was scratched out violently. Jules was clearly next. "Jules, please don't cry, we are going to get you out. Everything is going to be fine."

Jules sat on the cold tile floor. Her knees to her chest, arms wrapped around her legs with her head on her knees, softly sobbing. She knew this was her final day. She would soon join Jane and live every day in this fear tormented room. There was nothing she could do. It was like a final destination movie, the inevitable was coming for her.

Fog swirled around her as if it would devour her. The air felt so cold even though the fog from the hot water should have made her sweaty and gross. Then she felt the soft touch on her head. It caressed her head, lovingly, making you feel safe and petrified at the same time.

Suddenly, the water turned off, complete silence enveloped the room. The fog seemed to clear a little. Jules raised her head, wondering if it was over, maybe it just wanted to scare her. She stood up and looked in the mirror. Her swirled, shadowy reflection looked back at her, then it smirked at her and disappeared. Jules rubbed her eyes. She had to have seen things, there's no way she just watched her reflection disappear. She went to the tub and her stomach dropped. It sat full of water, with no stopper and yet it was not draining. A small ring bloomed in the center of the water, as though a finger had just touched the surface.

Jules stared. Another ripple. She couldn't look away. A single, wet hand print formed on the porcelain edge of the tub. She gasped and stepped back. And as she did, she heard the wet footprints on the tile floor.

Slap... slap... slap...

Jules heartbeat pounded in her ears and the hair on her body stood on edge. Then she heard a faint whisper in her ear.

RUN

Her chest started to race, yet her body stood frozen. She couldn't move. She couldn't scream. It was like she was having sleep paralysis. She had never been so terrified in her life. She could hear Brittany talking to her, but she sounded so far away. It was as if Brittany was in a different hotel room. A single tear streamed down her face.

Then she felt the push.

It was such a forceful shove. She hit her head hard on the side of the tub. The sound of her skull cracking echoed through her head. She grabbed her pounding head, her vision blurring. When she pulled her hand away it was glistening with red liquid. She was sitting on the floor, blood streaming for her scalp, scared out of her mind and yet still her legs would not move.

That's when she heard Brittany's voice. "Hey Jules, I called Brad. He's bringing one of his workers here. They are going to get the door open for you. They should be here any minute."

Jules' whole body seemed to let out a sigh of relief. She was going to be OK, stitches, maybe a concussion but she would survive. She went to stand up, excited, knowing they were on their way. As she stepped towards the door, her foot slipped on the wet tile floor. Her whole body seemed to move in slow motion. She felt her body slowly slide backwards, her other foot slipping out from underneath her. Her arms flailing to try to catch onto anything. Her back starting to curve as she felt herself going down. And then she felt the side of the tub hit her back. The pain was excruciating and sent shooting strikes of pain down to her toes that took her breath away. She opened her eyes to murky waves, realizing she too was underwater just as Jane had been. She was drowning and it was because of her own stupidity from slipping on the floor.

Chapter 11

Brad and the maintenance worker came into the room. They tried to budge the door the same way Brittany had. "I already tried that!" Brittany screamed out of nervousness and frustration. "I haven't heard any noise coming from the bathroom in a couple of minutes, you need to hurry."

The maintenance man worked quickly on the door, getting the last pin from the hinges. Him and Brad quickly grabbed the door and pulled it away. Brittany bolted into the bathroom, but what she saw would forever be burnt into her memory.

There was blood all over the floor and tub. A hand and leg lay limp over the edge of the tub, unmoving. As she ran to the tub the water had a dark red murky look to it, there was so much blood you could barely see through it. She reached in without hesitation, her hands slipping in the murky water as she grabbed Jules, praying she was not gone. She slid Jules lifeless body into her arms, red water trickling down her arms.

"No, no, no, no, no. Jules, you can't leave me. We were supposed to leave. Why did you have to go in the bathroom!" She screamed as she started to cry.

She could hear Brad in the background on the phone with the police. "We need an ambulance now! There's a girl not breathing. There's blood everywhere!"

Time had completely stopped. All she saw was Jules. Her face looked so calm, as she lay there lifeless. Her hair soaking wet and so red it looked as if she had dyed it. Her skin, usually glowing, was dull and lifeless. Brittany just kept crying, her chest burned, her hands shaking. *How had this happened? Why wasn't Jane enough?* So many thoughts went through her head as she held her best friend.

She felt a hand on her shoulder, but she didn't move to see who it was. She never wanted to let go of Jules. The moment she did, she knew she would never see her again. She was not ready for that type of completeness.

The once quiet twelfth floor was now buzzing with urgent footsteps and hushed, frantic voices. The paramedics arrived in a blur, two men and a woman, all in dark uniforms, their medical bags slung over their shoulders, faces focused but grim as they entered Room 1210.

Brittany didn't even hear the front door open. She didn't move until the paramedics were beside her, gently pulling her away from Jules.

"No!" she cried, clutching tighter. "Don't take her from me!"

"Miss," one of the paramedics said gently, kneeling beside her. "We need to check her. Please, let us help."

Her hands trembled as she slowly, reluctantly let go. The paramedic caught Jules' head and eased her onto the cold tile floor. Brittany backed up until she hit the vanity, her back pressing hard against it as she watched, breathless and broken.

The paramedics worked quickly. One placed two fingers at Jules' neck, checking for a pulse.

"Unresponsive," the lead paramedic said, shaking his head. "No pulse. Starting compression's." The rhythm of their movements filled the room, the pump of chest compression's, the slap of adhesive pads, the mechanical voice of the defibrillator counting down.

"Charging."

"Clear."

A jolt rocked Jules' body. Brittany flinched, covering her mouth with both hands.

Nothing. They shocked her again. Still nothing.

The paramedic tried one more time, voice tight. "Come on... come on..."

But Jules' chest didn't rise. The room had gone still again. One paramedic silently turned off the AED. Another slowly covered Jules' face with a clean white towel.

"No..." Brittany whispered. Her legs buckled, and she slid down the wall, hugging her knees to her chest.

"I'm sorry," one of them said quietly. "She's gone."

Brittany barely heard him. Her ears were ringing. Her heartbeat echoed louder than the sirens that still screamed faintly outside the hotel.

The paramedics exchanged quiet words, writing notes, radioing dispatch. The bathroom floor was soaked, the blood mixing with water, creeping along the grout in slow, spreading veins. One paramedic opened the window to release the steam and the suffocating pressure that hung in the room. But even with the window open, the air didn't feel any lighter.

Brittany remained curled in the corner, staring blankly at the towel covering Jules' face. The quick sparkle of a lipstick tube next to her lifeless hand. She was supposed to have made it out. They both were. All of this had started with a haunted room, a podcast idea, and the thrill of the unknown. And now?

Now it was death.

Now it was silence.

The twelfth floor had transformed into a crime scene. Yellow tape stretched across the entrance to Room 1210, casting long black shadows on the faded wallpaper. Uniformed officers moved with quiet urgency, speaking into radios and photographing every inch of the room.

Brittany sat slumped in a chair just outside the room, a scratchy hotel blanket wrapped around her shoulders, though it did nothing to stop her shivering. Her skin felt numb. Her brain buzzed with static.

A detective crouched in front of her. He was middle aged, clean shaven, with weary eyes that had clearly seen too much. His badge glinted under the hallway lights.

"Miss..." he paused, glancing down at his notepad, "Brittany, right?"

She nodded slowly, hollow-eyed.

"I'm Detective Plink. I know you've just gone through something traumatic, but I need to ask you a few questions, okay? I understand you and your friend were staying in Room 1210?"

"Yes," she croaked, her voice barely audible.

He scribbled something down. "And what led you to that room specifically? I was told you requested it?"

She hesitated. "We... we have a podcast. Paranormal stuff. We read about it online, a Reddit post. We thought it was just an abandoned room with a spooky story."

He nodded, flipping to a new page in his notebook. "Walk me through what happened tonight."

She took a deep breath, fighting the lump in her throat. "We were packing up to leave. Things had been... weird, but not dangerous. Then Jules saw something on the bathroom floor.

She went to check. I heard the door close. After that..." She shook her head. "It all spiraled. The door wouldn't open. She said the tub was running. She found a tarot card. The*Tower*."

The detective's pen stopped. "Did she say anything else?"

Brittany's voice trembled. "She said she loved me. She sounded like she thought she was going to die. I tried to get her out. Brad called you, but it was too late."

There was a long silence as Detective Plink scribbled notes. "And Jules never made remarks about wanting to end her life?"

"What?" Brittany asked, her head shooting up to look at him. "She loved life, she never would have done that."

"I have to ask these hard questions Brittany. And before this... you mentioned activity in the room?"

"Books moving. Pages flipping on their own. Messages in condensation. My name in a book that had always been blank... until tonight." Brittany wiped her face with her sleeve. "You don't believe me, I know. But you didn't see what we saw."

Plink's expression stayed neutral, but his eyes betrayed a flicker of something, curiosity? Unease?

"Miss," he said gently, "we didn't find any tarot cards in the bathroom. No book matching what you described."

Brittany blinked. "That's not possible. I held it. I *read* it."

Plink stood slowly, closing the notebook. "We're going to do a full sweep of the room. For now, we'll need to take you downstairs. An officer will escort you. Do you have someone you can call?"

"Yes," she whispered, staring toward the room that had stolen her best friend. "My mom."

He gave her a nod and stepped aside as a female officer approached.

As Brittany stood up, her knees buckling slightly, she turned for one last look at the door to Room 1210. It stood open now, just a crack, enough to see inside, where the lights had been turned off. The bathroom was just a shadow beyond the frame. And in the mirror, barely visible, nearly swallowed by the dark, she could have sworn she saw Jules. Smiling. Then gone.

Downstairs in the lobby, the cold reality of what had happened began to soak in. She sat on a bench near the fire exit, still wrapped in the same hotel blanket, her arms now pulled tight against her chest. Her hands were stained faintly pink, and no matter how many times she rubbed them against her jeans, the color wouldn't fade. There was this weird feeling that she wasn't alone though.

Detective Plink stood several feet away, speaking quietly with another officer. Their words were just out of reach, but their glances kept drifting back to her. Not with sympathy, no. It was something else now. Hesitation. Doubt.

A new officer stepped over to her with a Styrofoam cup of water.

"Here," he said gently.

She took it with a shaky hand but didn't sip. Her eyes were fixed on the reflection in the lobby's polished floor tiles. In it, she swore she saw someone pass near her, a woman, soaking wet but when she turned, the space was empty.

A chill ran through her. It was as if the hotel wanted to keep torturing her.

"Brittany," Plink said, returning with a careful voice, "we're going to take you somewhere safe for tonight."

She blinked up at him. "Somewhere safe? My mom's not coming? Did you get in touch with her?"

"Yes," he nodded. "We did. But you've been through something traumatic. And right now, you're not in a state to make any major decisions. We'd like to bring you to a hospital. Just for evaluation. You won't be alone. It's precautionary. Your mom knows where you will be and she will meet you there soon."

Her face contorted in confusion. "What? No. I'm not crazy. I didn't do this. I don't need to be evaluated. She... she was attacked by something in that room. It wasn't me, but whatever did take her was real!"

"No one's saying it was you," he replied, voice steady. "But you're seeing things that no one else saw. Things that, as of now, we haven't found evidence of. The book, the card, the lipstick, do you understand how that sounds to someone who wasn't there?"

"But it *was* there!" she shouted, standing abruptly. "Why won't you believe me?!"

The lobby went quiet. People turned to look, staff, officers, paramedics. The room shrank around her.

A female officer gently grabbed her by the arm.

"Don't touch me," Brittany said, pulling away. But she was tired. Her limbs ached. Her mind felt like it was peeling apart at the edges. Plink stepped closer. "You said yourself you were hearing voices. Seeing things."

"That doesn't mean I'm losing it," she whispered, voice cracking. "That means this place is *haunted.* Ask Brad, he can tell you he heard her voice, she must have been alive when he got there."

Another pause. Then Plink's voice, softer this time: "Let's get you somewhere warm, okay? Somewhere quiet. You'll get some rest. Maybe talk to someone."

They didn't handcuff her. They didn't need to. She didn't fight it. She was too tired to fight.

Two officers walked her to the cruiser and helped her inside. As the door shut, she looked up at the hotel, tall, unbothered, its glowing windows watching her like silent eyes. Room 1210 still burned in her memory like a branding iron. She was leaving without Jules. And somehow, she knew the hotel wasn't finished with her.

Chapter 12

Brittany sat in the cold sterile room, her body sitting on the hard unforgiving mattress. She stared at a blanket of white, the walls, the comforter, her clothes. Everything in the room purposefully thought out so you couldn't hurt yourself or craft a weapon. They weren't allowed to have top sheets because God forbid you could hang yourself from them. They only had a fluffy comforter that was too thick to tie around anything, and it was very small. It barely reached the edges of the bed. Her mattress cover was used as a fitted sheet. It was soft, but it zipped over the mattress and had a small padlock on it. That only left her pillowcase, and you couldn't do much with that.

She felt numb, how had this happened? Just days ago, she was sitting by a fire with Jules laughing about how scared they were by what was most likely squirrels in the woods. She couldn't believe she was now sitting in the psych ward, locked in her room and being evaluated for supposed hallucinations. As far as she was being told even their recording sessions from the trips to Devils Hopyard and the hotel were gone. It was as if they had never been there. The only thing anchoring her to reality was Jules lying in her arms, covered in blood and the only thing saving her from murder was the two men who pulled the hinges from the door.

She replayed those last few moments over and over in her mind. *Why had Jules gone into the bathroom? Why had the door locked behind her? And where the hell was the book?*

The officer who had visited yesterday had explained that they had a whole team search the room for the objects. They stated they spoke to Brad, the desk clerk, who stated that the room was not haunted. He stated we were the first people to stay in the room since they re-opened it after a tragic moment from years ago. When Brittany told the officer about the Reddit post he stated there was no such post and that they had even gone into Jules' phone history and no such post popped up.

She knew she needed to find out what was going on. She never made up that conversation with Brad. Her and Jules had both seen that Reddit post, and there most certainly was a book. How was she going to get out of here and find proof. She highly doubted they would just let her back into the hotel room. Brad was clearly not going to help her. Her mom didn't believe her and when she did come to see her there was always pity in her eyes and that condescending tone in her voice as she said, "This didn't happen Brittany. Tell them the truth so you can get help, and I can bring you home." The day they had evaluated her after the incident, Brittany's mom said she was acting erratic and was a danger to herself and others. She begged the unit to get Brittany help.

Brittany was stubborn though. She wasn't going to just nod along and let them gaslight her into doubt. She wanted to prove to them this was real so she could shove it in their faces. She replayed the night at the hotel constantly trying to think of anything that would give her a clue as to what happened and how to end this for good so no one else would die and Jules could rest in peace.

Knock Knock

Brittany watched a nurse enter the room. A young, short stocky brunette girl with her hair in a tight bun. She walked in with this fake smile plastered on her face that made Brittany's skin crawl. She noticed the small white cup in the nurse's hand. The nurse put the cup closer to Brittany as if she was offering communion. But Brittany clenched her jaw, she wanted to smack the cup out of her hand, watch the pills go flying, just to hear the girl scream.

"Here ya go Brittany. Take these and you will feel *so* much better." The nurse smiled wide, and her red lipstick has smeared onto her two front teeth like a creepy clown.

Brittany grabbed the pill cup and poured the pill into her mouth. She quickly hid it inside her bottom gums. She then grabbed the little blue water cup being held out to her. She quickly swigged it back. The water was ice cold and stung her teeth a little. She then stuck her tongue out and wiggled it around to show there was no pill.

"Thank you, darlin', you'll feel much better now."

The nurse shuffled obnoxiously out of the room. She hated when people didn't pick their feet up as they walked. The sound is so annoying and made her want to trip the nurse just to see if she would bounce off the floor like a rubber ball.

Once she clicked the door behind her, Brittany spit the pill out and placed it inside her pillowcase. Once the building went dark, she would use the heel of her shoe to crush it up and shove it into the tiles to look like grout, so no one would ever realize she was not taking them.

She didn't trust the nurses here. They all come in with their fake smiles and obnoxious customer service voices. Sometimes she hears them murmuring about her.

"That's the girl from the hotel."

"Yeah, the one that killed her friend."

"Don't look her in the eye, she'll kill you too."

It made her blood boil, but the anger she felt was intense, consuming. It didn't feel like it was entirely her. Like something festering, begging to let lose. Granted, she knew the atmosphere of this place and the condescending attitudes she got from everyone around her was attributing to her new mental state.

They wanted her quiet, her memory erased.

Chapter 13

It had been three weeks, but it had felt like forever since she had been placed here. She hated it here. She missed her home, her bed, her life.

The staff here were cold, but the worst was the red-lipped nurse, "the red bitch," as Brittany had started calling her in her head, who treated her like a wild animal in a cage. Cold eyes. Always watching. Always judging. Then there were the *shadows*, those godforsaken shapes that danced in the corners of her room at night, dark and wrong, stretching farther than they should.

But the worst thing... was the dream. She had a lot of nightmares in here, but this one came more frequently and was the scariest.

In the dream, she stood at the edge of a room, an endless void, swirling smoke in every direction. And in the middle, sat Jules, cross-legged, eyes wide with fear. Across from her was a woman in a long black dress, wrapped in a deep purple shawl. She wore a turban on her head, a single jewel in the middle. She was clearly a psychic of some kind. Jules would ask the same questions Brittany had once asked her, back in her bedroom. Only now, the questions felt twisted, like a ritual.

The psychic never answered out loud. She would simply flip

the cards. Brittany's cards from that night.

The Ace of Pentacles.

The Two of Cups.

Then, finally, the *Tower* card would fall from the deck just like it had that night with Jules in her room.

Except this time... the Tower card looked wrong. The art was burned in. Melted. And both of the figures, who were usually seen falling, were scratched out, violently and deeply, like someone had used a razor blade to erase their existence. Then, the card would burst into flames on the table, crumbling to ash as the psychic just sat there.

Jules would start crying as she mumbled over and over, "You're the Tower, It was you all along..."

Then the psychic would lean in, that smile growing wider than any human mouth should stretch. "You will return... and fall. I will have you."

And then Jules would burst into fire, screaming, her body consumed as if she were made of paper.

That's when Brittany would wake, drenched in sweat, her pillow soaked through. She'd be crying before she was even fully awake, heart thundering in her chest.

What if that really was Jules' fate? What if the burning never ended?

Knock, knock.

Brittany flinched. She looked up to see a woman in a stiff white coat standing in the doorway. Mid-40s, maybe older, mousy brown hair that laid stringy on her shoulders. Her face was long and narrow, lips permanently pressed in a scowl, it reminded Brittany of when her mom would tell her to stop crossing her eyes or they would stay that way.

"Brittany," the woman said flatly. "Let's go. It's time for

your therapy appointment."

Therapy. Right. Brittany stood up, wiping her eyes. The hallway outside was dull and clinical, as lifeless as the people who shuffled through it. As they passed other rooms, she caught a flash of someone familiar.

A girl. Dark hair, pale skin, sad eyes.

Jane? No. Not Jane. *Lindsay.*

The resemblance had always startled Brittany, but the more they talked during their "recess time" as the nurses called it in the common room, the more the similarities faded. Lindsay had her own story. One that felt too dark to be fiction. They had become close, well, as close as two patients numbed by medication and fear could get. They would sit side by side on plastic chairs by the window, sipping lukewarm tea as they shared fragments of themselves.

Lindsay would talk about her family and how they were no longer alive but never wanted to discuss how they had passed. Brittany would tell her about her mom and school, but she never went into private details, and she never talked about Jules.

Brittany was thankful that every week her mom would come for a couple of hours. During that time it gave Brittany a little sense of normalcy.

One day Lindsay finally told her why she was here, and about the voices she heard. "The Devil's coming for me," she'd whisper. Then she said that she started seeing him, "He dances around my bed at night, taunting me, scaring me, it's the Devil."

She claimed to wake up with sandy hoof prints around her bed. Claimed she saw him sometimes, just standing there, black as shadow, grinning with teeth too sharp. Horns protruding from his skull that swirled perfectly. He'd whisper the same phrase over and over.

"Fog and fire, fog and fire," he'd sing in a low, mocking tone.

"When one girl crumbles, the other will tire.

Take them all until I'm whole,

Then I'll have the world as my own."

Then she said he would disappear, but she knew he was never actually gone. She could hear him tapping the walls around her room. Over and over, faster and faster. She would cover her ears and close her eyes begging him to stop. Then she said everything would go quiet, but she knew he wasn't gone. Usually when she opened her eyes he would be hiding in the closet or in the curtains of her window, his yellow glowing eyes the only thing she could see, just watching her all night.

The scariest was the night she said she opened her eyes to him floating above her. "He smiled at me," she said, her voice cracking. "Like he loved the fear. He laughed menacingly and then wrapped his hands around my neck. I couldn't breathe. I tried to grab at his hands but they would go right through him as if he wasn't real. Then at the last minute he would let go."

Then he whispered in her ear, "Have you had enough?" She said she nodded and begged him to stop. He then grabbed her hand as he still hovered over her and told her to close her eyes. He told her that when she opened them back up, he would be gone. She told me that she closed her eyes, and felt this weird tingle throughout her body, and then she said her whole body started to tremble lightly. She woke up the next morning and said she wasn't herself anymore. She'd snap for no reason. Have thoughts that didn't feel like her own that she couldn't seem to push away. Rage that burned in her bones like wildfire. She told Brittany about the night she begged her mom for a priest, she knew she needed an exorcism. Her mom scoffed and told her she was being crazy. She kept begging, screaming that something was wrong. That she was seeing things and hearing things. She said her mom rolled her eyes, told her if she didn't stop this nonsense that she would give her a real reason to scream.

That same night, her stepfather came home, drunk as a skunk, talking about how pretty she was. Making references about how she had grown in many ways. He got closer to her, toying with her hair, and whispered, "I can fix your problem, I'll be your exorcist and put something else inside of you." Then he smiled and rubbed the back of his greasy hand down her arm. She was done, she could feel the anger raging inside of her. It wasn't her anger she felt, this burned hotter, her brain buzzed with hatred that wasn't her own. The whispers in her mind telling her to torture him. Burn him!

"I don't remember what happened next," she said. "I blacked out and when I came to, I was here. Police officers surrounded my bed questioning why I had burned the house down and killed my parents." She said she knew she sounded crazy telling them the Devil made her do it. "I knew no one would believe me." She said, a tear rolling down her cheek. "When I got here, all of the anger, and weird feelings left. My body didn't feel invaded anymore. It was as if the Devil had done what he needed to do and then threw me away."

Brittany held her hand and told her she believed the Devil was real and that she didn't need to feel alone.

She *knew* something dark was real. Something ancient. Something cruel. The weirdest thing she said though, was that the Devil had introduced himself as Zaron. She said it never made sense to her because the Devil had many names in the Bible but that wasn't one of them.

But hearing it made a shiver go down Brittany's spine. That name had been in her nightmares, had tormented her, and here Lindsay was saying it.

She never told Lindsay what really happened to her. She gave her a story, some past-life nonsense about being a witch from the 1800s, burned at the stake, reincarnated and terrified of fire. It was easier. Safer. She told Lindsay she would throw out matches and lighters stating they would be her end, and her mom would get mad. She said she would wake up screaming, telling her mom she was on fire, and that this would be her destruction. She would go on to explain her mom tried to get her psychiatric help but that help ended her up in here.

But Brittany knew the real truth. She was afraid if she spoke about the thing in the hotel room, they too would become part of this horror she was stuck in. Whatever had been in that hotel room had followed her here, and she refused to let anyone else be attacked by this thing and die. She saw it in the shadows at night in her bed. Heard it in the taps on her wall. Sometimes a tube of lipstick would roll out from under her bed. Other nights, the sink would gurgle like someone was drowning in it. She even heard the familiar thud, like a book dropping on the floor.

But when she looked? Nothing.

This thing was torturing her every night, subtle things to keep her in a paranoid state. To let her know that whatever was in that hotel room was still watching.

And worse? It seemed to be waiting. Waiting for what she didn't know, and that scared her the most.

Chapter 14

The office was sterile, beige walls lined with laminated posters about self-regulation and deep breathing. A fake Ficus stood limp in the corner, its dust-covered leaves drooping as if they too had given up. The fluorescent lights above flickered once, then again. Brittany flinched.

Dr. Cuttleman sat in a rolling chair across from her, legs crossed neatly, clipboard resting in her lap like a holy text. Her eyes, cold and calculating, skimmed over Brittany's chart before meeting her gaze.

"So, Brittany," she began, her voice clipped and smooth, "you've been here for three weeks. Would you say you're adjusting?"

Brittany blinked slowly. *Adjusting to what? The whispers at night? The phantom hands brushing her skin when no one was there? The taste of ash that sometimes filled her mouth for no reason at all?*

"I guess," Brittany said flatly. "I sleep. I eat. I scream. The usual."

Dr. Cuttleman scribbled something down. "Tell me about the screaming."

Brittany clenched her hands in her lap. "I have the same nightmare every night. A random woman sits across from my now deceased best friend. There's fire and I wake up screaming. It feels like it's me on fire when I wake up."

"And do you feel like this is guilt? Do you feel it should have been you who died?"

That question hit harder than it should have. *Always.* That guilt always lay heavy on her chest. She wished she had been the one to go into the bathroom. She wished she had been the one to drown. She felt like she was being watched from inside her own head, as if whatever was in the room knew exactly what she was thinking. Sometimes she swore she could feel something... moving just behind her eyes.

"I feel like someone left the door open in my mind," she said finally. "And something's... pacing in the hallway."

That got the doctor's attention. The pen paused.

"In the hallway?"

Brittany nodded slowly. "Ya know, of my mind. I don't know what it is. But I don't think it likes being ignored. It's trying to tell me something, pull me somewhere."

Silence settled between them.

Dr. Cuttleman leaned forward. "Brittany, I want to ask about the delusion, about the 'demon' you mentioned your friend Lindsay saw. Zaron, was it?"

That name sent a cold pulse through her spine.

"I don't know who he is," Brittany whispered. "Or why the name makes me feel this way, but when the name pops in my head, my whole body seems to tingle, and then I get these flash card images in my head of the hotel. But not from when we were there. It's older, the hotel when it was pristine, a bellhop in the elevator, two young girls sitting on the floor with their backs to me, a Ouija board, an old tarot deck laying scattered on the carpet, and then a shadow near the bookcase, and they flash over and over again and then they come to a dead stop and I just see Jules face, smiling, and then everything vanishes."

The lights flickered again. Once. Twice.

Brittany turned her head. For a second, she swore she saw a dark shadow standing behind the doctor, tall, formless.

Then it was gone.

Dr. Cuttleman sighed. "You're not in any danger here, Brittany. These things you see, the feelings you get. It's very normal for someone who goes through a traumatic experience. None of these hallucinations are real."

But Brittany laughed softly. It was the kind of laugh that sounded broken. Empty. "Oh, this is very real! You think padded walls and little chalky pills will stop this thing? You think your hushed voice telling me it's not real will cure me? He followed me from that hotel. I feel him in the vents. In the water. I dream of Jules burning every night. Jane screaming. And all I can do is sit and watch because I'm not strong enough. All of this is real."

Brittany looked up, tears suddenly hot in her eyes. "I think... I think he's trying to wear me down. And I'm scared he's winning."

The doctor wrote something down again. "You're going to get help in here," she said in that robotic tone of professional-ism. "With medication, and time, you'll learn to cope, you'll learn to put these thoughts in the back of your mind. One day you will wake up and realize it's not true."

But Brittany was already pulling away mentally. Because just then, a soft sound tapped through the vent behind the doctor.

Tap tap.

Her body went cold.

He's here.

Brittany's breath hitched in her throat, "Behind you," she whispered. "He's behind you!"

Dr. Cuttleman calmly removed her glasses, unfazed. "There's no one behind me, Brittany."

But Brittany had already risen from her chair, backing into the far wall, her hand flying to her mouth as the shadowy figure unfurled itself from the vent completely. It dragged down the wall, faceless, save for the teeth. Its movements jerky, as though flickering through different frames of time.

It didn't walk. It was just standing there. It leaned over the doctor, almost tenderly, like a lover preparing a kiss. And then, it turned its head to Brittany.

It saw her.

She froze. Her blood turned to ice. Its long fingers reached down... and plucked the Tower card from the doctor's desk.

Brittany gasped.

Dr. Cuttleman finally looked up, concerned now. "Brittany? What's wrong?"

The shadow held the card to its chest. Then bit down on it, ripping the image in half with those endless teeth. Ash fluttered to the floor like burned snow.

"Three deaths," the thing rasped. "You will all fall."

And with that, it slithered backward into the vent... the metal grating resealing like it had never opened.

Gone.

Brittany dropped to her knees, gasping for air. Tears blurred her vision.

"Brittany!" Dr. Cuttleman was at her side now, reaching for her. "You're dissociating. Focus on your breath. In and out. In and—"

But Brittany didn't hear her. All she could hear was the last whisper in her ear, almost lovingly spoken:

"You will all fall."

Brittany thrashed against the pale green walls of the therapy room, her screams ragged, animalistic. Her fingers clawed at her arms, her chest. The Tower card was gone. Ripped in half. Stolen. That... thing had seen her.

"It was here! It was real! He had my card! he took it!" she shrieked, stumbling backward into the corner of the room, her breath coming in frantic gasps.

Dr. Cuttleman pressed the emergency button. Within seconds, the door flew open, and two nurses stormed in, blue scrubs and latex gloves, already wielding the syringe.

"No, please, I'm not crazy!" Brittany yelled, tears streaming down her face, her vision warping from panic and exhaustion.

"It's just a reaction, Brittany," Dr. Cuttleman said calmly, too calmly, like she wasn't covered in shadow just moments ago. "We're going to help you settle down, that's all."

She backed into the farthest corner, shaking her head, gripping her scalp like she could squeeze the memory out of her mind. The syringe glinted in the flickering fluorescent light. Please," Brittany whimpered, "you don't understand... he's still here, tormenting me."

The nurses didn't pause. Hands grabbed her arms. She kicked, struggled, howled, but her body betrayed her, weak from sleepless nights, too drained to fight. The needle slid into her shoulder. A cold burn spread like ink in her veins.

"No," she murmured, her voice slurring already, "don't make me sleep..."

The ceiling above her began to melt into shadow. As the drug took hold, the last thing she saw was Dr. Cuttleman stepping closer, too close. Her face briefly glitching, flickering like a corrupted screen. For just a second... the mouth on her face smiled wider than any mouth should.

And then the world tipped sideways. Brittany collapsed against the cold tile floor, her breath slowing. Her fingers twitched once. Then stilled.

Silence.

A nurse pulled the blanket over her, another gently rolled her to her side, But just before her mind slipped into unconsciousness, she heard it:

Tap tap.

From inside the walls.

Then like a whisper in the wind...

"Almost time."

Chapter 15

Brittany woke up, her brain completely foggy. She wasn't feeling herself at all, her body felt heavy, and she wasn't sure how long she had been out. She heard her door open, and she looked up to see one of the nurses in the doorway. "Brittany, you are needed at group therapy. Here's some toast and milk. Eat it quickly, therapy is in a half an hour."

She dropped the tray onto the edge of Brittany's bed and walked out of the room. Brittany sat up, rubbing her eyes and trying to get them to focus. She was not hungry at all and after yesterday's session she really did not want to go to therapy, but in this place, you didn't have a choice. She got out of bed, her bare feet hitting the cold tile floor. Then she made her way to the corner of the room where her *bathroom* was. She didn't know if you could even consider it a room, there were no walls.

After finishing up, she looked in the mirror. She didn't even recognize the girl that stood before her. Her face was so much thinner now, the dark bags under her eyes, and her pale skin that had no color in it at all, she looked like a zombie.

She went back to where her breakfast sat on her bed, the toast looked very unappealing. She took a quick swig of the milk and forced it down. The milk was lukewarm and tasted a bit off, as if it had already started to go bad. Her stomach turned but she held it down. Then she heard the knock at the door.

Lindsay stood in the doorway with a smile on her face. "You ready for group therapy?" she said sarcastically.

Brittany sat on the cold, molded plastic chair, her back stiff and shoulders tense. She stared around the room, six other people sat in a circle around her. Dr. Cuttleman was one of them. All the people in the room were her age, late twenties, early thirties and they sat there numb, looking highly medicated and zombie like, as if all the color had been drained from them.

"OK guys," Dr. Cuttleman said. "Today we are going to go around the room and just talk. No specific subject this time. Whatever comes to mind just raise your hand and let it out. This is the vent session." She sat there, legs crossed, clipboard in hand, eager to hear us talk.

Everyone sat there not talking. No one stirred or acted like they wanted to be a part of the group session. You could hear a pin drop other than the occasional sniffle from one of them. One girl, she looked closest to Brittany's age, looked especially out of it. Her eyes were glossed over, her head kind of hung lower with her hair covering most of her face, her shoulders slumped. If Brittany tapped her, the girl was sure to fall right off the chair.

Brittany hated how they made everyone in here feel numb, in a comatose state. How were any of them supposed to vent when no one could barely think?

Lindsay sat next to her, fidgeting with the end of her sleeve. She looked especially uncomfortable today. Then she raised her hand.

"Yes Lindsay," Dr. Cuttleman perked up instantly. "What

would you like to say?"

"I figured I will go first, I just need to get this out and then maybe I will feel better."

Brittany felt the room shift, that quiet, heavy attention when someone started talking about something real.

Lindsay went on to talk about how today was the day her parents had died all those years ago. "I hate when this day rolls around, I swear I can see them in my room. I get visions of them standing near my bed, their faces extremely angry but they won't say anything. Sometimes I wish they would just scream at me, let the rage out, maybe then I could move on, but they just watch me. The next day they're gone again for another year, like clockwork. I hate this day, hate seeing them, hate the anger they still have for me, when I can't even remember starting the fire." Lindsay started to cry softly.

Dr. Cuttleman handed her a tissue, "Thank you Lindsay, I know it's not easy to talk about, but I am really glad you got it out."

Dr. Cuttleman searched the room for anyone else who wanted to talk. "Come on guys, it's good to get things out, it can help in the healing process."

Brittany felt something stir inside of her. Shame, fear, grief. All of it knotted together. She raised her hand.

"Oh yes, Brittany! I'm so glad you've decided to come forward. Please, the floor is yours."

Brittany hesitated, she didn't want to talk about any of the things roaming through her mind, but she knew if Lindsay was brave enough, she could be too. "I sometimes see the visions of the night everything went wrong." Brittany decided it was time to tell the truth about the hotel, what really happened. She couldn't keep up this charade about being a witch and being afraid of fire. "I see the hotel room, my best friend Jules laying on the floor and me begging her to wake up. I see her parents there shaking their heads in disapproval, knowing that I didn't keep their little girl safe and that their daughters young life is now with them. I sit on the floor and cry, begging them to forgive me for something I couldn't control." A tear fell down Brittany's cheek, and she couldn't keep going. She didn't want to relive the moment again. She remembered how sad Jules' parents were, their slightly see through bodies, with bowed heads, as they watched Jules' face get covered by the cloth. The sound of a body bag zipping still haunted her dreams.

"Thank you for that Brittany. We can always talk more about that on our one on one's. I feel like we've had a breakthrough, and I am very proud of you."

Then the girl from across the circle who had looked so out of it not moments ago raised her hand.

Dr. Cuttleman brightened. "Oh, girls this is Wendy, she just got here a couple of days ago. Please Wendy, proceed."

Wendy looked around the room nervously, her hands intertwined and her thumbs rubbing together like a cricket trying to make noise. She opened her mouth and then closed it again as if she was afraid to speak.

"It's OK Wendy," Dr. Cuttleman chimed in. "Take your time."

Lindsay offered gently, "You should share it. It might help."

Wendy sat there a moment longer and then finally spoke. Her voice so soft, you had to lean in closer to hear her. "I get visions that scared my parents, so they sent me here. They told me I was crazy and needed help they could no longer give. They said that I scared their friends because I would speak of dark things. I created fear in people, my parents said that it was not normal for a child to even think this way." Then she went quiet like she didn't want to get in trouble for expanding.

"This is a safe space Wendy, if you want to talk about the visions, you are more than welcome." Dr Cuttleman said to her smiling.

"I won't talk about the past ones, but I had a vision last night that I could talk about." Wendy said looking around the room at the other patients.

"Why yes I think that would be good for you to get them out." Lindsay said to her.

Wendy looked down at the floor as she proceeded to talk. "I had a vision of this dark tower, vines grew all around it, inside the tower a knight stood on the outside of the door, making sure whatever was locked in there couldn't get out. Two women sat inside, huddled together, scared and shaking. This weird dark fog swirled around them and at times the fog got so thick you could barely make them out. Then the fog would dissipate and there would be dark shadow figures surrounding them, there had to be at least twelve, they had no faces, and their bodies were hard to make out, but you could see the misty outlines of their figures, and their eyes. These neon glowing yellow eyes. Their eyes seemed to look right into your soul." She swallowed, her eyes still looking at the floor.

"You could feel the girls fear heavy in the room, it was as if it was a cloud that you could touch. Then another dark figure, larger than the rest and darker, came up from the floor and hovered over them. His anger was immense." Wendy's voice dropped lower. "The older woman screamed at him, "you shall never touch us, we are safe under this spell, you shall never feed off of our fear or sadness." As the woman screamed, a little boy came into focus around two of the dark figures, very young, sad looking, wearing a straw hat. The older lady screamed, "NO! Not him. Please." The dark figure laughed, "you can't save them all, you may have this one," he said sneering at the girl the older lady was hugging. "But this one is mine and so are the other two. Your warnings faltered, one has fallen and the other shall fall shortly." Then it laughed this horrible guttural laugh, "your tower shall soon fall my dear and once it falls your powers shall fall with it and you will be mine."

Wendy looked up from the floor and stared right at Brittany. Her lips curved into a smile that didn't belong on a human face. Then she continued, in a soft, singsong chant,

> *"the hollow ones creep, the hollow ones crawl,*
> *They crawl through the cracks of the darkest hall.*
> *They feed on your fear, they whisper your name,*
> *They twist what you see, they play their sick game.*
> *He takes your voice, he steals your cries,*
> *He paints your dreams with crawling lies.*
> *Round and round your mind they spin,*
> *Open the door and they crawl right in."*

Brittany just stared at Wendy, the hairs on her body stood on end. A shiver ran up her spine, and she knew something wasn't right. Who was this girl?The longer Brittany stared at her, she started to notice this dark mist forming around Wendy's chair, Brittany couldn't look away, it was as if she was in a trance. The fog got so thick, you could no longer see the girls' shoes. As Brittany's eyes scanned the girl, starting at her feet and making their way up, the mist seemed to follow as it swirled up Wendy's body. As she looked at Wendy's face, the girls' eyes seemed to glow a faint golden color. Her grin got wider, curling upwards as if she was the joker. Her teeth which were normal minutes ago, seemed jagged. In Brittany's mind she could hear

Wendy's voice whispering, 'Round and round your mind they spin, open the door and they crawl right in.' Brittany sat their completely frozen, her body trembling, her eyes tearing up as she quickly saw a vision of Jules bloody body lying on the floor.

"Okay everyone," Dr. Cuttleman said suddenly, clapping her hands, snapping the spell. "Let's wrap up for today. Free time before lock down."

Chairs scraped across the floor as all the patients started to scuttle away but Brittany sat frozen in the chair. The fog had lifted from her brain, and she knew if she tried, she could move but the words she had heard just moments before kept running through her mind. 'Open the door and they will crawl right in.' A single tear slid down her cheek. She was terrified, not because of the girls' story, but because somewhere inside of her, this felt familiar, it felt like she knew this story and knew those girls in the tower. She felt as if it was a premonition of what was to come for her. She knew there was a chance she was not going to make it out of this place alive, whatever was tormenting her was going to keep feeding on her until she completely broke. They had opened the door to that hotel room and now they were doomed.

"Hey Brittany, "Lindsay said interjecting Brittany's frozen state. "Let's go, we only have twenty minutes before lock down."

Brittany wiped the tear from her cheek and looked up at her friend. The tranceand fear seemed to fade away as if they had never been there, as if Lindsay was a good luck charm and had broken Brittany's spell. She got up and made her way to the big window area where they always sat.

As Brittany and Lindsay sat down, Brittany looked over at the table closest to her. There on the table sat a lonely chocolate pudding cup, completely untouched with no one around. It was as if no one else could see it but her and that it had been put there specifically for her to see. She turned to ask Lindsay if she could see it too, but then she quickly glanced again just to make sure she wasn't crazy and when she looked at the table it was empty. She looked around the room, but no one was close to them. All of the other patients were in the far corner of the room watching TV. No one held a pudding cup in their hand or was licking their lips as if they had just taken the last bite. She shook her head realizing she was probably just tired, and her mind was playing tricks on her from being scared earlier by Wendy's story.

Yet Wendy's chant still echoed in her mind and the chill on her spine seemed to be coming back.

Lindsay's looked over at Brittany, "I have to tell you something. I know you never told me about the hotel room, but Zaron told me. He told me what happened and how Jules died. He told me he needs you to come to the hotel. Said he's been waiting for you. That you were the key to the end."

"Who is Zaron? And what do you mean the end, the end of what?" Brittany asked, feeling like the ground beneath her was splitting and her head started to feel dizzy again.

"I don't know. He said Jules needed you. That you were going to help unlock something, a tower of some sort. He only showed me a flash photo, but it looked like something out of a fairy tale. Like where Rapunzel was locked up. Only it seemed darker, although I thought it was really weird that Wendy had just mentioned a tower. You don't think she is able to read my mind, do you?"

Brittany's pulse raced and she swallowed hard. "No, I think it was just a crazy coincidence."

Lindsay shrugged, "Yeah... you're probably right. But Zaron did say something about setting them free," Her voice sounding distant, like she was repeating something from a dream.

Brittany's mind flashed to the image of the tower with the girls locked up, the dark figures surrounding them. She knew she needed more answers, this had to be about Jane and Jules. Madame Zodo was warning her and was using these girls to get her message across.

"I know you're looking at me as if I really am crazy but that's what he said. Set them free. But he needs you to do it. He said Jules would guide you. I'm not really sure, it doesn't make sense to me."

Brittany's blood ran cold. A dull ringing filled her ears. "I don't know what the hell is happening," she said, her voice cracking, "but I need to get out of here. I need to get to that hotel. I think Jules needs me. I think you and Wendy were sent messages meant for me."

She was trembling. Her body vibrated with fear and urgency. "It's like whatever this dark thing is... it's feeding off me. Every day I'm here, it gets stronger, and I get weaker. It's using this place to drain me. To trap me. I won't let it, it can't have me or my friends."

Lindsay leaned closer. "Zaron said Jules would send signs. Hints. Little things to help you get to her. He said you'd understand when it was time. That this time, you would finally be free. No more fire. No more torment. I believe in you Brittany, you are going to get out of here, just listen carefully to the signs that they give you."

Brittany's entire body tensed. That word again. Fire. She could barely respond. Her mind spun, spiraling between the shadowy fragments of what she knew and the growing dread of what she still didn't. Could Lindsay be telling the truth? Or was this another twisted layer in whatever game the dark thing was playing? Was it Jules leaving the signs? The lipstick? The tapping? The book?

Or... was Zaron using Jules as bait?

Her head felt like it was caving in under the pressure. Her chest ached with grief and confusion. She didn't know who to trust anymore. She needed to figure this out, really put the puzzle pieces together and get the fuck out of this place.

"I need to lie down," she muttered, standing unsteadily. "I need to think. I'll talk to you tomorrow."

Lindsay didn't answer. She just watched Brittany leave.

As soon as Brittany's head hit the stiff, over-washed pillow in her room, she was out, her body finally giving in to the exhaustion that had been clawing at her for days.

But peace didn't come.

The dream was vivid. Sharp. But it wasn't her normal nightmare.

She saw a room, lit only by candlelight.

It was Jane who sat cross legged on the floor, her posture identical to how Jules once sat during their readings. And there, across from her, was the same lady again.

The scene was eerily familiar. The lady shuffled the cards. Jane asked the same questions that Jules usually asked, the same sequence of cards laid out.

And then, the final card fell.

The Tower.

But this time... it was perfect.

No melting. No scratches. No ash. It was as if the card was new.

Jane looked at the lady with fear in her eyes, "Madame Zodo,"

Jane asked, her voice shaking, "what does this mean?"

Zodo's eyes narrowed. "It will happen tonight," she hissed. "You need to run, Jane."

Jane leaned forward, panicked. "What will happen tonight?!"

And then Zodo disappeared into a foggy mist, leaving nothing behind but a faint scent of frankincense.

Jane screamed her name but as the last letter came from her lips she started to choke.

Jane's hands gripped the table, her fingers going white, as water came from her mouth. It started as a trickle and then started pouring out of her mouth as if someone had turned the faucet on full blast. Her face twisted in pain. Her lips turned blue. Her eyes bulged as she tried to breathe, trying to cry out. Then Jules sat next to her, watching her choke on water. Jules' eyes glowed yellow as she smiled, her lips turning up the way Wendy's had in therapy. Jules watched as Jane clawed at her own throat, blood started dripping from her nose and ears, and then her eyes got even bigger as she sat there completely frozen. Her head hit the table as water seemed to puddle all around her. In the far corner of the room came a whisper, 'Zaron is the key, Brittany. ZARON is the key!' and it sounded like the psychics voice.

Jules's head whipped in that direction, fog swirling around her dark and fast as if she was a tornado. "You will be mine," she whispered into the dark corner. "You can't hide forever bitch!" she screamed.

Brittany shot up in bed, her chest heaving. Her scream echoed off the walls.

"ZARON!" Brittany's mind shouted the word over and over. The name vibrated through her body like a detonation.

Madame Zodo had tried to warn Jane, but Jane wouldn't listen. It must be fate that she had met Lindsay. Zaron was coming to her through Lindsay, using her to warn Brittany. Were Madame Zodo and Zaron the same person?

Brittany stared into the darkness of her room, jaw clenched, fists tight. Brittany wouldn't be like Jane. She was going to get out of here some way and save Jules.

"I'm coming," she whispered into the shadows. "I'm coming for all of you."

Chapter 16

Brittany paced the room all night. Wendy's vision, the poem, and the nightmare running through her head. she needed more answers, needed to talk to Wendy. She needed to know if Wendy knew more or if she even understood what she was seeing in her visions.

As the lights turned on in the main room, she could see the red bitch standing at the nurse's desk, her hair a mess as if she forgot what a comb was, her wrinkled scrubs that fit too tight, her muffin top popping out from the sides of the shirt. She was fumbling with her keys as she tried to open the medicine cart. The nurse next to her, hands on her hips, waiting to do a narcotic count so she could go home.

Brittany kept pacing the room, she just wanted the red bitch to open her door so she could go talk to Wendy. She realized that by pacing her room, she looked like she needed extra medication, but she didn't care. She couldn't sit still, her friend's life depended on her getting answers and getting out of here and she knew Wendy knew a lot more than she was saying.

The nurse looked at Brittany, her eyebrow raising, then she turned to the red bitch and whispered something. "Great." Brittany said out loud to herself. "Now they are definitely going to want me to take extra pills, I look crazy. And I am talking to myself which is not helping my case." Brittany shook her head trying to calm the nervousness in her body and sat down on the edge of her bed, her foot now tapping on the floor. "Come on! Why does it take them so long to do their job." She hadn't even realized she was biting the skin around her fingers until she felt the sting. She pulled her hand away and saw the blood trickling down her finger. How hard had she bit herself? Then nervousness set in, what if her teeth were becoming jagged? She ran her tongue over her front teeth, but they were smooth and uniform.

Relief shot through her for a second and then the nerves set back in. She watched as the two nurses conversed at the desk, laughing and flailing their arms around, clearly in a very important gossip discussion. Brittany couldn't take it anymore. She quickly made her way to the window and slammed her fist on it several times. That got the nurse's attention, but they didn't seem very happy.

The night nurse came walking over and unlocked her door. "What seems to be the problem?" she asked clearly annoyed.

"I need my pills that calm me down, I seem to be having an episode." Brittany said lying. "Well, we do like you guys when you're quiet. Let me go get your nurse." She locked the door once again and walked towards the red bitch, pointing at me and laughing. The red bitch seemed to laugh as well and shook a pill bottle towards Brittany, as if taunting her. Anger started growing inside of her and yet the anger didn't feel like her own, it was as if someone else had taken over her emotions. Without realizing what Brittany was doing, her hand moved to her throat, and she made the motion as if she was cutting her own neck and then she gave her the finger.

The nurses face swapped from a smile to a scowl quickly. She wrestled with the pill bottle cap, trying to open it but failing miserably, her face getting redder with every try. The nurse looked over, pure rage on her face as Brittany stood there watching her and laughing. The other nurse grabbed the bottle and opened it up on the first try and chuckled. The red bitch glared at her and snatched the bottle. She shook two small purple pills into a cup and proceeded to shuffle towards Brittany quickly, her face full of fury. She had never seen her walk so quickly in her entire time here, Brittany was afraid she was going to run out of breath before she got to the door. She chuckled thinking of her having to stop her twenty-foot trek to her door, hands on her knees and bent over, trying to catch her breath. "Pathetic." Brittany said chuckling to herself.

The red bitch opened the door a crack and slid her arm inside the room, holding the small cup containing the pills. "Here, take these and then go sit the fuck down."

Brittany didn't feel as if she was in control of her actions and her words, it was as if she was just a puppet. "Aren't you afraid that with just your arm sliding in, I could just slam the door and break you?" She said with a crooked smile.

The nurse quickly pulled her arm away, accidentally dropping the cup. The two little pills scattered near Brittany's feet. "Now look what you've done, you clumsy heifer." Brittany said, anger now fully taking over her body. "You expect me to pop these in my mouth after you guys have been trudging through my room with god knows what on your shoes?"

The nurse's eyes grew, and she stood there completely stunned. Brittany could sometimes get agitated, but she never spoke like that to anyone, nor would she ever act this way to one of the nurses, they could shoot you up with tranquilizers and take your recess privileges away. "Excuse me?" the nurse said in a shocked tone. "Who do you think you are, you little shit?"

Brittany's lips curled into an evil smirk. "Your worst nightmare bitch! Why don't you go waddle back to your cart and grab me two more pills, you wouldn't want me to stay out of control would you?"

The nurse stood there, arms folded with a sour look on her face. Then she locked the door and made her way back to the nurse's desk. Brittany could see her talking to the other nurse and then they both got up and went to the cart. The red bitch bent down and opened the bottom drawer of the cart. "Shit!" Brittany exclaimed. "That's the tranquilizer drawer. What in the hell got into me?" Brittany sat there on the edge of the bed, her elbows on her knees and her face in her hands. Why was she acting out like this? It was as if something or someone was doing it on purpose so that she wouldn't be able to leave her room. Then her head lifted, her body froze. "It's you," she said into the empty room. "You don't want me talking to Wendy, do you? Afraid I will get answers and then I will have a clue on how to defeat you."

As she finished that thought the two nurses came to the door, a new male nurse standing behind them. They quickly made their way to her bed, the male nurse and the night nurse held her arms down. She wanted to fight, wanted to bite at their hands or kick the red bitch but she knew there was no point in trying. One way or another they were going to stick her with the needle. She needed to figure out how she was going to fight this medication so she could go talk to Wendy.

As the burn of the needle entered her arm, she felt the warm burning liquid enter her body. Almost immediately she felt this fuzzy feeling come over her, her mind got fuzzy, her arms and legs seemed extremely heavy, it was hard to even hold her head up. She tried fighting the feeling, but it was useless, she was going down and there was nothing she could do to stop it. She looked up to see the red bitch standing over her, her creepy clown smile on her face. "Who's laughing now Brittany?"

She felt them pick her up and lay her head on the pillow. Her eyes got even heavier, and she fell into sleep. Anytime they gave her this medication, she wouldn't be able to move, or think, or dream. It was as if she was completely out, dead to the world.

Chapter 17

When she finally woke up, her head was spinning. She slowly sat up. She had no idea what time it was or what day it was for that matter. She could see a couple of patients walking around the common area so she knew it couldn't be too late. She put her feet on the cold tile floor, nervous to try to stand with the way she felt. She slowly pushed herself off the bed and inch by very slow inch made her way to the toilet. Once she had finished, she felt a little more awake and in control of her legs. She needed to try to make it to Wendy's room so they could talk more.

She shuffled her feet to her door, feeling like the red bitch as she walked. She stood at the doorway looking out the window, scanning the room for Wendy. She didn't see her hanging out in the recess area, she figured she must be in her room. She slowly made her way to Wendy's door, the number 13 in big black letters right underneath the small window.

She knocked but heard no response, so she opened the door and walked in. The room was empty, Wendy nowhere to be found. "Hmm," Brittany thought out loud. "She must be in therapy."

As her eyes scanned the room she noticed a lot of drawings on the walls. Her eyes caught on one in specific and walked over to where her bed was to get a better view. Her breath hitched as she realized she was looking at a drawing of the Davidson House Hotel. The picture next to it was of the beautiful elevator doors, the next picture was of that picture in the lobby of Jane. Her eyes scanned the pictures faster, each of them a memory of Brittany's from the hotel. The leather book, Jules and Brittany on the couch, Brad, the bathroom, the ballroom, a beaded seeing eye necklace. The pictures just kept going, every picture she scanned made her stomach twist a little more. She didn't just have an idea of what happened that night, she knew everything. The bathroom even had a small tube of lipstick, the tube open to show you exactly what it was sitting in the middle of the bathroom floor. Every detail completely perfect and accurate.

The fuzzy feeling in her head completely gone now as anger took its place. Her hands and feet moved as though she had not been shuffling two seconds ago. She started ripping the pictures off the wall frantically. Her breath coming in quick fragments. Her eyes tearing up at every picture she tore down. Why did she have these, how did she know every detail? She sat on Wendy's bed, tears dropping onto the picture of her and Jules. She just kept mumbling the words, "I'm sorry Jules."

Brittany jerked up quickly, her heart racing as she heard a voice coming from the doorway. "Wow, I thought my drawings were pretty good, quite rude of you to just tear them down." Wendy said.

Brittany stood up and rushed at her, shaking the papers in her face. "How did you know! How did you know every little detail?"

"I honestly don't know what you're talking about? These images just come to me, and I feel compelled to draw them."

"Bullshit Wendy! You didn't think it was weird when you started drawing me?"

"Honestly, this girl looks beautiful, and full of life. She looks nothing like you."

"Fuck you, Wendy! I know that you know more than you are letting on. Why? What are you hiding?"

"I'm not hiding anything Brittany. I just drew pictures from my visions. I can't help that!"

"Wow, just going to keep playing dumb Wendy, that's real cute. How about you tell me about this vision you had. That stupid rhyme, the tower. What does it mean?"

Wendy shoved Brittany out of the way, "This is ridiculous Brittany, leave me alone."

Brittany could feel the anger coming back, the piece that wasn't her. Her head was pounding, her hands shaking.

Wendy ripped the pictures from Brittany's hands. "These are my pictures, no one told you that you could rip them down. What is wrong with you? You really are crazy!"

Brittany felt pure rage come over her, it consumed her. She slapped Wendy across the face and grabbed the pictures. Wendy stumbled back holding her cheek, tears welling in her eyes. Then Brittany pushed Wendy onto the edge of her bed and slapped her again before grabbing the collar of her shirt. Brittany got within inches of Wendy's face as she spoke angrily through clenched teeth. "I don't enjoy being played with Wendy. I know you know something and one way or another I will make you tell me."

Wendy spit, splashing warm saliva onto Brittany's forehead. The rage had completely overpowered her at this point. She punched Wendy so hard she broke the skin of her cheek, then she grabbed Wendy by the hair and dragged her onto the floor.

Brittany proceeded to kick Wendy in the ribs, screaming "I know you know more!" continuously. She heard Wendy's rib crack as Wendy screamed out in pain. Then Brittany squatted down, punching Wendy in the face as she screamed, "Who are you?" another punch. "Why do you know so much about that night?" another punch.

Wendy's face was bleeding a lot now as she choked on the blood pooling in her mouth, a small pool of blood collecting on the floor underneath her head. Brittany didn't know why, but she was loving this feeling, this anger she felt as she hurt Wendy, every time she punched her. This place was slowly making her more angry and violent every day.

Before Brittany could get another punch in, she felt herself being tugged, arms coming around her and dragging her out of the room. Brittany cackled as she was dragged backwards. She shook her fist that held a large chunk of Wendy's hair as she yelled, "You might be safe this time Wendy, but next time you won't be saved."

Brittany felt her back hit the hard floor as she was thrown into her room. Once again, two nurses held her down and she felt the painful jab of the needle and then the burning liquid entered her body.

Chapter 18

Jules came to slowly, her head was fuzzy and even though her eyes were still closed it seemed as if the room was spinning. She didn't know where she was. She didn't know what day it was. She opened her eyes but all she saw was darkness all around her. Her body shivered from fear, and she tried to wrap her arms around herself but the cold metal bite into her wrists and she heard the rattle of chains.The realization of having her arms chained made her body tremble even more.

She braced her hands on the cold ground and tried to stand up but realized that her legs were bolted to the ground as well. She searched her mind to try and figure out where she was. The last thing she remembered was Brittany crying and holding her in the bathroom, the blood everywhere. As she thought about the moment she realized she had not been watching from her body's perspective but as an outsider watching the scene unfold. She didn't know what happened after that or how she got into this place. All she felt was complete and utter terror. Jules forced herself to quiet her thoughts and just listen and see if she could hear anything else. There must be someone else here, even if it was just a guard. For a long time there was only silence, until the faint rattle of another chain echoed in the dark, but it seemed far off in the distance.

She tried to scream for help, but when she did, nothing came out of her mouth. She held her hand to her mouth in disbelief. She tried to scream again but there was only silence. Jules felt her stomach plummet to her toes and turn violently, and her mouth started to water. Jules was so confused. How did she end up here? Why couldn't she scream? Was this a dream, was she going to wake up and all of this was going to be over? Her eyes burned with tears as the nausea came on stronger and the shivering intensified.

Jules figured if she could get anyone's attention maybe they could help her. She slammed her hand on the ground, but no one thumped back. It was as if she was completely and utterly alone in this darkness.

then she heard the familiar sound that brought her back to the hotel room.

Tap tap.

She couldn't quite remember much about the room or what happened, she just remembered that there was a room that her and Brittany were in, they would hear tapping and whispering, and then she remembered sitting on the bathroom floor screaming.

Tap tap.

Her head swiveled trying to figure out which way it was coming from but all she could see was complete darkness. Whomever was tapping was purposefully moving around the area so she couldn't track it. She couldn't say hello, she couldn't do anything but sit there scared, her head on a constant swivel.

"Hello Jules" said a creepy voice that was grotesquely cheerful. "I hope you're comfortable because this is your new home."

Jules couldn't speak though she was not sure she wanted to, or she would have to hear this thing speak again. She couldn't understand why it was even talking to her. If it was the one that had put her here it knew she couldn't talk.

The chains trembled as Jules pulled helplessly.

The thing chuckled, amused by her silence, "Oh by the way, Brittany really misses you. I make her believe her loved ones are around her, really fuck with her mind. It's quite fun. She sits there screaming and crying, saying your name, wishing you were there. I love the smell of her sadness and her fear, It's exhilarating." The thing laughed, this horrible torturous chuckle.

"I can smell yours now too. I feed off of your fear. I feed off of your sadness. Every time you're scared I get a little stronger. I took your voice too. It gives you just a little bit more of an edge of fear, makes the fear more potent. I have to go terrorize Timmy now. Tata for now Jules, enjoy the dark."

Jules' breathing was ragged. She tried to calm herself so she could listen. She didn't know if the thing was gone. she couldn't hear anything, but she didn't hear him come in. She just felt watched at all times, as if eyes lurked all around her. This overwhelming sadness went through her entire body, yet she couldn't cry or scream. It made the sadness even stronger. She knew that was what it wanted. Yet she couldn't help the sadness that enveloped her entire body. She couldn't force herself to be strong like Brittany. *How had this become her fate? What did she do to deserve this kind of ending?*

Something slimy roll across Jules' foot. She jerked backwards and tried to push herself back, but she couldn't get far before the chains stopped her. The metal bit into her arms and her arms screamed in pain.

A high-pitched squeal broke the silence. She would know that sound anywhere from all the horror movies she watched, it was a rat. Her worse fear crawling all over her. She tried to shrink into herself as much as she could, her body shaking. "No, no, no" Jules said in her mind. She hated rats so much. Had she ended up in hell? She knew she didn't deserve to be here. She had always tried to help people and be a good person. Her mind tried to think of what she could have done but as hard as she tried to search her mind, all her memories had faded away.

"I can hear you, ya know." The eerie voice had returned. "You may not be able to actually speak but I can hear your thoughts. This is not hell, its Hollow Ground. You've made it to the scariest place ever. Worse than hell." It laughed deep and guttural. "Since you're searching for memories let me gift you one." The thing said.

***

Her mind flooded with the smell of popcorn and fried food. Laughter filled her mind, the sound of kids screaming in the background as the sound of a roller coaster rolled by in her mind. Then the vision came into view bright and colorful. She was standing next to Brittany. Brittany was throwing a ball towards a pyramid of milk bottles. She missed entirely and almost hit the middle aged man in the booth. She looked back at Jules laughing and shrugged, "how many points would you have given me if I'd hit him?"

"Oooh, 24 points. The stripes he's wearing make him worth more."

The guy gave her a rude look and they both started cracking up. Brittany threw the ball again and knocked every bottle off the table, they flew through the air and one knocked into the guys arm. "Oh!" Brittany shouted. "I should totally get a bigger animal for the extra hit."

"Alright wise guy, pick your damn toy and leave."

Brittany pointed to the huge pink unicorn half the size of Jules. Brittany turned to her, handing the plush animal over. "For you, my lady." Brittany said shoving the animal into Jules arms.

"Well how kind of you ya fine bloke." Jules said in a fake British accent, hugging it tightly.

They wandered around the fair stuffing fries, dough boys, and cotton candy into their mouths until they both felt like they were going to explode. "Oh my gosh Britt, I might actually die." Jules said clutching her stomach.

Brittany laughed hard, "seriously, I feel like I'm nine months pregnant." And then shoved one more piece of cotton candy into her mouth.

Jules laughed hard, "one more bite and you are literally going to explode, and I'm not going to carry you out of here in pieces."

"Oh yes you are, you're going to scoop all of me into your purse."

The girls giggled as they both walked to the entrance of the big top circus tent. Jules turned to Brittany with the biggest smile on her face. "This is my favorite part of this fair every year."

"I know, I love the acrobats. They're amazing."

The girls walked inside, the smell of hay, animals, and peanuts filled the air. The girls chose their seats quickly, excited to watch the show.The lights dimmed, and the music started, as the ringmaster ran into the middle ring. The spotlight beaming onto him with darkness everywhere else. The music playing lighter in the background. "Welcome ladies and gentlemen to the circus, where you will watch feats of strength, courageous clowns, beautiful acrobats defying gravity, and our lovely, bearded lady with the voice of an angel. Are you ready for the most amazing, magnificent, and colorful show ever!"

The crowd erupted in screams and clapping. "Well then let's get this show started!" The ringmaster spun and skipped out of the arena.The girls sat astounded as they watched acrobats flipping through the air, balancing on the high wire above, lions and elephants doing tricks that they should never be able to accomplish, and a woman with the most beautiful voice standing front and center.

At the end, all the performers came out as she was finishing the song, dancing around her and singing their hearts out, the lions stood in front of her all balancing on their hind legs, while the horses seemed to dance behind all of them. Then the music ended abruptly, and the lions roared loudly. The whole crowd including them all jumped up whistling and clapping loudly.

***

The sounds all faded, and all Jules saw was darkness again. The vision completely gone. Sadness filled her entire body once again, but it was deeper this time, though she was not sure how that was possible.

"Mmm, perfect." The voice whispered. "You smell amazing. I can feel myself getting stronger with every drop."

Jules' head bowed, her body shaking, her memories stolen, and all her energy completely depleted.

"I'll be back later to feed again. Later Jules"

And then complete silence once again.

Chapter 19

Wendy heard the sounds of the beeping before she even opened her eyes. As her eyes fluttered opened, she saw the machines around her, the white walls, and the nurse standing to the left of her jotting things down as she touched the screen of a machine.

She tried to move but everything hurt. She winced but that only made it hurt worse. Her face had its own heartbeat, her breathing came in short breaths that were painful, she felt completely broken.

Her memory of how she had ended up here was foggy, all she remembered was seeing Brittany in her room, then her shoving Brittany out of the way. After that it came in a blur, she just remembered seeing Brittany's eye. They were filled with so much anger and hatred. It terrified Wendy, she knew in that moment she had screwed up, she never should have touched her.

"Oh good," the nurse said turning to Wendy. "You're finally awake. You slept for two days."

Two days? Wendy was so confused. How the hell has she been out this long? "What happened?" Wendy struggled to say. Her mouth was dry and her throat hurt.

"You came to us after a brutal beating you got at the unit

you were in. The doctors thought you had a concussion, but we took a CT scan, nothing showed up. You were too out of it to do the normal tests we usually perform. It's good to see you talking though." The nurse did a couple of tests with a flashlight on her eyes, and then smiled. "You seem to be OK. I'll let the doctor know you woke up so he can check on you... I'll be back in a second with some Tylenol, I'm sure you head is pounding."

Wendy watched as the nurse walked out of the room and towards a nurses cart. She went to push herself up in the bed but her ribs screamed in pain. Her arms were no help either, they felt like Jello. She grabbed the remote to make the bed move up but as her head lifted it started spinning. Her throat got watery and her stomach turned.

She looked around the room frantically, knowing she was about to vomit. Nothing was close to her at all, so she leaned over the bed, her side burning with pain as she let it go onto the floor. Her ribs were now searing with pain as she wretched, nothing was coming out yet her body was still trying to force it.

Tears streamed down her face as she caught her breath. She laid back down on her pillow, terrified to move at this point. She wiped her eyes and then hit the call button for the nurse's desk. She heard the static as if someone had picked up the line, but no one talked.

"Hello?" She whispered, her throat burning as she tried to speak.

Then the light went out on her remote, the nurse on the other line hanging up. She hit the call bell again figuring it had glitched the first time, but the same thing happened. She dropped the remote and figured she would just have to wait for someone to walk by.

Her head turned towards the window to look at the nurse's desk, it seemed so dark and empty. No one was talking, no other machines beeping. The area was just busy a moment ago, where had they all gone?

She thought she saw something out of the corner of her eye move, but when she looked nothing was there. Her heart started beating faster which made her head hurt even worse. She really wished the nurse would come in with the Tylenol. Her palms were starting to sweat, and her stomach was turning again. She felt herself getting sick once again. She leaned over the bed and wretched but nothing came, just pain.

"Ooh, that doesn't seem fun." This creepy voice said from the corner of the room.

Wendy froze. *How could something be talking to her when she had just looked around the room seconds ago and nothing was there?* She slowly eased herself from the side of the bed, terrified to look near the corner of the room. As she slowly turned her head all she saw was the room. It looked darker, but normal. She figured she was just hearing things because of her head injury.

"Remember me?" It whispered, inches from her ear.

She didn't want to look, at this point she was absolutely terrified. Her hands were shaking as she grabbed the remote and hit the call button repeatedly. Someone had to come, even if it was just out of annoyance.

"You really think anyone's coming Wendy?" The voice said in a creepy cheerful tone.

Her hand was so sweaty, she had trouble holding the remote as she kept pushing the button. "What do you want?" She asked quietly, barely able to get the words out.

"I knew you would make Brittany mad, but I didn't expect this level of anger. She got you good."

Wendy froze, a memory flooding back as she now understood what the voice was. It was a Hollow One. The terrible creature who loved to torment others. "Why are you here? I did what you asked, now leave me alone."

"Oh darling, I will never leave you alone. You will always do my bidding, you may have worked your magic on Brittany but now there are others we can toy with."

"What? You told me all I had to do was anger Brittany. Get into her head and freak her out. Draw a couple stupid pictures. I did what you asked!"

"Yes you did. It was marvelous! That rhyme, perfection! She's still reeling. You should see it." The creature said, clearly enjoying himself. "But you will never be done. I let you live, but we made a deal. You were to do my bidding, and I wouldn't drag you to Hollow Ground."

"This is bullshit. I can't keep going through this. Getting beaten up by psycho people."

"You will do whatever I say!" The creature shouted, his voice echoing throughout the entire room. "Or I will take you down there, is that what you want, to be tortured forever?"

Wendy's head bowed, she knew there was no fighting this thing. She would be stuck doing its bidding until the day she died. "No, I will do whatever you ask."

"That's a good girl. I'll leave you alone until you can at least stand up. Then I'll be back, there's a little girl a couple doors down I've had my eye on. We're going to have some fun."

She heard the horrible chuckle as he disappeared. The room seemed to lighten a little, and conversations and machines beeping could be heard in the halls again. She couldn't live like this, being tortured this way. Either way wasn't good, but watching innocent girls break because of her, was breaking her heart. She had been a nice girl before this. She had a lot of friends and always made sure not to hurt peoples feelings, she never wanted anyone to be sad or angry.

She remembered the night she had made the deal, remembered how terrified she was, it was the worst night of her life.

* * *

Two months ago

Wendy sat on her bed with her tarot cards and a can of mountain dew. She loved flipping through the cards, asking the cards questions and seeing the response. It was like having a magic eight ball but with better answers. She never asked serious questions, just harmless one. Would she be popular? Would she make the gymnastics team? Would she end up with Charlie Brewsky? She always flipped the card and got an answer she was happy with, even if it was just how she interpreted the answers. Then she would giggle and ask the next question.

She took a swig from her soda and held the cards in her hand. She was feeling adventurous and decided to ask a different question. She knew she needed to really think about the question as she shuffled, manifest it into the desk. As she shuffled, she said the words aloud. "Is there anyone here who is no longer alive and wants to talk?" She was always curious about the afterlife and figured it couldn't hurt, it was just a card game.

As she flipped the card over, the tower card sat before her. She didn't know much about the cards meanings yet, so she opened the pamphlet that explained each card. As she read it, she wondered if because the card represented endings maybe it meant someone's life had ended. Wendy got really excited, maybe someone *was* here with her. Before she could ask any more questions to whomever was in the room, her ceiling light turned off and back on. Now she was a little spooked, she didn't care if this was a spirit answering her questions, she no longer wanted to play this game. She shoved the cards quickly back into the box they came in and shoved them underneath her bed. She was done playing with them.

That night as she was about to fall asleep, she thought she heard a board creak near the corner of the room as if someone had shifted their stance. She opened her eyes but it was too dark, her eyes weren't adjusted yet. A shadow seemed to run towards the door. She flipped her lamp on that sat right near her bed. Her eyes scanned the room frantically but nothing was in the room, everything was where it should be.

She turned the light back off, pulled her blankets up to her chin and closed her eyes tight. She had never been afraid of the dark, but something felt off tonight. Her heart skipped a beat as she heard the creek again, she gripped the blankets tighter and squeezed her eyes shut as hard as she could. A whisper came from across the room.

"Wendy."

Instinctively she opened her eyes to look. Her eyes caught on two yellow eyes that stared back at her. Her breathing became ragged, her heart racing. She knew there was nothing there a couple of seconds ago. She saw the eyes coming closer yet she couldn't look away. She blindly searched for the switch to turn her lamp on. As the eyes got closer her hand moved faster, pissed that her fingers were failing her.

The eyes were now right at the end of her bed. She felt the mattress give a little as if someone's hands had pushed down on it. She scrunched herself into a ball, her entire body shaking. Her hand finally landed on the lamp and she ran her fingers up and down the post looking for the switch.

She saw the eyes watching her, but she couldn't pull her eyes away. She felt the mattress moving, felt this thing crawling towards her slowly. Beads of sweat had now formed on her forehead that fell into her eyes and was making them sting, yet she couldn't close them. She felt if she even blinked, it would attack her. She felt the touch of something on her toes and she coiled them tight and scrunched into a ball even tighter. The eyes were so close to her she could feel its warm, sour breath on her. She could feel the thing almost on top of her yet she couldn't scrunch any tighter.

Her fingers felt the ridges of the round knob. She quickly turned the knob and the entire room lit up. Nothing was there. No eyes, no movement on the bed, and no sour smell. She scanned the room frantically, but nothing was out of place. Her stomach twisted and she wanted out of her room, but she was too afraid to put her feet down.

The light bulb smashed from her lamp and the entire room went dark again. Tears welled in her eyes and her body was shaking again. She heard this sinister laugh that seemed to echo around the whole room.

Her head turned towards the lamp hoping it was just a noise and it hadn't actually broken. Staring at her were the bright yellow eyes, so close to her that she could see the yellowish veins that were etched into its eyes. There didn't seem to be pupils, just neon glowing almond shaped eyes staring at her.

She jumped back trying to get away from it. Her hand slipped off the bed, realizing she was at the edge of her bed now. The eyes got closer and she again felt the mattress give.

"Please." Was all Wendy could get out, her voice so light she almost couldn't hear it.

"Please... what?" The voice whispered, its warm breath hitting her cheek, the sour smell turning her stomach.

"What do you want?"

"What do you mean? You called and I came."

Wendy was confused. She had not called on any creature to come to her.

"Mmm, you seem to forget you played a card game. Asked for someone to talk to you. Well, here I am."

Her mind went to her flipping through the tarot cards, asking that last question, seeing the tower card, then the light turning on and off. She had called to anyone, and this is what came. Her heart dropped to her stomach, this was her fault and she knew it.

"What do you want from me?" She asked in a shaky voice.

"Why, to feed off your fear little one. It's what I do."

"I'll do anything. Please don't hurt me."

She waited for a response, but everything went quiet, as if it was contemplating what she had said. After what seemed like minutes had passed it finally spoke.

"There is something you could do. I won't hurt you, but you must hurt someone else."

Wendy froze. She didn't want to hurt anyone, she was a nice person. She liked doing good and being helpful. She also knew she didn't have the strength to hurt someone. She was a peanut, shorter than all her classmates, with string bean arms and legs.

"What do you mean hurt someone else? Physically?"

"No. Not physically."

Wendy exhaled in relief. "OK, so then how?"

She saw the things eyes float closer, then she saw its jagged white teeth form into a smile. "I need you to become some- one's friend. Draw a couple pictures, make her believe you know something that bothers her, just confuse her a little."

"That's it? I just have to play a couple of mind tricks?"

"Correct. Granted, you won't be in the best place. But that's all. Just mind tricks."

"And if I don't?"

"Then I will kill you, and drag you down to a horrible place where you will be chained up and tortured. Your choice little one."

Wendy felt torn, she definitely didn't want to die but she hated the thought of hurting someone else, especially mentally. She had called on this thing, she had asked it to come. Her stomach turned as she thought about her parents and how devastated they would be if she died. She couldn't do that to them. Mind games would not kill anyone, they would only make you sad for a little.

"OK. I'll do it."

"Magnificent! I'll be back later. I've got some stuff to do."

Wendy didn't sleep at all that night, she was terrified it would come back and revoke the deal. She woke up the next morning to tell her parents what happened, hoping they would know what to do. She wasn't sure what she thought would happen but them saying she was crazy and sending her to a psychiatrist was not what she thought would happen. She tried explaining that night to the psychiatrist, but the lady felt there was an underlying problem.

The psychiatrist ended up calling child protective services or as she had heard the psychiatrist call it, CPS. She had the family investigated, assuming "her monster" had to be a sexual predator or that she was being beaten or neglected at home.

While her parents were being investigated, she tried to explain to CPS and the cops what really happened, not understanding at the time, that what she was saying made her look crazy and made her parents look guilty. They told her that the doctor had told them everything, and that she did not need to be scared, she would be safe now.

She ended up at the psych ward for evaluation. They put her in room 13 and gave her the new white clothes she was to wear from then on. They kept using the words schizophrenic and that she was a danger to herself. She felt like a prisoner and felt less safe than she ever had. She cried the whole day, not understanding how this had happened so quickly. She went from telling her parents what happened that night, to days later being locked away.

As she lay there in bed that night, she heard the whisper.

"Wendy."

She knew exactly who it was. That voice would forever be etched into her mind. She opened her eyes and looked around. In the corner of the room, she saw the eyes.

"That was quicker than I expected." The voice said.

"What? You did this? How? Why?"

"It was easy. I took the form of the psychiatrist, and it snowballed from there." The thing said in a gleeful tone, as if it was gloating.

"Why would you do that? You said if we made the deal, you

wouldn't torture me."

"This is the place. The girl I need you to play a couple of mind tricks on is here. I'll tell you exactly what to say and do, and if you do, I won't kill you."

* * *

Wendy recalled the group therapy session, the drawings she didn't understand but drew anyways, and then the fight. Brittany's angry eyes. She would never forget the eyes, so full of rage, but it didn't seem as if it was Brittany's rage, it was like someone had taken over her body.

She couldn't keep doing this, hurting people, and getting hurt in return. This Hollow creature would never stop. It was torturing her, just in a different way. She knew there was only one way to end this.

Wendy waited until nightfall, when the hospital would go quiet. There would only be one nurse to a unit and they would just scroll on their phone or watch TV, completely oblivious.

As the second shift nurse's clocked out, she saw the third shift nurse make her way to the break room to get her snacks.

Wendy waited. She counted the nurses steps and waited a little more. When she could no longer hear the footsteps at all she decided it was time to make her move. She swung her legs over the bed. Her knees buckled, barely able to hold her weight. She caught herself on the bedside rail, forcing her trembling legs to stand.

Once she felt she could move, she slipped into the dim hallway. The nurses station loomed just ahead. She quickly made her way to the desk, making sure not to trip or her still trembling legs. She crouched behind the desk and began searching for the keys. She flipped over papers, looked in drawers, flipped over clipboards. She hoped the third shift nurses were less likely to hide their keys since most people would normally be sleeping or out of it on this floor.

Then she spotted the nurses navy blue jacket tossed across the chair. She searched inside the pockets but came up empty handed. Her heart pounded in her chest. She dropped to her knees, eyes catching on the nurses leather purse underneath the desk. She yanked it open. Her fingers rummaged through the bag quickly, and her heart skipped a beat as she heard the jingle of keys. She dug deeper and pulled out the key ring only to see a dangling car fob. She threw them back into the purse.

She needed to get into the nurse's cart, she knew the neurological floor had certain drugs in the carts that other floors didn't, drugs that could make someone loose muscle movement and breathing. She shoved the purse back under the desk and froze.

She could hear footsteps making their way back to the unit. Wendy bolted for her room, nearly tripping as she dove back into bed. Her vision blurred, and her stomach turned. She wanted to vomit. She needed to fight that feeling. She did not have time to get sick right now, she needed to think. She grabbed the remote and rang the call bell.

"Yes Wendy. What can I do for you?" Came the cheerful tone of the nurse.

She hated that she would have to do this, but she needed to get into that cart. "I have a really bad headache. Can I have a couple Tylenol?"

"Absolutely. I'll be right there."

She saw the nurse stand up and roll the cart towards the room. The nurse stood outside her door, took the lanyard from around her neck and unlocked the top drawer of the cart.

"So that's where she had them." Wendy said to herself. They were around her neck the whole time. The nurse came in with the small medicine cup and water.

"Here ya go Wendy."

Wendy took the Tylenol and swished it down with the small water cup. "Thank you."

The nurse turned to leave the room. Wendy grabbed her pink hospital pitcher and *accidentally* dumped the entire thing on the floor. "Oh my goodness, I'm so sorry."

The nurse turned quickly, seeing water spreading all across the floor. "That's OK Wendy. Accidents happen. Let me go get some towels." the nurse quickly jogged out of the room towards the closet.

Wendy jumped from the bed quicker than she had ever moved, her feet hitting the floor without hesitation. Her body felt weightless, she was running on pure adrenaline. She grabbed the keys from the cart and unlocked the drawer of the cart. She rifled through the pill boards, not sure what she was looking for but knowing that she needed a pill board with enough pills in them.

She swore she could hear the nurses' feet shuffling. Panic seized her chest. She quickly grabbed a couple of boards, locked the cart, and ran back to her bed. She stuffed the pills under her pillow just as the nurse was making her way back to the room.

The nurse cleaned up the water and threw the soaked towels into the hamper. Then she smiled at Wendy. "Anything else you need love?"

"No. I'm good. Thank you. And sorry again for the mess."

"No problem. Have a good night."

The nurse pushed the cart back to the desk and sat down. Wendy heard the TV come to life and knew in a couple of seconds the nurse would be sucked in and wouldn't notice what was going on around her.

Wendy grabbed the pill boards from underneath her pillow and looked at the name, *Metoprolol.* She had no clue what that was for, but she figured if you take enough of anything it can harm you and hopefully kill you. She quickly popped the pills from the board, took a deep breath, and threw the heaping handful of pills into her mouth. Then she took a swig of water and swallowed them down. Wendy wasn't sure if that would be enough to kill her. She grabbed the next pill board and popped those out as well, then again threw them into her mouth and swallowed them down with a mouthful of water. She sat there for a second wondering if this would even work, as she seemed fine.

For a moment, there was only silence. Then the world began to tilt. Her heart fluttered, skipping beats like a dying engine. Her vision blurred, colors fading to gray.

Her limbs felt heavy, her breathing was becoming shallow, and then a strange warmth crawled up her neck.

It's working, she thought, just as the pounding in her ears became distant thunder. Her body slid deeper into the mattress. Her fingers twitched once, twice, and then went still. The room dimmed, the ceiling light fractured into streaks, and the world faded into darkness. The last thing Wendy heard was the faint sound of the television down the hall, then nothing.

Chapter 20

The next morning Brittany woke up feeling completely sick. Her head was pounding worse than ever, and she was nauseous. She didn't remember much about why she had been shot with that horrible venom this time. She remembered seeing the pictures in Wendy's room and hearing Wendy come in but then everything after was dark. She hoped Wendy was OK, blacking out usually meant something bad had happened.

Although now she knew that Madame Zodo was real, all those dreams she had in the past of a woman casting a spell and sitting in front of Jane warning her, the leather book, the weird feeling in the hotel, the lipstick, it was all real. She wasn't sure if Madame Zodo and Zaron were the same person but whatever was in the room with her must be trying to help her to get out. She promised the energy in the room that she was listening and that she would do whatever it took to get out of here and help the girls be set free.

Lindsay sat next to her for recess time, their same place next to the big windows, as they sat on the uncomfortable plastic chairs.

"Where is Wendy?" Brittany asked apprehensively.

Lindsay looked at her with worry on her eyes. "She's at the hospital, but then they are going to transfer her to a different facility. What happened Brittany?"

"I don't know. I remember going to her room. I wanted to know if she had any more information about her vision. I remembering seeing the pictures of the hotel night in her room and angrily ripping them off the wall, and seeing her in the doorway, and then everything went dark."

"You hurt her pretty bad. She has huge gashes on her face, she could barely breath, and she was bleeding from her scalp."

Brittany winced at what Lindsay was telling her. She couldn't understand what had happened to make her so angry. She was starting to lose control of her emotions and her actions. She knew it had to be this dark thing.

"Lindsay, I need answers, I think this thing is playing with my mind and my emotions. I don't feel like myself. I lose control so fast now. That's not like me."

Lindsay just stared at her, pity in her eyes but she also seemed scared, like if she got too close Brittany would get mad and beat her up too.

"I know you have heard the name Zaron many times, but did you ever hear the name Madame Zodo?" Brittany asked her.

Lindsay tilted her head, exhaustion softening her voice. "No... that name doesn't sound familiar. Why?"

Brittany shrugged, "I've had dreams about her, and when Jules and I were in the hotel room we were given her spell book. It's now long since gone because the police swear they never found the book or another book I tried to tell them was in the room. I know it was real though, Wendy drew pictures of both."

Lindsay's expression brightened. "A spell book? Brittany, I *swear* I've seen an old book in Wendy's room. She was reading from it and when I knocked on her door, she slammed it shut and tried to hide it."

"Can you tell me what it looks like?" Brittany asked.

"Better yet," Lindsay said, lowering her voice, "let's go get it. It must still be in her room. They haven't cleaned her stuff out yet."

The girls ran to Wendy's room. There was a box by the door and a stripped mattress. It was as if Wendy had been completely erased from the room. She used to have things her family brought, stuffed animals and family photos, and books piled on the bed. Brittany went to the bed and tipped her mattress up, thinking maybe she hid it there. Lindsay rifled through the box of things that had been packed near the door.

The psych ward rooms didn't have closets or places to put your belongings so there were not very many places to hide things, but after looking everywhere they found nothing.

Brittany was feeling defeated, she knew in her gut Wendy must have had that book at one time, she saw the drawing on the wall, the ones she ripped down. She shook out the pillowcase and papers fluttered to the ground. Brittany was staring at the drawings from the wall.

Somehow, she had found a way to hide them, which seemed weird because she thought Wendy had been taken away to the nurses' station right after the incident and then taken to the hospital. Who had hidden the papers for her?

She quickly grabbed the drawings, not wanting to leave the memories behind, not wanting to miss a clue and figured the pictures could help her.

"I'm so sorry," Lindsay said. "I know I saw her reading an old book, just like the one in the drawing you're holding."

"It's OK Lindsay, I wasn't meant to find it I guess." Brittany shrugged it off realizing she had failed yet again. As they were about to leave the room, Brittany heard the familiar sound on the wall the bed was pushed up against.

Tap tap.

Both girls froze. The noise had come from the wall behind the bed.

Brittany's breath caught. She quickly made her way over to that area and slid her hand in between the bed and the wall. She could feel something hard in the mattress, but how? The mattress cover is padlocked so you can't unzip it.

"Lindsay, do you have anything that could open up the mattress cover?"

"I don't. I won't take the chance in hiding anything like that. They check our rooms every day. You know if we hid something like that, we would get tranquilized, and they would lock us in our room for a week."

Brittany knew she was right, it would be too risky, so how had Wendy hidden something in the mattress cover? She slid her hand back and forth along the area, feeling for a tear in the cover. Nothing.

"We need to find something to open the lock up Lindsay."

Brittany watched as Lindsay rummaged through the box of belongings. "Oh my god, what about this!" Lindsay said excitedly holding up a bobby pin. "It fell out of one of her books when I was shaking things around."

Brittany jumped off the bed and quickly grabbed the bobby pin. She jammed it into the keyhole and twisted the bobby pin around, not quite sure what she was doing but knowing if she wiggled it enough, she could probably get it to open, but she was having no success.

"Let men try Brittany, I used to open up locks like this at home for fun, read about it in a book once and figured I'd give it a try."

Lindsay twisted the bobby pin inside for a couple of seconds and then Brittany heard the click. Lindsay quickly pulled the padlock off the zipper tags and unzipped the first part of the cover. Brittany quickly glanced out the windows, checking to see where the nurses were. The nurses were still sitting at the nurses desk, chatting away and scrolling on their phones, completely unaware of what was going on around them.

Brittany pulled the mattress away from the bed frame a little and then stood between the wall and the mattress. She unzipped the mattress cover a tiny bit more so she could reach her hand inside. She knew unzipping it all the way would be dangerous because there was no way she would be able to fully zip it back up in a hurry. Then the nurses would know they were tampering with it. She felt around but the book must have moved when she tipped the mattress.

Brittany's heart was racing, she needed the book but also didn't want to get caught looking for it. They could get into so much trouble if they got caught. "Lindsay, keep watch while I unzip the cover a little more."

Brittany knew if the mattress slipped, the nurse's would see the mattress through the glass door and it would give them away.

Lindsay discreetly stood in the corner of the room so she could see out the wall of windows and keep an eye on the nurses desk. Brittany tipped the mattress a little more. She had one hand holding the mattress still so it wouldn't slide on the floor as she was pinned against the wall. Her other hand slid into the mattress cover, arm deep in the cover, her neck pushing against the mattress. Her hand quickly moved around, feeling for the book. Her fingertips brushed against soft leather, she grabbed the book with her fingers, praying it wouldn't slide out of her grip. Just as she got the book up far enough where she could get a better grip on it, the book slipped.

"Are you fucking kidding me?" Brittany angrily said to herself. Sweat now beading on her forehead and her hands were sweaty.

"Hurry up Brittany, it's almost time for them to do their rounds."

Brittany tried to calm her breathing, she slid her hands down her plants to dry the sweat off, then she stuck her hand back in the cover. She was reaching as far down as she could, her neck pressing into the mattress hard, her arm pounding from the strain, her fingertips fervently moving around trying to feel for the book.

She felt the book again, the tips of her fingers just brushing it. She tried to push down further, the mattress giving all it had, her other hand shaking from trying to hold the mattress in place. The mattress gave just enough for her to pinch her fingers around the spine of the book and at a sloth's pace, slowly slid the book up. When she felt she had pulled it up far enough, she pushed the book into the mattress and slowly walked her fingertips down the book to get a better grip. She palmed the spine of the book now. Relief flooded her as she felt the book firmly grasped in her hand. She would not lose the book again, they didn't have time. She slid the book up and out of the mattress cover, being careful not to hit anything and make it fall again.

When she had it fully out of the mattress, she stood on the bed frame, her hands shaking, her breathing ragged. As she stared at the book memories from the hotel room came flooding back. Tears welled in her eyes as she remembered Jules sitting next to her, excitedly flipping through the pages.

"Brittany!" Lindsay shouted. "You wanna hurry so we don't get caught."

Brittany snapped out of the memory and wiped her eyes with the back of her hand. She zipped the mattress back up and slowly walked on the mattress and hopped onto the floor, then she pushed the mattress back up against the wall. "OK, let's go back to my room." Brittany said.

They quickly walked back to Brittany's room, trying not to draw tension to themselves, staring at the nurses' desk the entire time.

Brittany just sat on her bed, frozen, staring at the book.

"Are you OK Brittany?" Lindsay asked worriedly.

"I'm fine, just remembering something." Brittany said wiping her eyes.

Brittany opened the book and stared at the front cover. Madame Zodo's name was still lightly written there. Her fingers slowly rolled over the name, a single tear hitting the page, she had a small amount of hope knowing this book was real.

"Well, would you look at that!" Lindsay said, "Madame Zodo!"

Brittany opened the book to the page she knew all too well. There sat the communication spell that she swore she could recite without ever having to look at the words. She wondered how the book had ended up here. How had Wendy gotten the book? She flipped to the next page and a newspaper article sat there. Brittany's eyebrows furrowed. Had this been there the whole time and she just never realized because they never flipped the page?

The newspaper cut out was a picture of the woman she always saw. It was very clearly Madame Zodo. The newspaper headline said:

The Witch of Greenwich

Brittany read on as it talked about a woman, named Madame Zodo or as many knew her from her childhood as Jacqueline Zodo. She grew up not far from Greenwich, Connecticut in a little farm town. It was just her and her mom and a big farm. It went on to talk about Jacqueline's life growing up very poor and then cleaning houses for the wealthy. It stated that Jacqueline had a unique gift and was able to help people and comfort them in times of need. It also talked about how she could speak to the dead and cast spells for those who needed good fortune. She was the most famous witch in all of New England and people would travel thousands of miles to come see the Greenwich witch. If you were lucky, she would even help you expel bad spirits from your life with the help of her friends Lily and Charlie Buckhouser, the Demonologists of Stamford, Connecticut. "She was a lovely woman who only wanted the best for people." stated Poppy Wells, her best friend. It went on to say that she was an amazing person and would help as many charities as she could. She died in the late summer of August 2010. She left only her cats behind and her friends who called her family. She will be missed by all.

Brittany sat there, her eyes welling up, Madame Zodo was definitely coming to her from the grave to help her. She now knew that all of this was fate, she was supposed to meet Lindsay, she was supposed to find this book. She was listening and she would take all the help she could in making sure all of these wonderful people could finally be at rest and not stuck in that horrible hotel room.

"Thank you, Lindsay for helping me get this back."

"Of course. That's what friends do."

They hugged each other tight. "Alright Britt, I'm going to go back to my room to wait for rounds."

Brittany shoved the book under her mattress for the time being while she sat there thinking about how she was going to break out of this cursed place and get back to her best friend.

Chapter 21

Brittany's mom came the next day with snacks in hand. She sat on one of the uncomfortable plastic chairs, a nervous smile on her face, waiting for Brittany to appear. Brittany stood in her doorway watching her mom talk to Lindsay. She watched her mom's normal mannerisms, the way she laughed lightly and tucked a strand of hair behind her ear, no worries or care in the world. A sudden, irrational fury twisted in Brittany's chest. She didn't know why she was so angry, only that she didn't want her mom here.

Maybe it was the unfairness of it all, that her mom was off living a normal life while Brittany was stuck in this hell hole. Other than Lindsay, she was all alone with just her thoughts and her nightmares. She had asked her mom to bring her home so many times and every time she did her mom's response was the same, "Brittany you're doing so well here. The therapist says that every session you seem to be getting better."

What Brittany's mom didn't know was that she was not getting better. The shadows came more frequently, the nightmares seemed to get worse, darker, and scarier. Almost as if they weren't dreams but visions that had not happened yet. She would always tell the therapist she was fine, she knew now that telling the therapist how she really felt and what she really saw was only making her time here worse, and longer. During her sessions she now sat there with a smile on her face, acting as if everything was fine and that the medicine must be helping. Even though she knew she was just spitting it out every night.

She hated that her mom didn't believe anything she told her, and she knew that if she lived through this and ever had kids, she would never doubt anything they said. These dark things that came to you in the night were real, monsters could definitely live under your bed, and nightmares weren't always just dreams, sometimes they came true.

Brittany walked over to her mom, a fake smile plastered on her face. "Hey mom, great to see you, you look good."

"Oh sweetie, I have missed you so much. Your friend Lindsay said you guys are doing really well and have become very close. It's nice to see your opening up again."

"Oh yeah, Getting better every day." Brittany said wanting to throw up in her mouth.

"I brought you some of your favorite homemade cookies." Brittany's mom said, handing her the red plastic container. She hated eating the stuff her mom brought because it only gave her memories of Jules and them sitting in her room eating these as Jules would moan and dance as she stuffed her face. Now those memories seemed like a lifetime away.

"Thanks mom, can't wait to devour these back in my room." She tossed the tub onto the table and looked at Lindsay who was now giggling. Lindsay knew how much Brittany hated when her mom came. Yet Brittany could feel this overwhelming sadness anytime she complained about her mom to Lindsay. She knew she shouldn't complain because Lindsay had lost the only family she ever knew, but Brittany vented anyway. She knew her mom had the ability to take her away from here and just wouldn't.

Brittany's mom turned to her, pity lying in her eyes. "Are you sure you're OK today? I know this day must be hard for you."

Brittany's anger seemed to boil even more than it already was. "Really mom, let's just bring up the fact that it is Jules' birthday today. Every fucking day is hard in here!" She snapped. "You try eating the same slop every day, being locked in your room for hours on end with nothing to do but stare at the ceiling, and dealing with fucking heifers who shove pills down your throat to shut you up so they can go back to watching TV and fucking each other in the broom closet!" Brittany shouted, making sure her words cut like glass.

Her mom sat there, shock on her face and completely silent. "That's what I thought mom, you come here to make yourself feel better, make yourself believe you're doing the right thing by keeping your daughter locked away like a crazy person. All the while, your daughter is completely fine, you're the fucked up one!" Brittany said in a sour tone.

"How dare you, Brittany. I'm keeping you safe!" Brittany's mom shouted.

"Safe!? Safe from what mom? You? You scared of me or something? Afraid I'll drown you too like they said I did to Jules?"

"I don't know what the hell has gotten into you today, Brittany," her mom said rudely. "But I don't need this! Have a great day and swallow another fucking pill. You clearly need one."

Brittany heard the chair scrape across the floor as her mom quickly got up and walked to the locked door that led outside. Brittany heard the buzz of the door unlocking and watched as her mom left without ever turning back to look her way.

Tears filled Brittany's eyes. She was so sick of being pitied and judged and having people afraid of her. Her mom didn't even completely believe that she was innocent. She didn't want to see her mom ever again and hoped this would be the last time her mom showed up here. It only showed her what she was missing by being locked away, and bringing up Jules didn't help.

"You OK?" Lindsay said from across the table.

"Not really, I hate being here. I hate that my mom thinks I would hurt anyone. I hate that Jules is gone. I hate everything about this place and the people who work here who think they are better than us." Brittany looked over and saw the hurt in Lindsay's eyes. This place is really all she had. "But I really am thankful to have met you. You mean a lot to me Lindsay. I'm just really sad right now."

"I get it girl, especially with what day today is. Why don't we go to the library and see if we can research more about that witch."

"Sounds good, I need to take my mind off of what just happened."

The girls walked to the library, two nurses behind them the whole time, watching every step they took. They sat down at the computers and plugged in their codes to be able to log in. Everything they looked at was highly watched by the facility and would be questioned at the next therapy appointment if it seemed even a little off.

Brittany typed in the search bar, *the witch of Greenwich*. There were shockingly a lot of posts about her. All the articles were basically the same though, different news outlets telling her stories and the kind of person she was.

Brittany leaned over Lindsay's shoulder, glancing at the laptop screen. Her breath hitched the moment she caught the title of the article.

"The Suicide Hotel: Connecticut's Most Cursed Landmark."

Her stomach dropped. The bold headline pulsed like a wound on the screen, and the subheading was worse

"Inside the Haunted Room Where Tragedy is a Trend."

She blinked, her throat tightening as Lindsay scrolled down, revealing the rest of the article. The text sprawled across the page in cold, clinical paragraphs, dissecting the hotel's grim history like it was entertainment. Brittany read the names,

Jane Chapman. Jules Morgan.

Both listed beneath the tab labeled*victims.* The article didn't just report their deaths. It*sensationalized*them. It claimed the hotel was infamous for a "string of poetic suicides," reducing decades of trauma into some kind of macabre tourism pitch. It said Jane was an unstable woman with a flair for theatrics and then turned its attention to Jules. Brittany's Jules.

She kept reading, her jaw clenching tighter with every line.

"Jules Morgan, a young woman plagued by grief after losing her parents in a tragic car accident, reportedly became withdrawn, directionless, and emotionally unstable. Sources close to her say she expressed having no real purpose left in life."

Then came the final dagger.

"According to circulating rumors, her best, and only friend, a fellow paranormal enthusiast and podcast host, allegedly encour-aged Jules to stay in the haunted room as a 'sacrifice', unconfirmed reports suggest she referred to it as an ending worthy of a viral episode."

Brittany's vision blurred with rage.

"What the hell is this?" she whispered.

Lindsay looked up nervously. "I... I didn't want to show you. I stumbled across it while researching the property and..."

Brittany didn't respond. She scrolled past the first article and clicked on another, then another. Each headline was worse than the last.

"Room 1210: Suicide Pact or Marketing Stunt?"

"From Tarot to Tragedy: The Curse of Madame Zodo."

"The Spiritualist Who Killed Her Guests?"

They were dragging everyone through the mud. Jules, Jane, and even Madame Zodo. They called Zodo a fraud, an occultist, a danger to the community. One article described how a group of paranormal skeptics had visited her grave andtoppled her headstone, laughing as they claimed she'd cursed the hotel herself and would "keep taking souls until someone put a stop to her."

Brittany felt physically sick. Her chest heaved. Her fingers curled into fists.

"How could they write this?" she said, her voice shaking with fury. "How could anyone twist the truth like this? Jules wasn't suicidal. Jane wasn't crazy. And Madame Zodo tried to*help.* She tried to*warn them.*"

Lindsay sat back in her chair. "The internet doesn't care about truth anymore, it cares about clicks. And haunted suicide stories? That's good business."

Brittany stood, pacing. She felt the storm rising in her blood, a tremor that bordered on collapse. "She died in that room," she whispered. "Fighting something*none of them understand.* They're not even asking*what* took her. They're blaming her. They're blaming*me.*" She turned toward Lindsay, her eyes burning.

"We have to go back to the spell book. Now."

Lindsay blinked. "Wait… what?"

"There has to be something in there. A reversal. A protection rite. A way to fight back, even from the other side. Jules and Jane, they're not at peace. That Hollow One… it's still feeding off them. And if we don't act soon, it's going to drag me under too."

Lindsay hesitated. "You're talking about battling something *in the spirit realm.* We don't even know if that's possible."

"I don't care," Brittany snapped. "I *owe* them. Zodo tried to protect Jane. Jules died because of me. If there's *anything* in that book that gives us a chance to sever this thing's hold, even just a little. I have to try." She took a breath, forcing her body to steady itself. "I made a promise. And I'm not leaving either of them behind."

The girls hurried from the library back to the locked prison area they called home. They ran to Brittany's room, and she pulled the book from underneath her mattress. She flipped through the pages frantically, but it was just spells that made no sense. She got to the last page feeling defeated, but as she flipped it, there sat a handwritten letter.

My Darling Jane,

I write this vow to be with you for eternity. Though I still walk this world, I know my time shall come to pass on. You are the light I could not protect then, though I tried with all I had. The forces were stronger, crueler. But hear me now, Jane, I shall make it right in death.

I write this spell not of ink, but of blood. Once I pass from this realm, I will not leave you. I shall bind myself to your spirit, eternal and unseen. Even in death, we shall never be apart. I will forever look after you. I give you my vow, freely, fully.

So mote it be.

"Oh my gosh, Lindsay, she bonded herself to Jane, to keep her safe. Forever! But if that's the case, then are they trying to make sure I get to Jules because they can't keep her safe? Is she suffering in that room?" Brittany asked.

"I think so Brittany, but if this really is true, what is this thing? Madame Zodo feared it so much she bonded herself to Jane to keep them safe."

"I don't know, but I need to save Jules. She needs me, I know it." Brittany flipped through the pages once again, hoping there was a spell that could make her understand what this thing was and why it was so powerful.

Brittany's eyes drifted across the brittle pages, flipping carefully now. She reached the section of the spell book that spoke about creatures called the Hollow Ones. These were not spirits, nor demons, nor anything that had ever lived. They were empty vessels born from void and shadows, feeding not on flesh but fear itself. It went on to explain that the Hollow Ones held no true power of their own. They could not harm the living unless they were conjured and then fed. It was the spirits terror, the dread that burrowed deep in the persons heart that sustained them. Without fear, they were nothing. But once that fear took root, they grow stronger.

But one part of the passage was circled in red multiple times,

Among them walks one more cunning than the rest. A Hollow one unlike any other.

Brittany's stomach twisted as she read on.

This particular Hollow One has learned to think, to manipulate, to twist perception until reality bends to its will. It doesn't just feed on fear, it creates it. With a whisper, it can alter what you saw, what you thought. It can convince you of truths that were never real. It could trap you inside your own mind building panic until it bleeds into madness. It doesn't chase, it waits, it watches, and it can take many forms, making you trust them.

Brittany's hands were shaking, if this is true, she didn't know who she was supposed to believe. How was she going to fight this thing? No wonder Madame Zodo felt she needed to keep Jane safe even in the afterlife.

Brittany looked over but Lindsay was gone. *Was Lindsay part of this? Was she ever actually her friend? Was she Real?* Her heart pounded in her chest. How was she going to trust her own mind.

Brittany could feel the weight of the room shift and it was as if something ancient was watching her. Her pulse quickened, whatever she had just read about had burrowed inside of her bones and she knew she needed protection.

Desperately, she turned back to the book, her hands trembling. Before she could decide where to look, the pages began to flip rapidly, faster than her hands could follow. Then suddenly they stopped, the book lay open to a page titled,

Pure Protection

The instructions were written as if she was reading witchcraft for dummies,

Use your athame or if one is not present just use your minds eye to make a circle around yourself with clear intention. This circle is your sacred safe space.

Sit upon the floor, grounded, and let your mind clear, think of a time you felt most safe.

Keep that in your mind as you speak these words clearly and with conviction.

Brittany inhaled shakily, as she settled herself onto the floor. She closed her eyes, calling forth the memory of Jules and the smell of frankincense, the soft music playing, them laying on the floor laughing as though time stood still. The world around them could have been perishing but all they knew were things in the world at that moment were perfect.

She clung to that memory like a life raft and with a tear streaming down her cheek, trembling, but with determination she began to recite the spell,

"I call to those who walk the path of light,
Come now and stand with me in the night,
Help keep me safe, keep my spirit whole,
Left no fear pass through my soul.
Those who seek to breach my mind,
Shall be cast into silence, sealed and confined.
So mote it be."

As the final words left her lips, a warmth spread through her like invisible arms wrapping around her. The room didn't feel quite as heavy. The spell had taken hold.

* * *

The warmth from the spell still clung to her skin, but Brittany's mind drifted, no, *was pulled*, into a memory.

It began with scent.

Frankincense.

Soft and smoky, just like the kind Jules used to light on rainy nights. Then came the distant hum of music, the eagles, playing from an old Bluetooth speaker propped up on the windowsill. And then the laughter, hers and Jules', tangled together in a sound so full of life it made Brittany's chest ache.

They were back in Jules' room. The one with glow-in-the-dark stars still stuck to the ceiling. The one with cluttered bookshelves, an unmade bed, and the window that overlooked the maple tree.

Brittany sat cross-legged on the floor in her over sized hoodie. Jules sprawled beside her, face flushed from laughing too hard, a half-eaten cookie in her hand.

"Okay, okay," Jules said between giggles, brushing crumbs off her cheek, "but seriously, if you *had* to marry one, would you choose the Babadook or Slender man?"

Brittany burst into laughter. "Are you kidding me? That's the stupidest question I've ever heard, no question its Slender Man, he wears suits. At least he's got a sense of style."

"Oh my god, Brittany."

They dissolved into laughter again, Jules laughing so hard she snorted, which only made Brittany laugh harder. There was no fear, no shadows, no Hollow Ones or locked doors. Just them. Just light.

"I wish we could stay here forever," Jules said suddenly, her voice quieter now, serious. She turned her head to look at Brittany, eyes shining. "This moment. Just freeze it."

Brittany looked at her best friend, trying to memorize everything, every freckle, every curve of her smile, the way her hair fell in loose waves over her shoulder.

"I'd give anything to keep you safe," Brittany whispered.

Jules nodded slowly, her eyes softening. "You already do, Britt."

For a long time, neither of them spoke. The music faded to silence. The only sound was the rain, tapping gently against the windowpane. And then, something shifted.

The light dimmed. The stars on the ceiling flickered.

Jules turned toward Brittany again, but her eyes had changed. Gone dark, like ink spreading across paper.

"I'm still waiting, Britt," she said. But her voice wasn't quite hers anymore. The warmth vanished.

* * *

Back in the Present:

Brittany gasped, her body lurching forward as if breaking the surface of water. She was on the floor, the spell book still open in front of her. The protective circle held, but the memory, or whatever that had been, had cracked something inside her.

She wiped at her cheeks and found tears. Whether from grief, or fear, or guilt, she couldn't tell anymore. But one thing was clear: Jules was still reaching out to her, and Brittany had to find her.

Chapter 22

Jane sat motionless in the room that she had seen a million times at this point. To the living, it was four walls but to her it was a prison of whispers and shadow. Time no longer moved as it once had, minutes had stretched to years, it reminded her of how a dog must feel.

Then one night, the silence broke. She heard the muffled laughter of two girls right outside the room. She rushed to the corner of the room as they entered. She saw a brunette and blonde walk in squealing about how amazing it looked. Something about one of the girls tugged at her mind yet she could not remember why. They both talked about how they couldn't wait to stay here. The girls proceeded to try to talk to spirits using devices and she figured this was her chance to warn them to leave. She did not want them to be in this room and to fall victim to the Hollow One the same way she had.

She tried everything to warn them, flickering the lights, tapping on the glass, turning on the cold air, even knocking a book off the shelf. The cursed book, the book she once thought was curated just for her as a magical aspect to the room, but it only brought horrors. They did get spooked and ended up leaving the room but left everything behind. She knew this wasn't the end of them staying here.

After what seemed like seconds, since time made no sense to her, she heard the girls giggling again as they entered the room, but this time they seemed even more intrigued. She realized that she had failed to scare them away. She didn't want them to have her fate, and she knew that this hollow thing was stronger than them, they could not fight it.

She did everything in her power to scare them away, in desperation, she tried to write her story of what happened to her, her death, thinking it would frighten the girls enough to leave. The girls started packing their stuff up in a hurry. Relief flooded her.

But her relief came too fast as she felt the shift in the air, felt the darkness develop in the room. She saw the dark shadow starting to manifest by the bookcase. His yellow eyes glowing brightly and that horrible smile with the long-jagged teeth. She knew it was a matter of seconds before these girls would have the same fate she now held.

She didn't have any power in this room. She barely had the power to scream. She couldn't open doors for them or help them escape.

Yet the Hollow One couldn't terrorize her, and Jane didn't understand why. Why would he take her life just to leave her sitting in this hotel room forever. When he did see her, he would just stare at her, this feeling of pure fury would fill the room. He couldn't touch her, couldn't terrorize her, couldn't scare her.

Jane backed away into the corner of the room near the door, her heart aching for these two girls. He sat there, just staring at the girls, as if he was enjoying the show before he devoured them and then she heard him chuckle.

She heard his horrible slimy voice throughout the room,

"Finally… I will have my revenge. I may not have you, but she will do just fine, and one day I will find a way to get you back to Hollow Ground. You may have only been there a couple of days, but she can't keep you protected here forever. I can't wait to torment you again."

Jane flinched, thinking of how she had been tormented those couple of days, the fear she felt being chained up in the dark, not knowing what was around her, and her voice taken from her. She remembered the memories he would flood into her mind to break her down, memories of Betty, her parents, and the boy she let get away. They were times she knew she would never see again unless he was using them against her. This was her world now, a lifetime of being a terrorized spirit.

She saw her tube of lipstick roll to the middle of the bathroom floor. Jane prayed that the girl wouldn't see it and fall for his trap. The blonde girl stopped and stared into the bathroom, her feet moving slowly as if she was in a trance. Jane could only watch.

She saw her walk into the bathroom, the door slam behind her, she heard the scream, and then complete silence.

Jane watched as two men ran into the room and tried their hardest to open the door, but it was too late. The Hollow One had claimed her. Once the blondes' soul had been taken, the door finally gave in. The two men lifted the door off the hinges as the brunette ran into the bathroom.

Jane stood in the door watching as the girl held the blonde girl, crying and screaming her name. Jane also saw two older people standing nearby, their heads bow with sadness, knowing that must be the girls' parents watching their little girl pass on. Then the memory slammed into her. The nightmares she used to have of a blonde drowning, they were of her. She froze at the realization that she saw this coming long before Jules was born.

The next moment replays in Jane's head constantly. She saw the hollow one grab Jules spirit and drag her down. Jane tried to go after them, but she was contained to this room. She stood frozen, condemned to watch.

People came in taking pictures, rifling through the room, looking for evidence that she knew they would never find. The Hollow One made sure of that. Slowly, people started to file out until one day it was complete silence. No one came in, no one came out. They never did anything with the room. The room just waited.

Until one day, the air changed. It wasn't the Hollow Ones' dark energy that she was used to feeling occasionally. It felt comforting and loving, and familiar. And then this white light appeared in the room, and as the light faded, what stood before Jane was the lady that she had seen all those years ago in this very room. It was Madame Zodo herself.

The woman looked at her and smiled, and relief seemed to flood Madame Zodo's face. "Oh, thank goodness," Madame Zodo said. "The spell worked, and you are safe from Hollow Ground."

Madame Zodo crossed the room and hugged her tight. "The dark shadow you see is a creature. There are many of them and they are called Hollow One's. The Hollow One's feed off your fear, but there is one that is stronger than the rest. He can feed off your sadness as well. He is the one in this room. I had this horrible vision that you had died, so I cast a spell over you that tethered us for all eternity. I didn't want you to get dragged down there to be tortured for eternity."

They both sat there quiet for a minute, and then Jane finally spoke. "Madame Zodo, did Jules get pulled to Hollow Ground?"

Madam Zodo's head bowed for a minute, and when she looked back up, Jane could see the immense sadness in her eyes. "Hollow Ground is a horrible place. A place I would have never wanted you to go. You sit in a dark decrepit place chained to the ground, and they feed off of your fear little by little until you're nothing, your soul disappears forever. I didn't want that to happen to you. But I couldn't do the same for Jules."

Jane's tears caught in her throat, "Why not, you saved me?"

"Because I didn't know who she was. I would have visions of her and the other one, but their time period didn't make sense. I can't put spells on someone when I don't know who they are. I had to protect you, I had warned you that day, but it wasn't enough."

"So, if she is in Hollow Ground because of him, why am I stuck here?"

"He can't feed off of our fear or our sadness because of the spell. All he can do is make this is our prison so that we have to watch as others get consumed."

"What are these things? These Hollow Ones?" Jane asked nervously.

"They are the worst kind of things. Creatures who live under ground, made by the Devil himself. They are not demons, but creatures created from the Devils' anger. They must be summoned. They can never be fully destroyed but if you show no fear, they cannot feed from you. Most people do not have the ability to block their emotions so I give them protected necklaces that they must wear forever. They are summoned by foolish souls using tools to try to talk to spirits that they don't understand. They are very crafty. They love to play mind tricks and scramble your brain to believe things that aren't true. They can also take forms of people."

Jane's head bowed, realizing she was the reason this thing was in the hotel room. She had conjured it to this place, and she had dropped the necklace. She was also the reason Jules was now being tormented. "And the other girl, what will happen to her? She survived."

"I fear that it wants the other one too. These creatures do not like when their food gets away. The brunette you speak of seems stronger, braver. Hollow One's love to feed off people like that." Zodo paused for a moment, her eyes filling with dread. "I just have this horrible feeling that she's going to come back here and if she does, we are not going to be able to help her fight. We have no power here, nothing we can do to save her. We will watch her be dragged down to hollow ground as well."

They both sat in silence, knowing that if the hotel kept this room open, they would watch person after person be swallowed away and dragged to hollow ground, never to be heard from again, but to live in torment and fear until the day they no longer existed. And this was to be Jane and Madame Zodo's torture for eternity.

Chapter 23

That night, after the lights dimmed and the normal hum of voices from the nurse's desk had quieted, Brittany reached for the pill she stashed in the pillowcase. When she went to grab for it, it was gone, she felt only fabric. Her pulse quickened as her hand started fumbling all around the pillowcase. She shook it upside down frantically praying she hadn't lost it.

A card slowly floated onto the bed. Her breath caught in her throat and her hands shook as she stared at the card laying where her pillow once sat. There, face up, sat the tower card, but it wasn't how she remembered it. Now both girls were savagely scratched out. The name Zodo scribbled on the bottom in jagged ink that looked almost wet.

Her hand trembled as she picked up the card. Her thumb gliding against it, this was real, she could feel the texture of the card, could feel the indents from where the girls were scratched out violently. She knew she hadn't imagined all of this. They could try to erase her memories, gaslight her into believing this wasn't real, murmur behind her back. This card proved what she had gone through was real.

Brittany wasn't sure how she was going to make it out of the room, let alone the building. Her room was always locked and there was always a nurse behind the desk watching. Cameras were everywhere. She was very surprised her room didn't have a camera in it, although the wall with the door was all waist high windows with a glass door. She looked around the room, just a big white box with nothing other than a toilet and sink. No privacy whatsoever. She didn't even have a trash can in her room that she could use as a weapon. Everything they ate was finger foods, they weren't even trusted with utensils. She supposed she could slip the pillowcase over the nurses' head but that wouldn't be very easy considering she would see it coming. It's not like there was anywhere to hide in this room and surprise her. She laid her head on the pillow, and stared at the ceiling, contemplating how she would get out of here. Then she heard a tapping noise at the window wall.

Tap tap.

Brittany sat up but nothing was there. Then she heard it on the wall to the left of her.

Tap tap.

Nothing there. Then to the right where the toilet stood.

Tap tap.

She heard these sounds all the time but now that she knew about Jules, the hints, and Zodo, she listened a little closer.

There was this slight fog on the mirror, but it almost seemed like she was imagining it.

Then she heard the tapping from every wall at the same time. It reminded her of Lindsay's dream. The sound grew louder and faster and then stopped abruptly. Brittany quickly scanned the room on edge, waiting for the sounds to return. Just as her body was about to relax thinking it might be over, the entire bed shook violently.

She screamed and bolted for the door. Slamming her fists on the door and screaming. The nurse she hated, the red bitch, slowly stood up from her chair and looked at her. The rooms were soundproof so all she saw was Brittany banging on a door and her mouth open in a scream.

Brittany felt something tug on her shirt. She whirled around but nothing was there. This thing that shared the space with her was tormenting her. Trying to scare her enough that she would look crazy. No one would believe a crazy girl, and then she would be sedated again and be kept quiet.

The hair on her body was standing straight up as she felt the warm breath on the back of her neck and then a sour metallic smell.

"*Brittany.*" It whispered. She was so confused, she had done the protection spell. Why wasn't it working?

She whirled around and started banging on the door harder for help. The red bitch rolled her eyes and started to waddle her way to the door, shuffling her feet as she came.

"*Brittany.*" It whispered again from the right side this time.

Brittany turned and caught sight of a dark shadow near the sink. Brittany slowly turned her head fully to get a good look, but it was gone.

The nurse clicked the lock and slightly opened the door. "What seems to be the problem?"

"There's someone in my room." Brittany stammered. "It tugged on my shirt and keeps whispering my name. I know it's real."

"Yeah, sure it is" the red bitch said sarcastically. "Why don't you just go lay back down."

Then from somewhere in the room she heard her name again. "Can you please come check! I swear, you'll hear it!" Brittany pleaded.

"Ugh fine. Go sit on your bed and don't move." She flipped

the light switch on from her side of the wall near the door and walked in. "Well, there's really nowhere for someone to hide in this room. As you can see nothing is here," Her arm panned the room and then went to her hip. "Go back to bed Brittany. Or I'll get the doctor, and he will give you something to help you sleep." She shut the door and flipped the light off.

"Bitch!" Brittany muttered. She knew there was something here, lurking. She laid back down and tried to think of good times she had with Jules, anything to take her mind off what was in the room. Her eyes filled with tears thinking of the last time they sat and laughed together, dancing around the hotel room to Taylor swift.

"*Brittany.*" The whisper came for a third time.

"What?!" She snapped, sitting up. This time annoyed at the fact that whatever it was just kept tormenting her.

"*Come back.*" It whispered.

The sound of the whisper sent chills down her spine. She felt the side of the bed sink as if someone was sitting on it. A rancid stench of rot filled the air. She curled her toes up to her chest praying it wouldn't come any further. There was no way this was Jules. It didn't feel loving. Was this the Hollow One? Did he somehow make the protection spell not work? Had she only imagined she had done the spell?

She felt the mattress move as something started to crawl its way towards her and then she felt a burning pain on her side. Brittany screamed and ran to the door. Banging yet again for the unhelpful bitch at the desk. The nurse looked up with this look of annoyance like she was a toddler playing a game for attention.

Then the lights started flashing in her room. Brittany saw the nurse stand straight up and go pale. Her expression shifting from annoyance to fear. She waddled as fast as her short legs would allow but when she got to the wall, she noticed the light switch wasn't moving.

"Please." Brittany pleaded and banged on the door.

She saw the nurse fumble for the key. She sloppily tried placing it in the keyhole, missing every time. Brittany could feel the presence coming closer with each second. The tingling feeling growing stronger in her body, the closer this thing got the more her body trembled and the more her side burned. It was as if she was really on fire. She put her hand on her side and winced, certain this thing had cut her, yet the pain seemed to be spreading.

Finally, she heard the door lock click and the nurse pull the door open.

"I will give you a different room tonight. Something is clearly up with this light bulb." She muttered as she pulled Brittany out of the room. Brittany could tell the nurse was on edge, almost as if she had seen something but would never tell.

As she walked her out of the room Brittany turned to see if she could catch a glimpse of anything in the room. Nothing at all, just complete darkness.

She was brought to Wendy's old room, room 13. "Sorry." the red bitch said smiling. "This is the only empty room." The nurse unlocked the door and as they walked in Brittany could feel a heaviness in the room.

"Can you please at least walk me in the room and check it." Brittany pleaded.

"Really Brittany. This is ridiculous, I should've just given you the sedative," She sighed heavily and walked in. She slowly spun around the middle of the room as she said "see, no one's here."

Just then the nurse froze. She hands flew to her throat, and she gasped as if she couldn't get air. Her eyes were filled with fear and tears. She started wheezing and clawing at her neck. She bent over, her hands on her knees.

"Oh my god, are you OK?" Brittany asked worried.

The nurse wheezed one more time and then she looked at Brittany, tears running down her cheeks and mouthed the word 'help'. Her head twitched for a second and then snapped. She dropped to the floor, completely still.

Brittany staggered back, her breathing coming in gasps, her knees wobbled. What had she just witnessed? Then came the sound that haunted her every moment.

Tap tap.

Brittany screamed and ran into the hall. Her back crashing into the nurse's station. A chair fell to the ground with a loud bang. Another nurse came running over with a bag of chips in hand.

"What is wrong with you?" The nurse shouted.

Brittany just stood there, her eyes not leaving the red bitch's lifeless body. Part of her feared that if she looked away, the dead body would get up and come after her.

The nurse just looked at Brittany and in an annoyed voice shouted, "hello?!"

Brittany's shaky hand slowly pointed to the nurse laying on the floor. Then the nurse slowly made her way closer to the room, keeping eye contact with Brittany as if she would attack her once she got close enough.

The nurse put her hand to the door and stretched her torso around the door to peek at what Brittany kept pointing to. The nurse's breaths came out in ragged movements as she glimpsed at the lifeless nurse laying on the tile floor.

Her bag of chips dropped to the floor and scattered across the tile, She ran to the nurses body. Flipping her over she checked her pulse. "Come on, Vicky! Breathe!" She shouted, kneeling beside her colleague. She pushed on her chest a couple of times before checking her pulse again. She looked over at Brittany with disgust on her face, and with venom in her words, "What did you do?"

"I...I didn't do anything." she stammered. "She was standing there and then started choking and collapsed."

"You expect me to believe that!" The nurse screamed. Those were the only words she screamed out before she too started wheezing.

She looked at Brittany as she started coughing. Then she violently started coughing up chips, more than she possibly could have eaten. She kept coughing them up. Orange crumbs littered her white uniform, and a small pile formed on the floor in front of her shoes. Her eyes were as big as saucers as she grabbed at her throat. Brittany stood their frozen and petrified. What was going on? Who was doing this to them?

Then, as if out of a horror movie, she levitated a couple of inches off the floor, and was flown onto the sink. Her neck hit the side of the sink and the crack that came from her was sickening.

Blood seeped from where her head lay on the floor. Her lifeless eyes staring at Brittany. Brittany's stomach turned, the sight of this woman covered in orange mush and blood, the other lady's sour smell starting to permeate the air, coupled with this sickening fear was too much, Brittany turned from the woman and vomited.

Her head was spinning, her stomach hurt and she knew there was no way in hell this wouldn't be pinned on her.

She walked out of the room and slid down the wall. Her fate was sealed. She would be tried on all three murders now, she just knew it. Somehow they would pin Jules murder on her as well. She needed to get out.

It was the night shift, so she knew there were not many people on duty. These were the only two nurses for this unit. If she could get the keys she could sneak her way out. Brittany's face scrunched in disgust. She knew that would mean going back into that room and searching the nurses. She also knew unless she did this, she would always be plagued by whatever was following her. She couldn't go through this anymore.

She forced herself to stand up. She could do this. All she had to do was grab the keys and run. Then she saw the nurse's cart. She ran over to the cart, rifling through the drawers. After opening every drawer and starting to feel defeated she opened the last one. Sitting right in front, as if it was waiting for her was a sedation syringe. She grabbed it quickly. If either of these two nurses decided to come back to life, she would stab them.

She stood outside the door with the back of her head leaning against the windowed wall. She was terrified to face the room. She couldn't believe she was going to have to rifle through their dead bodies. Jules' face flashed in her memory, just quick enough to give her the motivation she needed. She turned and walked into the room.

She looked over to the nurse next to the sink. Blood dripped from the rim and into her face, leaving strips of blood on her cheek.

"You better not move," Brittany said, gripping the syringe tightly in her hand "I will stab you." She bent down and searched her front shirt pocket first but only found lip balm.

She threw it on the ground and heard it roll as she kept looking, a quick memory of the lipstick rolling from underneath her bed. She shook her head to erase the memory, now was not the time to freak herself out further. Her side pants pocket came up with a hand full of ketchup wrappers. What the hell was wrong with this staff? No wonder why they were all bigger. All they thought about was food. Brittany knew she was going to have to roll her. Her keys had to be in the other pocket. She was extremely heavy, at least three hundred pounds of dead wait. She grunted as she tried to push her. The nurse didn't budge. Brittany got on her knees, not realizing she had knelt right in the blood. She put her hands underneath the nurse and grunted as she tried to yank her onto her back.

Her hands slipped and she stumbled backwards and fell to the ground. The nurse was covered in blood and was slippery. Brittany sat there, her body trembling, she was exhausted and terrified, her body wanting to give up. She knew that giving up was not an option. Brittany forced herself to get back on her knees and put her hands back underneath the nurse, grabbing a hold of her shirt, she yanked harder. The nurse's body rolled onto her back with a loud thump. Brittany's hair was now in her face and without thinking she slid her hair up and out of her face. Blood smeared the top of her head. As her hand slid into the last pocket she heard the jingle.

"Yes!" She said in relief. She frantically shoved her hand in and gripped metal keys. She pulled on the keys, but they seemed to be stuck in the lining of the pocket. She pulled harder hoping she was not going to just break the key ring. She needed to get these keys out quickly. One more final tug and she heard the stitching of her pants rip. Then the relief came over her body as the keys slipped free. "Oh, thank god!" She thought.

She clambered to her feet and started to rush for the door but paused. Sitting at the threshold of the room was a chocolate pudding cup. It was a sign from Jules. She was helping her get away. "Ya know," she said into the air. "You didn't have to scare me half to death, I would have willingly found a way to get the nurses into the room. But good job on the grotesque part."

She walked into the common area but had no recollection of how she had got into this unit, so she wasn't sure how to get out. There were three doors and all of them said exit, but exits to what? Other areas of the hospital. An actual exit. Or straight to guards. Brittany needed to be really careful. One wrong door could send her somewhere she really didn't want to go. Sweat dripped down her forehead as she frantically looked from one doorway to the next.

Then the familiar sound came from the door to the left.

Tap tap.

Alright Jules, I'm listening. But before she left this place hopefully for good, she needed her book. She ran back to her room and slid the spell book out from under her mattress. Then she ran for the exit. As she walked closer to the door she stopped at Lindsay's door. She peered in, Lindsay was curled up in bed sleeping softly. It was as if everything that had happened thus far with the nurses had been sound proof, not one single person in their rooms seemed to have stirred. She was going to miss Lindsay. They had grown close these past few weeks and now the only friend she had. Brittany hoped Lindsay would be OK soon, and that whatever was haunting her would leave her alone once Brittany ended whatever was tormenting her from room 1210.

She walked over to the door slowly, trying not to catch any

other workers attention. There were five keys on this ring. She really hoped one of them opened this door or groping a dead woman would have been for nothing. She tried the first key in the keyhole. Didn't fit. Next one. Didn't fit. At the last and final key she prayed it would work. It slid into the keyhole. She heard the soft click as she turned the key. One part down but now she had to hope no alarms would go off when she opened the door.

She slowly turned the handle and pushed the door open inch by inch. Nothing went off and the hallway was empty. Brittany sighed, realizing she may actually get out of here. She spun and closed the door as quietly as she could.

When she turned back around, the hallway was dark and silent. The only sound was the beeping of machines coming from the rooms. Brittany quietly walked past room after room. Everyone was asleep in their beds. No TVs were on. No lights of any kind. Not even a fan for noise. If it wasn't for the machines she would have sworn time had paused.

She got to the end of the hallway and saw a neon sign for the lobby.

Just then she heard the ding of an elevator and the doors sliding open. Light chatter filled the hallway she needed to go down. Her back pressed against the wall and she prayed they weren't coming this way. She waited, holding her breath as if they would hear her. The chatter got quieter as she heard them going the opposite direction. The relief like a calming blanket surrounding her.

She peeked around the corner and nothing. Complete darkness and silence. As Brittany started walking, she could see the double doors that led outside. She looked left to right making sure no one would see her but the only person in view was a guard. He was sitting in his chair, his head slumped to his chest snoring softly. The sound of soft white noise from the monitors behind him.

Brittany tiptoed as quietly as she could toward the doors hoping she wouldn't accidentally trip and wake him up. As she got close to the doors, she heard the hiss of the motor, and the doors slide open softly. She looked back at the guard, holding her breath, her heart thumping in her chest, her hands shaking.

She kept tip toeing towards the door til she felt the pavement underneath her shoes. She knew she wasn't even close to being out of the woods yet. She still had a ways to go before she would be invisible to any workers. She slowly started jogging down the small pathway that led to an open parking lot for the employees. If anyone was in their car on break, she was screwed.

She scanned the parking lot quickly, car after car, but no movement. No lights were on in any of the cars and everything around her seemed quiet.

Her heart was racing as she swiftly walked past the cars to the forest in front of her. Once she hit the dirt she took off, running for her life. Trees whipped past her. She needed to get as far away from this place as possible.

Her chest was burning as she pushed through and kept running. She wasn't far enough away. She needed to get farther. Her eyesight was starting to tunnel, and her legs felt like Jello. She couldn't pass out. She wasn't far enough away. In the distance she could lightly hear a siren coming from the hospital alerting everyone that something had happened.

That was her cue to run even harder. Her feet seemed to float as she ran even faster, but as she looked back to make sure no one was behind her she felt her foot catch on a root, and then she was airborne. She felt the earth underneath, hard and fast as her body slammed to the ground. She tried to suck in air but nothing, she couldn't breathe.

The wind had been knocked right out of her chest. She started clawing at her neck. The only thought going through her mind was this is how she was going to die. This was the creatures stupid plan all along. It wanted to kill her too. She was the last puzzle piece, and this was how it was going to take her out. It was giving her a hope of making it out of the ward just to off her in the woods.

And then she gasped. Brittany clutched her chest as it burned but she was breathing. She rolled over and onto her knees as she knelt on all fours breathing heavy. She needed to catch her breath and then keep running.

After a couple of minutes, she held onto a nearby tree and stood, her legs were completely Jello. She could barely stand on them, let alone run. She slid down, her back to the tree.

She was alive. Bloody, muddy and in the form of Jello, but alive.

The forest surrounded her, quiet, dark, and endless. Just her and whatever it was that led her out here. She didn't know where she was going, but she knew she wasn't safe yet. She sat beneath the tree, her back pressed against the bark as she tried to steady her breathing.

Then she heard it, it was faint but unmistakable, she heard her name being called. Her heart was pounding and the nervousness set in as she realized she was probably getting caught. She crouched lower, her fingers digging into the damp earth. They were going to find her and take her away again. She had fought so hard to get away, she knew she was so close to getting to the hotel only to be captured.

She could see a faint shadow of a figure coming toward her but as the figure got closer, she noticed it didn't seem to be moving with authority but with urgency and she felt this familiarity.

She heard the voice call out again. "Brittany! Please tell me that's you."

"Lindsay?" Brittany asked wearily.

"Oh, thank goodness, I found you." Lindsay said stumbling towards her. "The guards are going crazy! They found the bodies. They know you're missing."

"I figured it wouldn't take too long," Brittany said. "I need to get back to the hotel."

Lindsay dropped to her knees beside her, "you look like hell by the way."

Brittany gave a quick chuckle, "feels worse than it looks."

"I can help you. We aren't too far." Lindsay said. "But I know you must be tired. I'll sit with you for a minute, let you catch your breath."

Brittany was so thankful to see a comforting face. She was happy she wouldn't be alone in this but at the same time she didn't want her only living friend to be caught in the cross hairs of whatever this being was. She didn't want to lose Lindsay as well.

"How did you get out?" Brittany asked, very confused, since she knew what she had to do to get out of there.

"There was so much chaos, they never saw me slip out. I knew you would need a friend, I had to get to you." Lindsay held her shaking hand, and they sat there in pure quiet for a minute as Brittany regained her strength.

Brittany leaned her head against the tree, grateful for a

moment of peace. Then Lindsay broke the silence.

"Britt… what makes Jules so special to you?" Lindsay asked.

Brittany just stared at her for a second confused. That was an odd question, they had talked about Jules quite a bit and she had told her about Jules' parents and losing her in the hotel room.

"I mean, we've talked about this before. I figured you kind of know why." Brittany said with a questioning voice.

"I know you guys were close, but to go somewhere that you know you could be sacrificing yourself to save someone who is already dead. That seems crazy."

Lindsay wasn't wrong Brittany realized, she did sound crazy, but Jules was her best friend. Regardless of her state of living now. "Maybe… but I promised her I'd keep her safe forever," Brittany said. "That means even in the afterlife. There's a chance she's still being tormented, and I can't let that happen. She needs to be free. She's dealt with too much sadness in her life to be stuck in sadness still. That promise doesn't expire."

"You know," Lindsay said leaning in closer. "I heard that he had them all chained up in some dungeon and feeds off their fear and that Jules is his biggest source of power right now but that he's still hungry and he says that he could feed off you forever."

Brittany went still. "How would you know that? Did Zaron tell you about that in your dream?" Then anger hit her and she didn't care how Lindsay knew. "Why would this help me right now?" She questioned angrily.

The kindness in Lindsay's eyes vanished, her lips turning up into a cruel smile. "Oh, come on, it's kind of funny. You say you're this strong girl who is so brave," Lindsay said sarcastically. "Yet he thinks you'd make the biggest fear meal.

So, what is it, Brittany. Are you brave or just a big baby?"

Brittany swung her head quickly to look at Lindsay. "What the fuck? What is wrong with you?" Brittany said.

Lindsay just let out this horrible wretched snicker of a laugh. "You'll never make it to her. He's going to consume you before you make it to the hotel. He can smell your stench of fear and it's only getting stronger."

Brittany was so tired, her body barely able to move but she dragged herself through the dirt, away from the thing, there was no way this was Lindsay.

The thing only laughed louder.

"What are you and where is Lindsay?" Brittany said holding back tears.

"You're so naive, you wanted friendship so bad because you're so afraid of being alone that you clung to the first girl that showed you any sort of affection in that place. Lindsay was never real. I made her up. I like screwing with your reality, breaking you down slowly, watching you wherever you are without you knowing. And I would say I did a damn good convincing job. You ate up every second of it. I gave you that comfort."

Brittany clutched the tree, trying to drag herself back faster. "There's no way you made her up. She was real. I hugged her, I could see her, I trusted her."

"I am the most powerful Hollow One there is," It hissed. "You really think I couldn't take the form of some mousy little girl? Please, I can do anything." The thing said in a mocking tone.

Brittany closed her eyes. This had to be a dream. This couldn't be real. This couldn't be happening. When she opened her eyes, it was gone but she could hear light laughter all around her, tormenting her, enjoying every minute. Slowly feeding off her fear.

She scrambled to her feet. She needed to get to the hotel.

Chapter 24

The forest was too quiet. Not peaceful. Not calm. Wrong.

Brittany's sneakers crunched against the underbrush as she stumbled forward, branches clawing at her arms like skeletal fingers trying to pull her back. The moon offered little help, just a faint glow through the thick canopy above. Everything smelled like damp earth and something older... like mildew and rot. She didn't know how far she had run. She didn't care. She just knew she needed to get to the room.

As the adrenaline began to wear off, a new fear settled in. The kind that didn't come from screaming ghosts or flickering lights, but from being truly, terrifyingly alone. she wished Jules was here. She knew she couldn't trust her own mind anymore. Everything she believed was fake.

The police didn't believe she had nothing to do with it. Two people were now dead in a hospital, and now she was a fugitive. The hopelessness set, even if she found the truth, even if she proved Jules didn't take her own life... no one was going to believe she was innocent. This wasn't going to end well for her.

Though she knew the ending for herself, she knew she still needed to help Jules and set Jane and Madam Zodo free. They deserved to be able to rest in peace. She had to get to that hotel and somehow get in that room.

She just kept walking, though the forest pressed in around her, disorienting and dense. She had no clue which direction led to the hotel, but the sirens from the hospital were growing dimmer with each step she took.

Then she heard the familiar sound that seemed to get her out of trouble.

Tap tap.

It was the sound of tapping on a tree, like a woodpecker. At this point she wasn't sure it was Jules helping but she wanted to believe it was her. She wished she had a way to warn her about the Hollow One playing his tricks. She followed the tapping from one eerie tree to the next. Her legs still felt wobbly, and it was hard getting through some areas where the hills felt like mountains. She grabbed onto whatever vines were growing nearby and pulled herself along.

Just when she thought there was no way her legs could carry her anymore, she felt this weird strength come over her. Her body had this tingling sensation as if her whole body was on pins and needles. It was as if Jules was here, in her body, giving her strength. Her legs no longer felt tired. She felt focused and more determined than ever. As she walked through the forest, she no longer had trouble walking up the hills. She didn't need the ivy to pull herself along. She walked as if she knew exactly where she was going.

As she got to the top of the hill she saw the clearing, the farmland seemed to go for miles. Mowed fields ready to be made into hay bales. As she got closer, she saw the white farmhouse in the distance, the sagging roof and the chipped paint. The farmer who clearly takes better care of his land than he does his home. She saw the big red barn that she knew had probably seen so many animals come and go, farm equipment that has been there since the farm came into existence that would never work again, cobwebs in the corners older than her, and a scarecrow tucked in the corner somewhere that never actually scared the crows.

She looked around the farmland, a huge tractor sat in the middle of the field, a baler attached to it. A mower sat near the farmhouse. Huge tires piled up near a stonewall. Then she saw it. Off near the trees in the shade sat an old 1970s white Chevy truck. It looked beat up, rust on the wheel wells, the truck separating slightly from the bed, dust covering the windshield. As Brittany got closer, she saw the hay bales in the bed of the truck, clearly ready for work tomorrow. She pulled on the driver side door handle and to her relief the door popped open. Dust and hay covered the inside of the truck, coffee cups and old candy wrappers thrown on the passenger side floor. It smelt like an old truck too.

She hopped inside and saw the keys sitting in the ignition. She hated what she was about to do, this farmer is clearly very trusting and knows no one would come on his property. He probably knows all his neighbors, and they probably watch out for each other, calling if something seems a miss, but she needed the truck, she needed to get to the hotel. Once there, she will do what's needed to be done to help Jane and Jules. She will bring the truck back, apologize profusely for stealing their property, she will tell them what happened and hope they understand.

She turned the key, and the truck came to life. It purred loudly as an old work truck does. She was so thankful that the truck was way out in the field and not close to the house. She put the truck in drive and slowly crept down the field, following the tire tracks embedded in the mowed grass. She came to the dirt path and drove for about a mile before she hit a paved road and then shestarted to drive. She had no idea where she was going but she hoped if she kept going straight, she would drive into an area she knew. She drove for a couple of miles, but noticed there were no houses anywhere, just endless trees, the forest stretching on as if it had no intention of letting her go. Brittany started worrying, maybe she was really out in the middle of nowhere, maybe civilization wasn't for hours. She looked at the gas gauge and got more worried when she saw a little less than a quarter of a tank, she wasn't going to get too far depending on where she was.

She finally saw a house come into view. At least she was seeing more than forest. She was thankful because that meant she was closer to town, but she was very nervous knowing she was driving a stolen truck. If she were to get caught, they wouldn't just give her a ticket and send her on her way. Not to mention she broke out of a psych ward and two nurses were dead.

She drove a little further, the houses were getting a lot closer together now. She was so hopeful that she would soon see a landmark that would make her realize where she was.

She got to a stop sign and her stomach started turning. There were three different ways she could go, one of them would lead to town but the other two would probably lead to more houses, more forest, and farther from the hotel. There were no signs for direction, she needed to go off her instincts.

It reminded her of the game her mom and her would play when they would take their Sunday drives. Her mom would ask her which way they should turn, and they would drive wherever the roads took them, Brittany the GPS. Brittany would always choose the way that looked the most interesting. She recalled the one time they played this game, and they were driving past a cute ice cream shop and mini golf area. Brittany's mom surprised her by stopping and said, "Well Britt, guess this is where the road took us." Brittany was so excited and hoped they would keep finding cool stuff like that on their Sunday drives, but most of the time it was just beautiful scenery or farmland.

Brittany decided she was going to play that game in hopes it would magically bring her to the hotel or at least to somewhere she knew. She turned left. As she drove the houses got a tiny bit closer together, and the road seemed to get a little wider than your average back road. Then she drove past a cute mom and pop diner. She knew she was getting close to town and her heart skipped a beat realizing she might find her way.

A mile down the road she could see a gas station in the distance. She could see cars and a yellow blinking traffic light. As she got closer to the blinking light, she saw Dunkin' Donuts, and a Dollar General. Her heart skipped a beat as she realized she knew exactly where she was. She had driven through this intersection so many times with Jules when they lived in Connecticut. She was only ten minutes away from the hotel.

She wanted to hit the gas and fly there but she knew that would draw too much attention. she needed to stay calm. She came to the blinking light and a cop rolled to a stop to the right of her at the intersection. Her heart started racing, she knew if she got stopped, this was all over. She would get arrested and maybe have a life sentence. No one would believe she didn't kill those nurses, or Jules for that matter. She would get thrown into prison without a second thought. The jury would get one look at her, hear her story and say she was crazy. Maybe she would end up back at the psych ward with nurses who would now fear her, treat her horrible because their friends had died. Would she get stuck with Lindsay, which she now knew wasn't actually Lindsay. She would be tormented for life, watched like a hawk, she wouldn't even be able to go pee without someone standing in the room, she'd probably be handcuffed at all times, drugged so she was numb and slow.

Her heart was racing as the police officer looked in her direction, and her eyes went wide. There's no way he doesn't know, he could probably read her reaction, knew she was guilty, knew her face from the news and knew she escaped.

Her hands went sweaty, her mouth went dry, and her head started to spin. It was all over, she would never help Jane and Jules.

But just like that, the cop car drove down the road, pulled into the Dunkin' Donuts and made his way to the drive thru. Relief flooded her entire body. Now she needed to calm her shaking hands and legs so she could drive without wrecking the truck.

She slowly pulled away from the blinding light, turning right to go towards the hotel. She knew how to get there like the back of her hands. She made the next right, then made a left at the second stop sign. Then stayed straight for the last seven minutes until she came to a winding mile long driveway. She pulled slowly down the driveway. She was so close, now was not the time to freak out and doing something reckless and end up veering off the road.

As she got to the end, she could see the hotel coming into view. All fifteen stories, just staring at her, watching her, waiting for her.

She was finally here, but she knew she needed to find a way to sneak in. Most people knew her face, they knew what happened that night with Jules and they would know that she was not supposed to be coming back here. She drove to the back of the hotel and saw a door, hoping it would be unlocked.

She got out of the truck and walked to a plain metal door at the back of the hotel. It felt out of place with how the rest of the hotel was adorned. All the doors were magnificent and mysterious. Except for this one door. Brittany grasped the knob and to her relief it was unlocked. She was completely shocked. This was too easy. She stepped through the door to a dark, musty basement. The floors were concrete, and spider webs etched the ceiling. She could faintly see a small staircase that led to another normal metal door. As she got closer, she could make out the wording on the door. Staff entrance only was written in red, flaking letters.

Her hand touched the cold metal knob and she was again shocked when it turned effortlessly. She peeked her head out slowly and looked into a hallway. It was quiet and dark. Even though it was nighttime it still shocked her that there were no sounds at all. Her feet hit the carpeted floor and for the first time in a long time she felt she may actually help the girls. She started walking down the hallway towards another white metal door that read stairs. She quietly made her way to the door.

As she opened the door movement caught her eye. She stopped and put her back to the door hoping she wasn't seen. It was a girl in a black dress with red heels walking up the stairs. Yet what confused Brittany was the heels made no noise. It was as if she was floating up the stairs. Her curiosity got the better of her, and she peeked up the stairwell, but nothing was there.

Tap tap.

Brittany's hands shook as she grabbed the railing.

"OK Jules. I'm listening." She whispered up the stairs.

As Brittany quietly climbed the stairs, she would randomly see the flow of the black dress or catch a glimpse of the women's shoes rounding the next level of the spiral staircase. Her whole body was shaking, she really hoped this was Jane she kept getting glimpses of and not something or someone else.

She finally reached the door with a big red number 12 on it, and she froze. How was she going to get into this room? She didn't have a key card. What if someone was in there? What if she got caught trying to get into the room? I'm sure there are cameras in the hallway. As her thoughts spiraled, she was starting to doubt this was going to be possible.

Tap tap.

She closed her eyes and breathed heavily. "OK girls. I understand. I'm coming."

She shook her head trying to calm the fear and thoughts running through her mind. She grabbed the handle and slowly opened the door to the 12th floor. As she peeked out it reminded her of the hospital. It was eerily quiet. No sounds, no lights. It was as if the world was on pause. She stepped onto the carpet, the birds staring at her with their ominous look. It sent shivers down her spine as memories flooded back from when her and Jules walked these halls for the last time.

Tap tap.

"You are being quite pushy, ya know." She said chuckling softly to herself.

She quietly made her way down the hall staring at the numbers on the doors as she passed. 1206, 1208, and then she stopped dead at the golden numbers on the door in front of her.

1210.

Her heart was racing, her knees turning back to Jello, sweat forming on her forehead. Was she really doing this? What if she too didn't make it out? Her mind was buzzing, and she could feel her eyesight tunneling and the dizzy feeling in her head.

"Brittany" she heard the whisper from the other side of the door. The same whisper from inside the psych room.

"OK you can do this, just open the door, Brittany." She told herself. Her hand wrapped around the knob. It was wet. She pulled her hand away and noticed a dark red smear on the palm of her hand.

"Oh my god, oh my god, what the fuck." She whispered to herself as she rubbed her hand on her pants panicking.

"I can't... I can't go back in there. I'm sorry Jules..." She whispered as if whatever was on the other side of the door was listening and could hear her. Her eyes filled with tears as she realized she had failed. She was too afraid to go back in. She couldn't face the memories locked away in this room. She didn't want to face whatever had taken Jane and Jules lives. She always prided herself on how brave she was, but she no longer felt brave. She was a coward.

"I'm so sorry Jules. I'm so sorry." She choked out as tears spilled down her cheeks. "I can't... I can't face seeing where you took your last steps, your last laughs, you last breath. I can't."

She slid her back down the wall and curled into herself. Her shoulders shaking slightly as she started to cry. She had come so far and yet when Jules needed her the most she had froze, she was a failure.

Tap tap.

She looked up at the door and saw the door slightly creak open.

"Brittany," a female faintly whispered. "Please help me."

She stared into the sliver of darkness coming from inside the room. As she continued to stare inside, she swore she saw a quick glimpse of red heels pass by. A tube of lipstick rolled out the door and lightly tapped into her hand. She just stared at the tube in disbelief. Where had it been this entire time when the cops supposedly combed the whole room? Was someone actually in there, waiting for her, toying with her? Was the Hollow One inside waiting for her? Or was she going to walk into the room and officers would be sitting on the couch waiting to bring her in for the murders? The fear of those thoughts kept her frozen in place, just staring at the tube of lipstick laying at her fingertips. Then she heard a laugh. It was quick but she would know the laugh anywhere. It was Jules.

"Jules?" She whispered into the cracked door. "Jules?" She whispered again. Nothing. No sounds. No more laughs. Just eerie silence.

She stood up, determined. She needed to know if Jules was still stuck in this room. She needed to face her fears and walk in. She counted to herself, three, two, one.

She pushed the door open and walked inside.

Chapter 25

The room was dark, a thick heavy feeling permeated the air. She flipped the light switch on and stared around the empty room. The couch sat empty, beds made perfectly, nothing out of place. She looked towards the bathroom. The door had been rehung and sat closed, memories from within sealed tight as if in a tomb.

But the air... it wasn't right. It pressed against her skin, like the walls themselves were holding their breath. She stepped in further, the carpet muffling her footsteps. She had been given so many clues this whole time but now it was as if the room was frozen in time. No tapping, no mysterious apparitions, no more clues falling into place.

She sat on the couch hoping something would come to her, or that she would remember something from that night that could help her figure out how the Hollow One got here. Where had it come from? Why was it here? We're all these clues that Jane had supposedly been giving them that night all just been a ploy to get Jules into the bathroom? How many times had it killed?

Thump.

Brittany looked over at the bookcase and then the floor. There on the floor sat the book the police swore wasn't real.

Brittany swallowed hard and got up from the couch. She grabbed the book with shaky hands. The leather smooth on her fingertips.

The spine read something completely different now.

The beckoned.

Brittany just stared at the words, frozen. The book always seemed to be a premonition. She sat there, fingers clutched tightly around the book, as hot tears streamed down her cheeks. What had happened that night? Why was Jules taken and not her? They promised to always be together but at this moment, in this suffocating silence, she couldn't even feel Jules' presence.

With trembling hands, she sat the book on the table, she curled up on the couch not knowing how to fix this, or how to help any of them. She was defeated. If this Hollow One really was trying to break her down and devour her soul so that he could become even stronger he was doing a great job. She wanted this thing to just take her now so she could be with Jules. Then she felt the anger surge again. Why hadn't it taken her yet? Was she not good enough? She stood up, grabbed the book and hurled it at the wall.

"Hey asshole! What are you waiting for? If you're so big and bad why the fuck haven't you taken my soul yet? You scared of me just like everyone else seems to be?" Brittany screamed into the empty room.

The radio turned on and Taylor Swift's music quietly played throughout the room. The song they used to dance to all the time. Brittany froze, and her heart dropped into her stomach.

"Jules?" Brittany said in a shaky voice on the verge of tears. "Please... if it's you, give me a better sign so I know it's you."

But nothing came. The radio played the song but that was

all.

Brittany sat back down on the couch, hands covering her face and sobbed, loud, aching cries that filled the room. She cried for what seemed like hours into a room that had never been this quiet, ever.

Brittany's eyes felt heavy, exhaustion hit her hard and no matter how hard she tried, she could not keep her eyes open.

She felt the cushion beside her move, and she jolted up but when she looked nothing was there. She touched the cushion but there was no indent, or any evidence that anyone had just been sitting there.

A door creaked open to her right. Brittany turned her head slowly in that direction, terrified of what she would see. Jules came from the bathroom, her hair wet, her favorite night shorts and a tank top on.

"Hey Britt. What's up? You look like you've seen a ghost?" Jules said laughing.

"Jules?" Brittany asked, rubbing her eyes as if it was a mirage and if she rubbed hard enough it would go away.

"No, Santa clause." Jules chuckled. "Yes, it's me, who else would it be? God, I thought you would never wake up. You took a nap a while ago. wasn't even sure we would get to investigate this place."

"What? What day is it? How long have we been here?" Brittany asked shaking.

"Are you high? It's July sixth. We've been here for like.... What, three hours tops."

Brittany stared down, noticing she was not in her white clothes from the psych ward, but the clothes she wore the night they came to this room."Jules, I had the worst nightmare of my entire existence. You died, and then I was sent to a psych ward where I was being tortured by a horrible creature. I thought I'd lost you."

Jules Chuckled. "Damn girl, no more fast food for you before we investigate anywhere. That's what you get for inhaling tacos."

Brittany laughed weakly, a sob still caught in her throat. It had all been a terrible nightmare. Jules was alive, she was fine. The nurse's were not dead and the creature didn't exist. Brittany's body started to relax but then her eyes caught on a familiar object. The book she thought she had thrown in her dream was now sitting on the table. "Hey Jules, did we take this book out?"

"Yeah, you started reading it and fell asleep mid page."

Brittany stared at the book, she was so confused. This book had always been empty. How could she read a book with no words? She flipped the book open, and the title of the book read,

Timmy found his home.

As she flipped the pages they were all filled in. Words on every single page. She flipped to the beginning of the book and started reading about a little boy named Timmy who had got lost in the woods, he talked about how cold it was, snow covered the ground, and he was shivering. Timmy watched as the sun set, still not finding his way home. As time passed, he felt his body losing energy, he was shaking so badly from the cold and his fingers and toes burned. He felt his eyes get heavy, felt his body drifting into sleep. When he woke up, he was no longer cold, or scared. He walked a little more and saw a little girl with bottles in her arms. He could hear calves calling to her. He watched her feed the cows and enjoyed as she read to him. Timmy was always sad though, he could hear his family calling to him, they always seemed so close. When he would run outside, they were nowhere in sight. This happened every day like a movie on a loop. And every day he would go back to this little girls' room, tired and sad, feeling lonelier than ever.

One day Timmy came inside after hearing his parents but not finding them. He got to the little girls' room and felt comfort as he saw her sitting on her bed reading her book. Oh, how he loved when she read the voyages of Dr Dolittle. It was his favorite. He sat down in the corner, but she didn't acknowledge him. He tried to call to her, but she didn't respond. It was as if he was completely invisible to her. He came back for a couple of days but always got the same response. He was now even lonelier than before. He couldn't find his family and now the little girl who befriended him, could no longer see him. He walked to the barn and sat with the cows. Out of the corner of his eye, a dark shadow appeared. He feared, knowing there were dark things in this spirit world that could harm him. He tried to get away, but the darkness seemed to creep faster towards him. As he ran faster, there was suddenly only darkness, and this horrible laughter had surrounded him. He feared whatever creeped in the darkness had now caught him. He felt a tug on his shirt and as he turned this large dark shadow stood before him. All he saw was yellow eyes and long sharp teeth. He tried to scream but it dragged him, feet firstinto the darkness of the woods. The next thing he knew he was enveloped in darkness. Chains held him in place, he couldn't scream or speak, it was as if something had taken his voice from him. He was stuck in this dark prison, and there was no way out. He could hear other chains rattling near him, but no sounds came from anywhere. Were there other spirits chained up down here who couldn't get away?

Timmy sat there terrified. He didn't know how he ended up here, he just didn't want to be alone. Now he was more alone than ever. He heard the laughter first. Then the voice. "Well hello Timmy. The thing said in a slimy voice. You were never meant to be mine. Yet death freed you from the order of men. Now you belong to Hollow Ground, where you will be tormented for eternity. I'll never refuse a free meal."

"Who are you?" Timmy said, his voice shaking.

"I am the worst part of fear little one, I twist your thoughts, your feelings, your life. I make you more scared than you've ever been and sadder than you can imagine and then I feed off that."

Timmy's eyes burned with tears and he felt a lump in his throat. He swallowed back the feeling and forced himself to speak. "Why?"

"Because that's what I do. You call to me, I feed."

"I didn't bring you here!" Timmy shouted.

"No but your cute little friend did, she played a dangerous game with a board. And now... here you are."

Timmy calmed himself and breathed lightly, thinking good thoughts of his friend. If he wasn't scared it could not feed and maybe then he could find a way out.

He opened his eyes, and he was home. In the house he grew up in. His room looked exactly the same, he scanned the room, everything was in its place. He could hear his mom downstairs. He ran down the stairs as fast as his legs would carry him. "Mom!" He screamed.

"Timmy! What seems to be the problem love?"

He didn't say a word. He just hugged her tight. He would never let her go. He could smell her perfume, and the flower she always put in her hair. He could feel her arms wrap around him tight. He was home and safe. His father came through the door, a turkey dangling by it legs in his father's left hand. "Well son, you gunna come help me with this so your mama can start supper?" His father raised the turkey up high so he could see it.

"Yes papa," he said hugging his mom one last time before running outside to help his father dress the bird. His father looked down at him and smiled. "I'm proud of you boy. You are learning quickly."

When they finished, his father patted him on the head, "love you son. You've done good. Now go inside and wash up and do your reading for school."

Timmy smiled bright, he was so thankful it had all been one awful dream and as he walked inside the house, everything was dark. Slowly the kitchen started to fade as if it was just a painting and the paint was melting away. "No. No. No." Timmy said, his heart caught in his throat. He could feel the tears welling up ready to explode.

"Mmm, perfect. You smell amazing. This is what I do, this is your eternity." Timmy felt the energy zap out of him and his head went limp, his body felt heavy and then his eyes shut.

Brittany snapped the book shut. "What the hell kind of story is that?" She muttered.

Jules came towards her holding a Red Bull can. "Here babe, you look like you could use some energy."

"Thanks Jules." She grabbed the can and cracked it open. As she took the first swig, she heard Jules and froze.

Jules' voice, casual, and amused drifted towards her. "How'd ya like the story? Pretty crazy right? God Timmy was a good one! He made me pretty strong."

Brittany's can fell to the floor. "Wh... What did you say?"

Her voice barely audible.

"Damn, it's so easy to scare you puny humans. Oh no the poor little boy is stuck forever. Let's cry about it." The thing I thought was Jules said.

"Jules?" I said shaking.

"Oh honey," It said with a wicked grin, voice twisting, "I love the way you smell when you're scared Brittany. Let's keep this game playing shall we. What should I do next to scare you? Should I be her dying in front of you this time or something worse?" It said laughing and then slowly dissipated.

Brittany jolted awake shaking and gasping for air. The room was dark other than the light she had turned on when she had first arrived. No Red Bull can sat pooling on the floor. The bathroom door was still shut. It had only been a dream. A terrible vivid nightmare.

Then she looked at the coffee table. There was the book, the one she definitely remembered throwing when she had her tantrum. Her hands shook as she opened the cover.

There, looking her in the face was the same title.

Timmy found a home.

She slammed the book shut, her heart racing, her body shaking. She didn't know what reality was and what wasn't anymore. This thing was toying with her. Scaring her at every turn, fueling her up until he was ready to devour her.

Brittany went to the bookcase and started ripping the books off the shelves. There had to be an answer in here somewhere. One by one, the books flew from the shelves, hitting the floor with dull thuds. Dust filled the air, stinging her eyes but she didn't stop.

She was breathless, sweating, trembling with fury and fear when she noticed something small and metallic. Buried behind a book was a bracelet. Her breath hitched, it was the bracelet she had given Jules when they were twelve. She remembered that moment like it was yesterday.

* * *

20 years ago

Middle school cafeteria

Jules sat at the lunch table, swirling the peas around the tray with her fork. Her shoulders were hunched, as if she were trying to disappear into her hoodie.

Brittany walked up to her laughing, "You do know if you don't eat them, you won't be strong enough to beat up Jennifer Lakewood."

Jules looked up at, caught off guard and chuckled. "Please, I could easily beat her up. She's a string bean. She won't be able to pick on my bush of a haircut anymore."

Brittany laughed, "it's not that bad Jules. You look like a young napoleon dynamite, and it'll grow out quickly."

Jules stuck her tongue out and Brittany sat down next to her. "Here Jules, have my pudding cup."

Jules eyes lit up and she smiled and grabbed the pudding cup quickly out of her hand. She ripped the foil top off and started dancing as she popped the first spoonful in her mouth. Brittany adored her best friend and loved seeing her happy, even if just for a moment. She lived with her aunt and uncle now and she always said she was fine but sometimes Brittany could feel the sadness she carried.

As Jules scraped the last bit of pudding from the cup, Brittany cleared her throat. Jules looked up and saw Brittany holding a small silver bracelet with half a heart on it.

Jules smiled wide, "for me?"

"It's a friendship bracelet. I've got the other half." Brittany said as she held up her other arm to show the same bracelet.

Jules stared at the bracelet with glassy eyes and then grabbed the bracelet. She threw her arms around Brittany in a tight hug. "Thanks Britt. I hope we are friends forever."

"Always!" Brittany said. Then they linked there pinky's together and laughed.

* * *

Back to the present

Brittany held the bracelet in her hand, she was not going to cry, she was going to stay strong and figure out how to defeat this horrible thing.

Then, from deep inside the bookcase, a whisper came. "Do you want her back?"

Brittany didn't move, she just stared at the bookcase for a moment, frozen. Then she finally spoke, "you don't think I know you're just playing with my mind?"

"You want to hear her laugh, her touch, her smile as you made her feel loved like family? Give me what I want, and you can have her back."

"No!" Brittany whispered. Her voice cracked but she held her tears in, "you can't make her come back, she's dead. And she's not yours to give back."

"That's what you think. They're all mine, and so are you. You just need to accept it."

"I will never accept it. You can't have them. I will figure out how to get them back." Just as Brittany said it, she could hear laughing come from inside her head. "Get out of my head!" She screamed.

"Oh honey, I'm not in your head. I'm in your soul. I've already taken hold and slowly I will take every bit of you." It said laughing manically.

"Get out of my head!" Brittany screamed, her voice raw.

The shadow didn't answer, but the silence it left behind was worse.

She held the bracelet in her hand tighter. She would not let this thing keep taking pieces of her, screwing with her head and heart.She walked over to the bed and saw the tarot card sitting on top of the comforter. The room was silent, but not still. The air trembled, thick, and heavy, like a thunderstorm was coiled just above the ceiling.

Brittany sat on the edge of the bed, the Tower card trembling between her fingertips. The artwork stared back at her with too much familiarity. A jagged bolt of lightning. A crown flying off. Two figures tumbling headfirst from the flames. Jane and Jules.

She traced the figures with her thumb. The lines looked almost... scorched. Burned into the card, not drawn, and the tower, so tall, so straight, so solid. Still standing while everything else fell. Her eyes fixed on it. Her breath caught. It wasn't the girls who were the focus. It was never about who fell. It was about what remained. "The tower doesn't fall," she whispered. "It holds."

Her fingers gripped the card tighter. She was the tower. She had stood through it all, the blood, the deaths, the whispers, the tapping. She'd survived. She'd endured. And now she was at her peak fear.

A creak broke the silence. She looked up. The bathroom door was open now. She didn't remember hearing it move. But there it was, wide enough to cast a long shadow into the room.

And in the doorway stood Brad. Calm. Smiling. His hair was neatly parted. His hands at his sides. But his eyes… they were wrong. Too black. Too still. Like something ancient was staring out from behind them.

"You see it now," he said, voice soft, smooth. "You were never the one falling, Brittany."

She couldn't breathe. Couldn't blink.

"You," he whispered, stepping forward, "were the tower all along."

Brittany backed away instinctively, the tarot card still clutched in her hand like it might shield her. Her breath hitched as the air grew heavier, like the walls were pressing in, like gravity was changing. "Why?" she managed to choke out.

Brad tilted his head, as if the question amused him. "Because towers are strong, but when they come down, they come down hard and it's amazing."

She stumbled backward until her calves hit the bed frame. Her knees buckled. "I don't give you permission to take me," she whispered, shaking her head. "I will never let you in."

Brad stopped mid-step. "Oh sweetie, you already did, didn't you?" He nodded toward the card still trembling in her fingers. "You listened to the taps. You followed the trail. You came back. You opened the door. It was never Jules leading you here. She wasn't the one leaving you clues and making you feel safe."

She looked down at the card again. Her name was fully

written now, beneath the two scorched-out figures. But it wasn't just written. It was moving. The ink swirled like a living thing, the letters crawling along the parchment.

"No," she said firmly. "No. I'm not yours."

He sighed. "You're already mine, Brittany. You've been mine since the first time you entered the room and decided to engage with what you thought was a lost soul you could speak to. I mean, I guess technically you were responding to a lost soul that I imprisoned there, but you guys ate it up. My favorite was when I started making you guys see Jane throughout the hotel. The fear that set in smelt delicious."

Suddenly, pain lanced through her skull, white, hot, and immediate. She dropped the card, clutching her head as something unseen pushed into her thoughts. Her own memories flickered like broken film: Jules screaming in Room 1210. The whispers in the hospital. Brad letting them interview him. The creepy image in the elevator. It had always been him.

"I love taking the form of people and not just my true figure. People are so gullible. I show up as a sweet guy looking to help you guys or that mousy girl, and you trusted them. No questions asked." He said laughing.

"What did you do to Brad?" Brittany asked.

"That's the best part," the things said sneering. "It's just like your beloved Lindsay. They were never real. I made them up. That Reddit post and the articles online at the hospital, my handy work as well. You guys were so easy."

Brittany's memory flashed to sitting next to Lindsay. Lindsay was the one that had found all those horrible articles dragging the girls through the mud. She knew exactly where the book was hidden. She seemed to know everything that scared Brittany. Her heart ached and fear filled her body. She had not even been talking to a real person. Every time she confided in Lindsay, she was really confiding to this thing.

Then her body felt wrong, pins and needles that started at her scalp and slowly took over her entire body. She felt like she was full of static, like something was vibrating beneath her skin trying to get *in*.

She screamed in agony and fell to her knees. "Get out!" she shrieked. "You're not me! You're NOT ME!"

The shadows in the corners of the room pulsed. The overhead light began to buzz, then pop, then go dark.

Brad knelt in front of her, his smile serene, his voice like a lullaby. "You don't have to fight. That's the beauty of collapse, once it starts, there's no stopping it. Don't you want to be with Jules?"

He touched her forehead with two fingers and the room shook. Brittany's eyes rolled back. Her jaw locked. Her chest heaved like something was climbing up from her ribs, but she wasn't done. With the last ounce of strength she had, she shoved herself backward, breaking his touch. Her back slammed into the wall. Her breathing came in choking sobs. "No," she said again, teeth clenched. "You want a vessel? Find another."

Brad straightened slowly, no longer smiling. "Brittany..." he said, voice deepening, not calm now, not patient. "You *are* the vessel. I've been waiting so long for someone like you. I have been preparing you for months."

Then came the tap.

Tap. tap.

But this time... it came from the inside of her skull.

She screamed. Her scream echoed off the walls, high, ragged, desperate, and then... silence. She collapsed to her knees, trembling, teeth clenched so tight she thought they'd shatter. "Stop," she whimpered. "Stop..."

The air in the room shifted, not colder... but *wrong*. Dense with something ancient, sour, heavy like smoke that never fully clears. From the corner of her eye, the bathroom door creaked wider.

And standing in the threshold...

Jane, Jules, and Madame Zodo.

Blood matted Jane's curls, running in rivers down her face. One of her arms was bent wrong, her wrist twisted unnaturally like a broken doll. Jules stood just beside her. A bloody gash on her face. Her shirt soaked with blood. Her eyes completely black. Madam Zodo stood next to Jules, her face looked as if she had been burnt in a fire, large patches of her hair were missing. Her black dress tattered and dirty.

"Jules?" Brittany choked out. "Please... help me."

The girls just stared in complete silence as if they were frozen. No comforting looks, or flickers of recognition. Not even sadness.

"I'm still here!" Brittany sobbed. "Please! I don't want to go like this. I'm not ready!"

Her vision blurred. Her limbs no longer felt like hers. Her hands twitched against the floor. Her fingers were numb and the feeling was creeping up her arms.

Brad took another step forward, his voice curling through the air like smoke. "Let go. There's nothing left to fight for, at least if you let go you will see them again."

And maybe... he was right. She saw it all again in flashes, her and Jules on the hotel bed, laughing at something stupid on TV. Sneaking into historical cemeteries after dark, watching as Jules would always slip trying to get over the stone wall. Their first recording session, wearing matching ghost sweatshirts, tangled in wires, Jules whispering, *'What if something actually answers us?'* And then jumping as the floor creaked. Jules laughing so hard she snorted during their first podcast. And then hearing Jules whisper, *'We're in this together, forever.'*

Brittany's breath caught. The pain in her skull deepened, like claws dragging across her brain. The burning pain returned on her side again, then spread quickly to her back. She cried out, her body arching, as the pain deepened. When she lifted her shirt, her flesh was blistering, glowing red and alive as if invisible hands were branding her from within. The stench of scorched flesh filled the air. She was burning... just like in her nightmares.

And then... Another voice. Soft. Shaking. But it wasn't Brad's. "Fight it."

A small object clattered to the floor beside her and made her forget everything that was happening.

A necklace. The *seeing eye necklace*. Jane's necklace. She had read about it in the curated book at the hotel and she had seen pictures of this necklace on Wendy's wall.

It shimmered faintly in the dim hallway light, the eye in the center staring up at her, unblinking. A whisper curled through her ears, not from the demon, but from *Jane*. "Fight, Brittany."

Brittany's fingers reached for it, slow and trembling. The moment her skin touched the charm. A burning warmth spread through her hand and up her arm.

Brad hissed, staggering back into the bathroom shadows.

The lights above snapped bright.

And for the first time since entering Room 1210... Brittany felt *something* inside her fight back.

The warmth from the necklace surged like lightning through

Brittany's veins, igniting her nerve endings. She gritted her teeth and screamed, not in fear or pain, but in defiance.

Brad snarled, no longer bothering to pretend he was human. His jaw cracked open far wider than it should have, splitting with a sickening sound as rows of jagged, uneven teeth glistened in the dim light. His eyes flared an unnatural yellow, burning through the haze as fog began to coil around his body. The air between them thickened, warping, groaning, as if the room itself was struggling to contain whatever monstrous thing had just stepped forward wearing Brad's skin.

"You *don't* get to win," Brittany growled, clutching the necklace tighter.

But the demon had already buried itself too deep. Her body jerked violently. Her head snapped back. Blood trickled from her nose. Her vision blurred as something inside her *pushed*, like hands trying to rip through her skin from the inside.

"Brittany…" Jane's voice came again, distant, and soft. "Don't let him take you…"

She slammed backward into the wall, her hands loosening, the necklace clattering across the floor. Brad lunged forward like a shadow given shape, fingers stretched and clawed.

"No!" she shrieked, diving for the necklace. Just as his hand grazed her shoulder, her fingers closed around the charm. A shock wave burst from her chest, invisible, but powerful enough to send Brad flying back into the bathroom mirror, cracking the glass in a spiderweb pattern.

The necklace pulsed with a strange, golden light now. Brittany gasped for breath, every inhale feeling like knives in her lungs. She dropped to her knees, pressing the necklace to her heart.

The creature screamed from the bathroom, a sound that

didn't belong in this world, shrill and layered like a chorus of dying things.

Brittany's lips trembled as she began to chant, words that filled her mouth like instinct, "Evil spirit standing tall, its time you make your greatest fall. Return to the ground thou evil plight, I banish you with good and light."

The light from the necklace flared.

Brad convulsed, black smoke writhing from his mouth and eyes.

"You're not real," Brittany said through clenched teeth. "You're what's left after fear. You're nothing. And I'm not your vessel."

As the Hollow One lunged again, the eye on the necklace blinked once. Then went dark.

Brad dropped mid charge, slamming to the floor like a puppet with its strings cut. He twitched once... then lay still.

The room was quiet again. Too quiet.

Brittany didn't move. Her whole body shook. Blood dried in a line down her neck, and her hands wouldn't unclench from the necklace.

In the shattered mirror... her reflection was alone.

But the hallway behind her was no longer empty.

Jules and Jane stood there once more. Still broken. Still dead. But smiling.

But their smile wasn't *right*.

Brittany's body froze again, breath catching in her chest. Jules' smile was wide... too wide. Jane's head tilted slightly to the left, the skin of her neck still split where it had once been crushed. Their mouths moved, but no sound came out.

She blinked. They didn't.

"Jules?" Brittany whispered. Still no answer.

Instead, Jane stepped forward, barefoot, toes leaving faint wet prints on the carpet. Her gown still soaked from the bathtub. Brittany's stomach turned when she realized: the water was still dripping off her dress.

Jules followed, her red lipstick smeared across her cheek, as if applied by trembling hands after death. Her eyes flicked to the necklace Brittany clutched, then up to Brittany's face.

"Am I..." Brittany started, voice hoarse, "...too late?"

The girls just stared.

Behind them, in the cracked mirror, Brad's body began to move. Not his limbs, *his shadow.* It peeled from beneath him, climbing the walls and ceiling, shaping itself into something tall. Unnatural. Watching.

The light above flickered. Then both Jules and Jane opened their mouths at the same time and screamed. No words. No names. Just one long, distorted wail that sounded like all three of them were burning alive. Brittany dropped the necklace, clamping her hands over her ears, but the sound *was inside* her head. Like fire ants crawling under her skin. She screamed back, trying to drown them out.

"You're not them!" she howled, backing into the corner.

The ghostly figures dissolved like smoke into the air, their final echoes twisting into cruel laughter. The laughter deepened into a low growl, not human. Not of this world. It rumbled through the walls like the very bones of the hotel were reacting.

The Tower tarot card, still on the floor, caught flame without warning. The edges curled inward. Then the floor beneath Brittany cracked, and the door slammed shut.

Brittany's knees hit the floor hard, the impact jarring, but it didn't matter, the pain inside her was worse. It was like her blood was boiling. Her fingers bent backward on their own.

Her jaw locked in place. Her back arched so sharply it felt like it might snap. A searing heat spread through her spine, each vertebra lighting up like it was being branded. He was breaking her completely.

Her eyes rolled back. Black veins spread across her skin. Her chest heaved as if something was trying to *crawl out* of it. Her whole left side seemed to be burning even hotter, and spreading through her like venom forged in Hell itself. She screamed, but the sound warped, twisting into a demonic growl as the entity took hold.

Then a memory flooded in. Soft. Gentle. So sudden it almost hurt. Jules' laugh echoing inside their tent. 'If we die tonight,' she'd giggled, 'at least we're doing it together. They had held hands under that stupid sleeping bag, fingers laced tight, shivering not from fear but from how *alive* they felt, and in that moment, Brittany felt the last piece of her slipping away.

Just as she was about to give up for good, Brittany felt something grab her hand. She cracked her eye open as much as she could, but nothing was there. Still, her fingers curled instinctively around it. The air felt thick, electric. Like Jules was right there beside her.

Fight.

The word pulsed through her like a drumbeat. Another memory, no not a memory, a name, slammed into her mind.

Zaron.

"You can't defeat me," The Hollow One said. "I've fed on many, I'm too strong now for your puny necklace. It doesn't hold enough power."

The beads shimmered on the floor, she realized they weren't protection. They were false hope. A trick. Just enough to make her *think* she had a chance. Just enough to make her *tire out.*

The realization split her soul open. Pain ripped through her body like fire being poured into her mouth, her nose, her ears. Her throat burned as if she'd swallowed a coal. She tried to scream, but nothing came out.

Zaron.

She *had* to say it. Something in her gut made her realize if she said his name, this would all end.

Her eyes streamed with tears as every nerve in her body fought against the inferno inside. Her tongue felt like stone. Her lips trembled.

Another flash, Jules again. This time, her face covered in blood, but her hand still outstretched. Still reaching for her.

The tent.

Their bond.

Their promise.

And then...

Brittany's mouth cracked open, barely more than a whisper at first, like wind squeezing through a crack in the wall. "Z-Z..."

The pain surged, one final wave, trying to drown her, but she *grabbed back.*

"ZARON!!!"

Her voice tore through the room like a bolt of lightning, echoing off the walls. The light bulbs exploded. The bed rattled violently. From the bathroom doorway, the shadow form *twitched*, convulsed.

His blazing yellow eyes snapped towards her, the twisted smile finally slipping from his face. The scream that erupted from him was not human. It started as a low, guttural growl and twisted upward into a shriek so piercing it seemed to split the air apart. The lights shuddered and the sound carried the weight of a thousand tormented voices crying out through him. The floorboards beneath him splintered open, and the creature was yanked downward into the darkness below.

Silence fell heavy in the room as Brittany's knees gave out, and she collapsed, gasping for breath.

The moment Brittany screamed the name, it was as if the entire room exhaled. The darkness that had curled its fingers around her soul retreated, slowly, angrily. The air shifted. Lighter. Cleaner. The oppressive weight lifted from her chest and for the first time in what felt like hours, maybe days, she could breathe.

She collapsed to the floor, her body shaking. Every nerve ending buzzed with aftershocks of pain. But inside her? Pure stillness. Peace. She was still here. She remembered reading in Madame Zodo's book that his name held power. She knew if she got his name out, she might be able to free them.

She didn't remember closing her eyes, but when they fluttered open again, distant voices buzzed around her, hurried and anxious. The police. They found her lying on the floor, pale, cold, and unmoving. One officer dropped to his knees, pressing trembling fingers to her neck. "She's alive," he shouted. "Call it in. We've got a pulse."

Then the world began to fade again. This time not into a cruel, suffocating darkness she had known before, but into something softer. A gentle, merciful pull that drew her down into a quiet, healing sleep.

Chapter 26

Two days later

Brittany woke in a hospital bed.

No restraints. No locked doors. Just the sterile smell of rubbing alcohol and fresh linen. She blinked twice, clearing her vision.

She felt a hand on hers, rubbing the back of her hand softly. She turned her head and saw her mother was there. Eyes red. Hands wrapped around Brittany's like she was afraid to let go.

"You're safe," her mom whispered, voice breaking. "You're in a real hospital, sweetheart. Not... not that place."

Brittany's voice cracked. "How?"

"The police saw everything. The security cameras showed the nurses... they were attacked. But you... you didn't do anything. You just stood there. They ruled their deaths as suicides. The footage cleared you. Completely."

Tears welled in Brittany's eyes. A different kind of release now. Relief. Brittany swallowed and winced. Her throat felt like someone had rubbed it raw with sand paper. She went to sit up and winced, her side erupting in pain.

"Oh, be careful sweetie." Her mom said. "They had to graft your side from skin on your right side. The doctor said you had third degree burns, but they have no idea how."

Brittany's vision blurred as she remembered feeling the searing pain in the hotel room. Her stomach turned, the smell of her skin searing reentering her nose. She needed to be alone. She was not ready to explain how the burns occurred fearful it would end with her back at the asylum. "Mom, can you get me some water?"

"Of course, sweetie."

Brittany watched her mom leave the room, praying this was not just a dream and that her mom would walk back through the room.

And then, something shifted in the air. Brittany looked towards the door and caught a glimpse of Jules standing in the doorway, smiling. Jules lifted her hand to the glass window, as her heart bracelet twinkled on her arm. Brittany knew this time it was real. Jules was finally free. Jules waved goodbye and vanished, as if she had never been there.

Brittany leaned back onto her pillow, her chest rising with a breath that felt earned.

She had fought. And she had won. Then she felt her bed give way next to her. She opened her eyes and saw Jules lying beside her.

"Thank you, Britt, you really did keep your promise of always keeping me safe."

Brittany's eyes filled with tears. "Always." That was all she could get out.

Jules held her best friend's hand. "I finally get to go see my parents again. Thank you. I love you so much Britt." She felt her hand get squeezed a little tighter. "Goodbye for now, but just know, I'll always be with you."

"Always." Brittany said and they linked pinky's one last time. Then Jules disappeared. Brittany lay there smiling, finally at peace, a final tear sliding down her cheek.

* * *

In room 1210

Madame Zodo stood in the center of room 1210. The oppressive heaviness in the room was gone. The shadows no longer whispered. And beside her stood Jane and Jules. They were all finally free. Their forms glowed softly, and there was peace in their eyes.

Jane turned toMadame Zodo. "Thank you so much for always keeping me safe in here. Otherwise, I know I would have been chained up like the others."

Madame Zodo smiled gently. "Call me Jacqueline girls, and I would have done anything to keep you safe. This was my fault in the first place for not getting you out when I realized what it was in the room. But I am amazed at how strong you are Jane, screaming to Brittany, she never should have been able to hear you."

"I honestly don't know how I did it, I just used every bit of strength I had and prayed it was enough. And don't ever blame yourself." Jane said her tone soft but firm. "Just because you know something's wrong doesn't mean the people you warn will always listen. Sometimes we can't see how things will end until it's too late.

Jules nodded, "We think we are invincible, that bad things only happen to other people."

Jacqueline just stared at the girls happier than she had ever been. The girls had fought so hard and endured so much. She was proud of them.

Then the girls said their goodbyes to Jacqueline, "I think it's time to go." Jules said to Jane.

Jules smiled, "I'll see you on the other side, Jacqueline."

And then the girls vanished, finally able to be set free of the room and move on. Jacqueline stood there taking in the quietness of the room. Enjoying the fact that there was no more darkness in the room.

Jacqueline took one last lingering look around the room, her fingertips brushing the wall as if offering a silent farewell. Every shadow, every scar in the plaster held memories she was ready to let go of.

Gratitude and sorrow tangled in her chest, thankful she would never have to see these walls again, yet aching for what had been lost in them.

With a final breath, she let go. Her form shimmered, dissolving into the still air, and as she faded, one thought carried her onward... *may I find them, wherever they are now.*

* * *

Two months later...

The hotel room lay in absolute silence, too heavy, too still. Then, from the dark corner of the bookcase, came a low, throbbing hum. The old leather-bound book shuddered where it rested. Its surface rippled, alive with something that shouldn't be.

Slowly the cover began to burn from within, the scent of

scorched leather filling the room. Letters carved themselves into existence, glowing with an unholy light.

Johnny's final attempt.

The glow pulsed once, then dimmed to nothing. Silence crept back in, but it didn't last. From somewhere deep in the shadows came a faint laugh, promising that the story was far from over.

Afterword

Thank you so much for reading Room 1210. I truly hope you enjoyed stepping into this world as much as I loved creating it. Writing this book has been a lifelong dream and a passion that has lived in my heart for years. Because of readers like you, that dream has become a reality.

If there is one thing I have learned through this journey, it's this: **never let fear win**. Do not let doubt or the opinions of others keep you from chasing what sets your soul on fire. Do the things that scare you, explore the world, take chances... and if you have ever wanted to write a book, *write it*.

To everyone that encouraged me, cheered me on, and reminded me to keep going when I felt nervous or unsure, thank you from the bottom of my heart. If you enjoyed this story, it would mean the world to me if you left a review on Amazon. Your words help this book reach more readers and keep my dream alive.

With love and endless gratitude,
Jill Norris

Author Note

Jill Norris has always been drawn to the shadows where history and the supernatural intertwine. A devoted horror enthusiast and lifelong seeker of the unknown, she channels her real-life experiences as a paranormal investigator into her writing. When she isn't exploring haunted places or uncovering eerie legends, Jill co-hosts a paranormal history podcast where she and her friend blend dark humor with bone-chilling stories from their investigations.

Her fascination with witches, spirits, and the mysteries beyond the veil began in childhood. An age when curiosity often blurred with courage. That same wonder and unease inspired the haunting world within Room 1210, a story born from whispered legends, strange encounters, and the thrill of wondering what might be watching just beyond the light.